The Holiday Ex-Files

USA TODAY BESTSELLING AUTHOR

JENNIFER PEEL

Dedication

To Adeline Jane—you make every season magical.

One

OKAY, EX-FILERS, IT'S October. We all know what that means. The holidays are upon us. I know, it gives me the shudders too. Many of us will feel compelled to couple up, but just remember that while it's easy to crop a mistake out of a photo, hearts and souls are an entirely different matter. So be safe out there. And I'm not talking about safe sex, though that is important too. Actually, think abstinence with a capital A. *Better to be safe than sorry. Like really, really sorry. Remember, one might be the loneliest number, but there are worse things than being alone—even during the holidays. (See my list of things worse than being single under the pinned posts and highlights.) But if you must indulge in coupledom this holiday season, please visit my website at www.theholidayexfiles.com for the best poses and photo arrangements in case, or should I say when, you have to crop out those pesky exes.*

As always, I will be here winter, spring, summer, and fall to remove them all.

Lots of love,

Cami

P.S. Don't forget about the Halloween Bash at the Civic Center in Aspen Lake to benefit the women and children's shelter. You can donate online or in person.

P.P.S. No couples allowed.

I read over my post for the day, did a quick spell-check, and clicked publish. I set my phone down on my nightstand, ready to pick up my laptop and get to work. I know working in bed isn't good for my musculoskeletal system, as my mom loved to point out, but I was most creative in bed. Wait, that didn't come out how I wanted. What I meant was I did my best work in bed. Oh. My. Gosh. Forget the whole bed thing. I work best when I was comfortable.

I went to reach for my laptop but stopped when Neville, my shih tzu and the only man allowed in my bed, narrowed his eyes at me. I'd seen the look before—he'd inherited it from my mother. The look said, "Cami, honey, all this helping people shun relationships and the holidays isn't healthy. You used to be such a happy, sweet girl. Maybe you should talk to someone. Would you like some cheesecake?"

I always took the cheesecake. As for the other advice, I filed it under It's Too Painful, Let's Not Go There. And as far as happy and sweet went, I wasn't unhappy, and perhaps I wasn't as sweet as I was before *the incident.* I was more like artificial sweetener sweet. It almost tasted like real sugar, but you knew something was missing. That pretty much summed me up—something was missing. More like something was stolen.

That was okay though. I was okay.

I scratched Neville's head. "If only you knew the whole story, buddy, you wouldn't be giving me that look. You'd be cheering me on. But it's just too much for your virgin ears. Well, that is if you are a virgin." I wasn't exactly sure. I'd adopted Neville after *the incident* almost three years ago, and Neville was already four by then, which meant he was twenty-eight in people years, which meant he was the same age as . . . well . . . *the him* at that time. Which might explain why Neville needed anxiety meds. He'd probably had an incident too. Regardless, he didn't need the gory details. Besides, I kind of sort of already told the entire world about it; well, most of it at least. Some pain was better off private.

I swore Neville shrugged before curling up and closing his eyes. If only my mom were so easy to appease. She would have given me cheesecake and a lecture about the beauty of love and the holidays. She might have even serenaded me with "Have Yourself a Merry Little C-word." (I refused to say or even think the once-beloved word.) It had happened during the annual Jenkins Fourth of July lake party this past summer. To make it worse, my entire family—all one hundred and fifty of them from my five brothers, their spouses, nieces, nephews, aunts, uncles, cousins, grandparents, and I think some random strangers looking for free food—all joined in. If that wasn't enough, they sang ten more C-word songs like they were herald angels leading us to the baby Jesus, all while fireworks exploded in the star-filled sky. I had tried to escape but they all surrounded me like they were doing some sort of intervention. They probably were. But I'd held strong and refused to sing any of my old favorites. The entire time, I repeated in my head the lyrics to "Love Stinks." *This thing they call love, it's going to make you cry.* Truer words had never been spoken.

A loud sigh escaped. I needed to work. I grabbed my laptop, ready to edit the photos I had taken for an upcoming listing at my father's real estate firm. I should mention it was *his* father's too. Yeah, that was awkward. A word of advice: don't ever date a coworker, especially when he's the son of your father's business partner. Really, just don't date. Here's another tip: don't marry *him.*

I had just pulled up the file I needed when someone loudly knocked on my door. I say someone but I knew who it was by his knock that sounded like the beat to Queen's, "We Will Rock You." I looked at the time. What was he doing here at nine in the morning? I threw my baby-soft pink comforter off me, startling Neville so badly he yelped as if he was in pain. The poor thing was afraid of his shadow. Maybe I should talk to the vet about upping his meds.

I picked up Neville, as he was too afraid to jump off my plush king-size bed, which had a good dozen pillows on it. The more pillows the better, as *the him* used to make fun of them. And the frillier the better, as *the him* didn't like frill either. My room looked like a ruffle factory had exploded all over it. I wasn't exactly proud of it, but it was mine, all mine.

I padded across the cold hardwood floors in my tiny one-bedroom condo that I'd spent way too much money on. That's what I got for living in a ski town, my hometown. It was worth it though. I loved Aspen Lake. Unfortunately, so did everyone else, it seemed. Real estate prices were out of control. I would never say that to my father. He loved this sellers' market. Thankfully, my side job brought on by *the incident* and my Photoshop skills made living in my favorite place possible. I could at least thank my ex for that.

I took my time getting to the door. I stopped and turned up the thermostat. It was kind of chilly. Lows were getting down into the thirties overnight now. Then I headed for the kitchen and filled Neville's dog bowl up with his specialized food and his bottled water of choice—FIJI. He loved the good stuff. I set Neville down and let him enjoy his food.

Meanwhile, he kept knocking and knocking and knocking. He'd moved on to Mac Miller's "Knock Knock." I let him do one more chorus of it because I liked the song. Then I moseyed on over to the door. I stood in front of it, contemplating whether I should open it. I didn't understand why he kept coming around this past year. I knew what he wanted, and he could email me his request. But, I knew I would eventually grow tired of his knocking—and I knew he would never leave—so I opened the door in all my jeans and hoodie glory. My sandy-brown hair was up in a messy bun, and I had only gotten around to moisturizing my fair-skinned face. That was about as fancy as I got when I was editing.

On the other side of the door stood Noah Cullen. Yeah, like those *Twilight* vampires. He was just as beautiful as them too, except he didn't sparkle—other than his shiny white teeth. I bet he'd bitten his fair share of women. His skin was far from granite; instead he looked to be kissed by the sun, which highlighted the barbed wire tattoos wrapping his muscular biceps. I swear he wore a tight T-shirt every day just to show them off, even if it was twenty degrees outside. His dark, tousled hair curled just above his ears completing the classic bad boy look—the kind of bad boy girls loved. But not this girl. Though my heart was in a deep-freeze, I did see the appeal.

He flashed me a brilliant smile. "You answered a full five minutes quicker than last time. It's almost like we're friends again."

Ouch. That stung, but I didn't let it show. If he only knew how much I hated giving up our friendship. But he was a painful reminder of his best friend. And of too many good times I couldn't bear to remember. And most importantly, he was too much a part of *the incident*. He'd helped me pick out the infamous *tree* (yeah, the one that starts with a C) and had decorated it with me, all because *the him* was too busy, but apparently not too busy to well . . . never mind. I flung the door wide open, knowing he'd invite himself in anyway.

"You got *Ben*"—my voice always made some weird strangling noise whenever I said my ex's name—"in the divorce. Don't you remember?"

He slid in and shut the door before I changed my mind and asked him to leave. "I'm suing for joint custody now."

He had a knack for making me smile. And judging by his smirk, he was proud of that fact.

I wiped the smile off my face and sighed. "What are you doing here?"

He tugged on a loose strand of my hair like he was one of my big brothers or something. That was weird. I didn't need another big brother. Five were plenty enough. "Come on, Cams, you know you love it when I drop by unannounced. I'm the only person who likes the crappy coffee you make."

I rolled my eyes at him. "Hey, don't hate on the instant coffee."

"I would never. You're the only person I know who buys coffee that tastes like nuts and citrus and comes packaged like tea bags."

That made it sound plain weird, but with some half-and-half and sugar in it, it was golden. "I suppose you want a cup."

His answer came in the form of sauntering toward my tiny kitchen, which was in serious need of a renovation. The old oak cabinets, a throwback to the nineties along with the mauve countertops, were almost as old as me, a ripe old twenty-nine. I had to remind myself I was living in one of the most sought-after towns not only in Nevada, but in the United States. And I could see the ski slopes from my balcony, so the place being so outdated was a small price to pay. Someday, I would get around to all my plans for my little home. Someday, when I quit thinking about the perfect place I used to call home. The place where all my dreams died.

Noah went straight to Neville, who was now taking his dog food out of his bowl a piece at a time and barking at it, as if each morsel were a vicious killer. Yep, he was special that way. I told people he did it because it was part of his DNA given his ancestors had to hunt for food to survive. Except, shih tzus were bred to be royal lapdogs, but I was still going with it.

Strangely, Noah was the one person besides me who didn't send poor Neville into cardiac arrest. Noah knelt next to my pooch and scratched his head. "Hey, buddy, how are you?"

Neville reveled in Noah's touch, rubbing his puffy, white teddy-bear cheeks against Noah's knee.

"You still need to meet your girlfriend, Luna." Noah glanced up and gave me a pointed look.

I leaned against the counter with my arms folded. "Sorry, Neville's not into golden retrievers." He was afraid of his own tail. A dog as big as Luna would send him over the edge. Although she was a beautiful dog—I'd seen her in plenty of pictures. "Besides, I just read that J.K. Rowling has reportedly said that Neville and Luna don't end up together after the end of the series." I had never figured out why Noah decided to name his dog Luna. When he'd gotten her several months ago, he'd asked me who Neville's girlfriend was in the *Harry Potter* series. Neville never really had a girlfriend, but he'd crushed on Luna.

Noah shrugged. "I have a feeling they'll eventually find their way back to each other. As it was meant to be." His ice-blue eyes bore into mine as if he were trying to tell me something meaningful. He was acting strange lately. I had a hard time believing he really cared if our dogs hooked up. I didn't even think that was physically possible, even if Neville hadn't been neutered.

"Whatever you say." I turned and opened the cupboard near the sink to grab two mugs.

Noah stood and made his way to me, which only took a couple of steps in the tiny U-shaped kitchen. He acted right at home as he grabbed two bags of coffee from the bamboo tea bag holder I kept them in.

"What are you doing up here anyway?" I asked.

Noah lived in Carson City, which was about a half hour from here.

"Besides annoying you?" He placed a bag in each cup like we were doing an old familiar song and dance together.

"Yes, besides that." I filled up the cups with steaming hot water from my faucet's instant hot water dispenser. One of the highlights of my little place.

Noah opened the ancient white refrigerator door and pulled out a carton of half-and-half. "Not that annoying you isn't reason enough, but Mara needs me to give her a quote on some work she wants done for an upcoming listing near here." Noah was the best contractor around and could fix anything. He did a lot of work for Jenkins & Scott Realty. You know, my dad's and *his* dad's realty firm.

Mara was my best friend, confidante, and ex-sister-in-law. Yep, Mara was Ben's sister. Thankfully, I'd gotten her in the divorce. Some relationships were thicker than blood, even those of siblings. But don't tell my brothers that. That being said, it was hard having my life so intertwined with my ex's. I couldn't say enough about how it was never a good idea to fall in love with your dad's business partner's son. When my dad's real estate firm merged with the Scott family's firm ten years ago to create Jenkins & Scott Realty, I remembered my dad saying big things were on the horizon. Who knew then how big? And awful. Everyone thought it was kismet that Ben and I ended up falling for each other. We were treated like the crowned heirs who would see to it that the kingdom remained strong for generations to come. If I had only known the prince would be royally unfaithful. At least I got Mara out of the deal—the best real estate agent out of the bunch if you asked me. And the best friend a girl could ask for.

I bobbed my coffee bag up and down. "I think she mentioned that."

Noah poured the perfect amount of half-and-half into my cup before reaching for a pink packet of sugar and handing it to me.

I couldn't help but smile at him when I took the sugar. We were acting like an old married couple. I pushed that thought out of my head. The thought of marriage in any form, to anyone, made me feel itchy all over—like a bad case of poison ivy. I shuddered and scooted away from Noah. Not like Noah ever thought of me that way. In fact, I knew the main reason for his visit. It was always the same thing.

I grabbed a spoon out of the drawer nearest me and stirred my coffee to perfection. "So, who do you want me to crop out of your photos this time?" I tried to keep the snark out of my voice. After all, it was my specialty and what I was famous for. Let's just say catching your husband having sex under the *C* tree with one of his clients, now wife, kind of does crazy things to you. Like making you stay up all night after *the incident*, cropping him out of all your wedding photos, and perhaps making a few where he was holding his bloody head in his arms while I shoved it full of wedding cake. In my state of shock and dismay, I had done the only thing I could think of—I'd posted those babies online with the caption: *Came home early from a business trip to surprise my husband, instead I got the surprise of my life when I caught him decking someone else's halls under our tree. 'Tis the season to be salty. Falalalala.*

I still had a hard time wrapping my head around the response that post got. It had now been shared millions of times, to my ex's and his influencer wife's dismay. For me, though, it had become a lifeline. When people began sharing their own terrible breakup stories with me and wondering if I could do the same thing to their wedding photos, or any photos with exes in them, it helped me deal with my own excruciating pain. More like mask it. At least it gave me a new side job since I couldn't bear to keep doing lifestyle shoots for families. Even though I was good at it. Like really good. I had gotten so many requests to crop out exes that The Holiday Ex-Files was born.

I lovingly called my fans and clients the Ex-Filers. There were even Ex-Filers chapters across the country now. Most of them had monthly get-togethers, like a support group. I started one here too. We mainly held charity events like the Halloween Bash that would support the women and children's shelter. A lot of the holidays now gave me a rash, but Halloween was acceptable because for one night I could pretend to be someone else. Someone who didn't wish her life had turned out differently.

Noah did a sidestep to remove the distance I had placed between us. When he stood so close, I was reminded how tall he was. He had a good six inches on my five-feet-nine frame. Our heights had made us good basketball players. We'd both played in college. I got a good whiff of him too—he smelled like sugar and spice. Basically, he was a big snickerdoodle. A long time ago, I'd asked him for the name of his cologne because it was yummy and I wanted to buy some for his pig of a best friend. Noah's response was, *"It's my natural scent, I call it stud muffin."* I knew then he was a player. Add in a string of girlfriends a mile long—who all wanted to gobble him up, leaving not a crumb—and his status was firmly cemented.

With a big grin, Noah reached into his jeans' pocket and pulled out a flash drive.

"You know, flash drives are so 2010. You could email me the photos or upload them to the cloud on my website."

"I could, but I love seeing the way your emerald eyes narrow and judge me. And the dulcet tones of the lecture you always give me warms my heart," he teased me.

I scrunched my face, totally judging him. "I just don't get it. I swear you have a new girlfriend every two weeks. Why bother taking pictures with her? You could just delete the photos. What do you do with all these photos of yourself when I'm done editing them, anyway?" Sure, he was beautiful, even conceited at times, but I'd never thought of him as someone who worshipped himself.

"Why do you care so much?" he said with such a smirk.

"I don't, it's just now that you're thirty-two, don't you think you should slow down? Maybe try monogamy." Not like I condoned coupledom, but how many women did he need to date? More like how many hearts did he need to break? "Or even try being single. It's not a bad life." Well, it could be at times, but I wasn't going to mention it.

He cringed at the mere mention of the word *single*. "Don't worry, I already know who the future Mrs. Cullen will be." He wagged his perfectly arched and trimmed brows. I had to say, I admired his grooming habits.

I stepped back, shocked. "You do?" He'd never talked about getting married. There were going to be a lot of disappointed women.

"Yes, ma'am." He tapped my nose.

"Who is she? Do I know her?"

He nodded.

I started thinking of all the women I knew who could be possibilities. There was Deidre, another realtor from the firm. She was cute and perky, and definitely into Noah. She'd even made up repairs for the houses she'd listed just to see him. Or maybe it was Isla—she was a friend from Noah and Ben's college days who I was sure always wanted to be more than a friend. Then there was Annika; she was in my Ex-Filers chapter, and she and Noah went to homecoming together in high school. "Don't leave me in suspense."

He held up his mug as if he were toasting me. "I'm afraid you're going to need to be suspended for a while longer. She's a work in progress."

I did narrow my eyes at him like he accused me of doing earlier. "You make her sound like a house you're renovating. Is she not good enough for you yet?" I snarled. He sounded just like Ben, who I was never good enough for. I could still hear him in my head: *Cami, you have such a great body, but your clothes are too baggy. Cami, don't wear heels; you look too tall next to me. Cami, maybe you could put a little more effort into your hair. We have a reputation to uphold.* Shamefully, I had jumped through every hoop for him, hoping to live up to his expectations. Through it all I lost myself, and then I lost him too.

Noah inched even closer and set his mug down. He tilted his head and studied me. In his eyes I saw the same look I'd been getting for the last few years. It said, "What happened to you?"

I gripped the counter, willing myself not to tear up. I knew I wasn't as sweet as I used to be. A few years ago, I would have never lashed out at Noah. Sure, I would have teased him for all the women he was dating. In fact, I had tried to set him up several times with Mrs. Right, because in reality, Noah was a good person. He'd even tried to help me pick up the pieces after I'd caught Ben cheating on me, but I'd pushed him away. I kept on pushing too. But for some reason, he wasn't willing to let our friendship go. He really should. I knew I didn't deserve him after the way I'd treated him.

"Cams," he said my name so sweetly, "I could never aspire to be as good as her. She's the most incredible woman I've ever known."

"Oh." I dropped my head. I felt like such a jerk. "I'm sorry, Noah." But then I remembered his flash drive. My head snapped up with, yes, my judging eyes. "Why date these other women, then?"

"Because she intimidates me and I don't know how to tell her how I feel," he sounded so vulnerable as he pressed the flash drive into my hand. His warm, calloused hand engulfed my own while his intense gaze held me in place. We are talking, like, my parents had just caught me skipping school intense, which I had never been found guilty of doing. Not to say I hadn't skipped school, but that was another story.

I swallowed hard, not sure where this was all coming from. Noah was getting weirder all the time. This woman must really have some hold on him. I didn't think he could be intimidated. He had a reputation for being untouchable but oh so desired.

Noah leaned in with his signature I'm a demigod smile. "Besides," he whispered, "I would have to think of another way to annoy you."

I slid my hand out of his, curling my fingers around his flash drive—half-irritated, half-touched that he still bothered to annoy me. In the process, for a split second, I realized what a comfort it had been to hold his hand. I missed that kind of affection. Even the platonic kind Noah and I used to share. But I'd made a solemn vow to myself. We are talking unbreakable-curse-level solemn, that I would never take comfort in another man again, not even a friend. Especially not a man who was in love with an incredible woman. I would never give that woman any reason to doubt how Noah felt about her. She deserved at least that much. My only hope was that Noah didn't break her heart. But the odds weren't in her favor. I felt sorry for her already.

Two

OKAY, EX-FILERS, HERE'S your 'how to rock the single life' pro tip for the day: If you are having a hard time sleeping alone, sleep in your bed diagonally. Not only does it give you the illusion of taking up more space, but when you turn your head, you're not met with an empty pillow next to you.

Lots of love,

Cami

I sleep like this every night now. It is totally genius.

I clicked publish before turning back to my new favorite show, *Cosmetics and Crimes*, and my favorite person, Mara.

Mara and I had a standing weekly date where we ate Thai takeout and watched YouTuber Zoe Moore while she did her makeup and talked about serial killers. It was a bit morbid, but it was fascinating. And I learned a lot—like how I could make my ex disappear without a trace. Not that I would, but honestly, some of these female serial killers had all the luck. One killed like five husbands and never got caught. I bet each one of those husbands was a cheater. Of course, I would never have Ben knocked off, but I'd had visions of what it would have been like if my beautiful tree, all ten feet of it, had come toppling down on Ben and Claudia. I could hardly think of her name without some vomit rising to my throat. I'll tell you this, it was a marvelous sight picturing them pinned under that tree with a few glass ornaments stuck in Claudia's perfectly chiseled butt.

Maybe I needed therapy. Yikes.

"Please pass the cashew chicken," Mara interrupted my evil thoughts.

I handed her the carton and swapped her for the mango sticky rice. Once we were done filling our plates, we both curled our feet beneath us as we sat on my pink velvet couch. Yes, it was another purchase I wasn't particularly proud of. It looked like I lived in a giant dollhouse. Ben's cheating did things to me. When I'd furnished my little place, all I'd thought of was what Ben would have hated the most and I went with it. And I think I wanted some of my innocence back. I was all of twenty-three when I'd married Ben. I'd thought I knew it all back then. Back when I believed in forevers and love. And . . . I rubbed my flat stomach. I couldn't think about it.

"Ooh, I like her flame eyes," Mara commented. "Do you think I could pull it off?" She batted her gorgeous hazel eyes at me.

I was grateful once again for Mara saving me from myself. "Totally. You could do it for the Halloween Bash and come as Aries."

She dipped her chin. "You think I should come as a flying ram?"

"A flying ram on fire," I corrected her.

She tossed her head from side to side, making her shiny brown hair with the perfect amount of caramel highlights swing like she was the star of a shampoo commercial. The Scott family had some serious beauty genes. Admittedly, my ex was gorgeous too.

"You know, I kind of like it." She giggled.

I set my food down and googled Aries costumes on my phone. Several mythical ram's horn headpieces popped up. I showed Mara my findings.

"I'm totally doing this. Do you think you could do the flame eye makeup?"

I watched Zoe's technique on the screen. "I think so."

"Perfect. What are you going as?"

"I'm not sure yet." I popped a spicy shrimp in my mouth. Sadly, in another lifetime it seemed, I would have had my costume picked out in July. Ben's too. He actually loved all of our couples costumes. Not thinking about it.

"By the way, your post was freaking hilarious yesterday. And your engagement is incredible. I can't believe you're up to a million followers. You have more than my sister-in-law now," she growled, "though I use the term loosely. How Ben stays married to someone who refers to herself in the third person constantly, I have no idea. If Claudia Cann, you can," she mocked the catchphrase of the woman we loved to hate.

Claudia Cann was a fitness guru and influencer. We are talking, she wore a wide-brimmed hat everywhere, type of influencer. She was also ten years older than Ben and everything he ever wanted. Shorter than him, more glamorous than me—with her golden-blonde tresses that always looked perfect, even during the workout videos she constantly posted. All that working out meant she had a killer body. She didn't even look close to her age. I swore she'd sold her soul to the devil or the collagen gods. No one should look as good as she did. She was so beautiful it hurt, like knife-in-the-heart hurt.

The thought of her had me feeling sick to my stomach. I set my plate of food on the coffee table.

Mara did the same before rubbing my arm. "I'm sorry, Cams, I shouldn't talk about her."

"It's not your fault. It's been almost three years. I should be over it already. Besides, it's not like we can avoid her. You're related to her."

Mara grimaced. "It's the worst. Last week at my parents' house, she announced she's starting her own line of action wear called Claudia's Collection. Tagline, *If Claudia Cann Wear It, You Can Too.*"

I snort laughed.

Mara's eyes lit up. "That was my mom's and my reaction too. Claudia didn't appreciate it and literally smacked her butt before walking out."

"That probably hurt her hand." She had buns of steel.

Mara gave me a sympathetic smile. "Cams, you're a million times better than her. My brother is an idiot, and honestly miserable—which he totally deserves."

I perked up a bit. "Why is he miserable?"

She gave me a look that said, "Duh."

"He's married to a narcissist for one. For his birthday, she got his car wrapped with her picture and logo on it."

"What? Are you serious? His precious Audi TT is covered with her? How did I miss that?" I bet he freaked, which made me ridiculously happy. He'd bought that car when we were married, and every day he would wipe any bit of dirt off it with a cloth baby diaper. He talked to it like it was a person. He'd say things like, *Looking good, Audrey.* Yes, he'd named his car.

"I've been waiting for a time like this to share that little gem." She took my hand. "You have to quit comparing yourself to her. She doesn't deserve the honor. Who cares if she can bench-press twice her weight and eats seaweed every day for lunch? Who wants to live like that?"

"Obviously, your brother."

"Nah. He just likes the free advertising she brings to the table. I hate that he keeps beating me out every month as top salesperson. I blame her for incessantly pushing him on her followers like she's sponsoring a homeless child who needs help. He needs help all right. Like a mental evaluation."

"Yeah," I whispered. Then why did he choose her over me? I always wondered.

"Cams, come on, you're better off without him. Without romance period. Look, you even stopped watching Hallmark C-word movies cold turkey." (Yes, my best friend even played along with my sick game of never naming the forsaken holiday I used to be crazy about.) "That alone is a victory." Mara hated all things Hallmark and romance in general. I probably should have come around to her way of thinking a long time ago. Admittedly, once a upon a time, I was a hopeless romantic. Sometimes I missed that girl.

"I don't want him back." I meant every word of that. "It's just, I gave him so much of myself and it meant nothing to him." I cleared the emotion out of my throat. I was never crying over him again. Ever.

Mara took my hand and squeezed it tight. "That's not true. As piggish as my brother is, I believe he loved you. He just didn't know what to do with someone as good as you. And it's not like my dad has been the best example of how a man should treat a woman," she snarled.

It was the worst-kept secret that Jay Scott was a philanderer. Poor

Kellie, Mara's mom and the best mother-in-law I could have ever asked for. Why she stayed with him, I have no idea. Even Ben used to wonder. He'd even promised me he would never be like his father. He hated how much his father had hurt his mother. Ben was a liar and a chip off the old block.

Mara waved her hand around and squirmed. "Anyway, let's not talk about them. We have serial killers to learn about." She let go of me and grabbed her food.

I reached for my laptop. I had several clients waiting for me to vanquish their exes, at least in their photos. If only I knew how to do it in real life.

Mara was used to me working while we watched TV. I was a good multitasker.

Neville came out of his hiding spot in my room, jumped up on the couch, and settled as close as he could to me. He didn't care for humans other than me and, well, Noah. Which reminded me. I pulled up the photos I had downloaded from Noah's flash drive. Technically, I shouldn't show them to Mara, but I'm sure Noah knew that I would. And it's not like he was heartbroken over all the women he was doing couples photo shoots with. Though he should be. Wowza.

I stared at Noah's latest victim. To say she was stunning was an understatement. We are talking ebony-skinned goddess with the most alluring bronze eyes. And her flowy dark hair was to die for. They were a gorgeous couple. The location was fantastic too, the nearby state park from the looks of it. The turquoise water of Aspen Lake shimmered in the background with the mountains looming in the distance. The photographer did an amazing job of using natural light. The mountains were glowing, as was the couple. Maybe Noah was part vampire after all.

I tilted my head, looking at every angle of the shot. I missed doing photo shoots. Especially those satisfying moments when, like this photographer, you caught the light just right.

After I fangirled on the artsy shot, I turned my laptop toward Mara. "Noah's latest."

Mara had just shoved a large bite of cashew chicken in her mouth, so when her jaw dropped it wasn't a pretty sight.

"Stunning, right?"

Mara realized her mouth was hanging open and started to chew. While she took a moment to get her bite down, I kept wondering why the beautiful creature in the photo didn't make Noah's cut. It must be some woman he was in love with.

Once Mara swallowed her food, she grimaced and even growled at the screen. "That looks so fake. He's not even touching her."

Like I said, Mara was pretty anti-romance, but looking closer at the "couple," she wasn't wrong. "Well, it makes it easier for me to edit her out."

"Isn't he using your services like every few weeks?"

I nodded.

She peered closer at the screen. "I swear it looks like he randomly grabbed the closest girl around just to have his photo taken with her. They look so bored."

I bit my lip, wondering if I should say something. I kind of had a theory that I knew wouldn't be popular with Mara. But I thought she should know. "I think I might know why."

Mara grabbed her Diet Coke. "Do tell."

"Well . . . Noah told me yesterday that he's already picked out his future bride."

Mara's eyes widened as she raised her drink to her mouth. "Really? Who?"

I gave her an uneasy smile. "He didn't give me a name, but he said I knew her and she's incredible, but she intimidates him. So, I've been thinking about who I know that fits the description. And well . . ." I bunched up my shoulders. "The woman who made sense was you."

She spit out her drink, and it went all over my floor and coffee table. She spluttered while grabbing napkins out of the takeout bag. "Me and Noah. No way. There is a rule about not dating your brother's best friend, and I plan to keep it." She sopped up her mess.

I set down my laptop and helped her clean up, though my sudden movement scared Neville. He ran back to my room.

While I patted the coffee table dry, I braved pressing the issue. "I don't know. Think about it. He knows you're off-limits, and let's admit it, you are insanely incredible and a tad intimidating. I mean, you love serial killer shows."

She waved her hand all around. "No. No. No. He sees me as the annoying kid sister. Besides, he's a man whore. And once you've been out with one, that's all it takes to swear you off men."

I gave her a sly grin, knowing she meant her ex, Heathen Steven. "So you're saying that not even Noah Cullen could tempt you?"

"Tempt me, sure. Which is why I've always kept my distance. I could see myself totally taking advantage of him, you know, to irritate my brother, but then I'd hate myself in the morning." Her eyes got a little dreamy.

I giggled. "You do like him."

"Uh, that's not only a no, but a hella no."

"Hella no?" I smiled.

"It's like next-level hell."

"I'll remember that." I tossed a wet napkin in the bag.

She sat back and eyed me, an aha moment appearing in her pretty hazel peepers. "You know, it could be you."

I spat out a huge laugh. No way did Noah want me. We were hardly even friends anymore. Besides, everyone knew I was planning on staying single until death did I part. "I was married to his best friend." I hated to say it out loud, but since she was my maid of honor and his sister, it was pointless to pretend otherwise.

"Yeah. That would be messed up."

"Totally."

Mara shrugged. "It's probably some obscure woman you met like one time."

"I'm sure you're right." Because I definitely knew she was wrong about Noah wanting to marry me. What a ridiculous thought.

Three

Happy Sunday, Ex-Filers. Here's your 'how to rock the single life' pro tip of the day. When attending family dinners, always make sure to wear sweats or anything with elastic waistbands. And don't be afraid to wear a dirty or wrinkled T-shirt. Make sure whatever it is, it says you don't care about your appearance. This will prevent your well-meaning mother or other relatives from inviting potential dating candidates. This advice is especially golden for holiday dinners. Not only do elastic waistbands act as a deterrent to suitor prospects, but they also allow you to eat second and third helpings and still feel like you can breathe. Note: If your sloppy appearance doesn't turn them off, you can try one of the following, which have worked wonders for me:

Ask them what their favorite song is and burp it out for them. Not only is it disgusting and a total turnoff, but you will delight your nieces and nephews to no end.

If you can't burp on demand like yours truly, start talking to yourself and make sure to answer. Make it sound like you're murmuring and plotting. I promise you will never see someone leave so fast.

Now go forth and make me proud.

And just remember, if you fall victim to one of your mother's schemes, I'll be here winter, spring, summer, and fall to remove them all.

Lots of love,

Cami

I smiled at the post, while sitting in my car outside my parents' house, before I clicked publish. I had so many good memories of me chasing off the men my sweet mother had tried to throw my way during the monthly Jenkins Sunday dinners. My proudest moment had come when I'd burped out all eight minutes of "Stairway to Heaven." The guy, I couldn't even remember his name, only picked that song because of its length. My poor mother was mortified, while all my brothers and their wives stared at me in horrified fascination. My father just shook his head at me the entire time. Some of my older nephews chanted my name, egging me on. I needed ten throat lozenges and a nap afterward, but it was totally worth it. The best part was when—whatever his name was—excused himself to use the bathroom after I was done and never came back. That was the last time my mother ever tried to set me up again.

Admittedly, I felt bad for my mom. She'd wanted a daughter so badly. After every one of my brothers' births, she would tell my dad, *There's a girl coming to us, I just know it.* Then I came and made her the happiest woman alive. She had so many hopes and dreams for me—and for herself. She'd been writing to me in her journal since she was fifteen. Little notes on how to navigate life from my teen years all the way to college, marriage, and having a family. She had tips and tricks for everything, from how to make a dollar stretch to how to deal with stretch marks. The dearest woman ever had even written a special journal for me on how to make breastfeeding work. I rubbed my chest. If she only knew how much I wanted to put that knowledge to use. How I'd thought I was going to get the chance.

I shook the soul-crushing memory out of my mind. It was time for me to face my family once again for the aforementioned Jenkins monthly Sunday dinner. Otherwise known as total chaos. Between all my older brothers and their wives, there were seventeen grandchildren now. My siblings were doing their best to singlehandedly keep OshKosh B'gosh and Huggies in business. Not only that, but they dipped into my savings monthly, because what kind of aunt would I be if I didn't bring presents for all my minions, as I lovingly called them. This month I had personalized T-shirts made for them that said, *I LOVE MY BAE (Best Aunt Ever).* My older nephews, twelve- and thirteen-year-old Corey and Ryland, probably wouldn't appreciate them, but they had to at least wear them once today so I could get a picture of all the minions together in the best shirts ever.

I threw my phone in my purse and grabbed the handle of the paper bag full of T-shirts. I took a deep breath, readying myself for the chaos my mother insisted on thrusting upon us every month. I knew it was a good thing. Family was important. And I loved my family. However, I always showed up a bit late, so that everyone was already there. It made it easier to get lost in the crowd. I still felt like when everyone looked at me, all they saw me as was Ben's ex-wife, a cheated-on spouse. Don't get me wrong, I knew they all loved me. Heck, when my brothers got news of what Ben had done, they'd all shown up at our place. Within thirty minutes they had packed all my belongings, then helped me move into the little apartment I'd rented until I knew where I was going to land permanently. Chandler, my oldest brother and lawyer, even represented me in my divorce.

With one last deep breath, I heaved myself out of the car into the nippy fall mountain air. My parents' secluded mountain estate with gorgeous lake views always made me smile. It was my mom's dream home. A beautiful four-story with a wall of windows on the side facing the lake. She called it her slice of heaven. She'd dedicated the lower level to her grandchildren and called it the Babe Cave. It was as if an indoor playground collided with a movie theater, complete with a snack bar. What I wouldn't have given for a place like that as a kid. I would give even more to have some kids of my own to enjoy it. But I was a born-again virgin, and was I ever a believer. It was going to take some divine intervention for me to change my mind about it. Which reminded me, I needed to book my "December" vacation to the Virgin Islands. I'd been going there the last couple of years over C-day, hoping to soak in all the virginity I could get. And you know, run away from the holiday I used to love most. The holiday where I'd lost all the magic in my life.

But I was okay. Totally not unhappy. I helped people rid themselves of painful reminders. And I gave great tips on how to be single.

Case in point: I was wearing sweatpants. Even though my mom hadn't tried to push anyone on me in a year, I wasn't letting my guard down. I even brought throat lozenges with me in case I needed to burp anything out. I wasn't exactly proud of that skill I'd acquired during my college years, but I would use it to my advantage if I had to.

I trudged in, soaking in the smell of pine trees and the perpetual aroma of campfire. I loved that smell. There was something so comforting about it. It reminded me of camping trips with my family and simpler days.

When I walked in, it looked like a child's birthday party gone wild. All I saw was a sea of noisy children running around, with various toys and balloons, in the open and spacious great room. I half worried they'd tied all the adults up somewhere and were reenacting *Lord of the Flies.* Thankfully, three of my brothers—Derek, Seth, and Kellan—appeared, each with a toddler in their arms, and they looked to be unharmed.

The minions were alerted to my presence, and several of them rushed me. They always knew I came bearing gifts. Soon I was surrounded like I was their goddess and they had come to worship me. It wasn't a bad gig. I knelt and let them all pile on me. Corey, Ryland, Anna, Teddy, Emily, Jacob, Alexa, Bradley, Collin, Sarah, Michaela, Toby, Melody, and Aubrey. My brothers set their toddlers, Saylor, Evie, and Lisa Marie, on me too. I was groaning under the weight of them all. The older kids were getting huge.

I succumbed to the weight and ended up on my back, hardly able to breathe, but happy. Death by minions wouldn't be a bad way to go. I kissed as many cheeks as I could and did my best to save the little ones from the crushing weight of the big ones. Thankfully, parents started showing up and extracting their kids.

Kellan, who was just older than me, held out his hand to help me up. I always had to suppress my smile around him. He was the "special" one in our family. An Elvis impersonator who lived in Vegas with his Priscilla Presley impersonator wife, Tonya, and their little girl, Lisa Marie. Kellan went all out with the black, slicked-back hair and sideburns that would take a lawn mower to shave off. At least he wasn't wearing one of his many rhinestone jumpsuits today. However, he was wearing a T-shirt with a big Elvis head surrounded by pink hearts.

I took Kellan's hand. "Well, thank you very much," I did a horrible impression of the King of Rock and Roll.

Kellan chuckled. "You need to work on that, sis."

"I'll put it on my list." I gave him a side hug, once I was on my feet. "How was the drive?"

He and Tonya drove the over seven-hour trip once a month to stay for the weekends we had family dinners. The rest of my siblings lived in either Aspen Lake, Reno, or Carson City. Not one of them worked for my dad, Daniel, which was super disappointing to him. That kept the pressure on me to keep taking photos of listings for him. He was so proud of some of them, he'd hung them on his home office wall. It's not that I didn't enjoy my job at Jenkins & Scott Realty—it was some of the employees. Not that I saw Ben often. He lived on the California side of the lake, managing one of the offices there. In his opinion, the California side was much better. What did he know? His wife loved to say, "Claudia Cann can only do California." Internally I gagged thinking about her and her stupid third-person sayings.

I just needed to stop thinking about her, period. I focused back on my minions. I grabbed the bag and went to hand T-shirts out to them, but was interrupted when a surprise visitor strolled in the front door without knocking.

Noah walked in like he was one of the family. Even some of my minions ran to him and hugged his legs. It was kind of adorable despite his love of annoying me. In years past before *the incident*, he frequently came to the monthly Sunday dinners, but that seemed like a lifetime ago. I had no idea why he was here today.

While he should have been distracted by the barrage of minions and my brothers making their way toward him, he made sure to grab my attention. He raised his hand and mouthed, "Hi."

I tilted my head. I was pretty sure he was wearing the exact same outfit he'd worn in the last two photo shoots I'd cropped his exes out of. Fit-me-right jeans, a button-up he left untucked, and a charcoal blazer. He looked like he had walked off a *GQ* cover. I could only imagine how stunning the woman was that he'd done yet another photo shoot with. Seriously, he needed to slow down. These poor women. Unless, that was, he had finally convinced the mystery woman to go out with him. But would he do a photo shoot with her so soon? Or maybe he wasn't doing a photo shoot. Either way, I still narrowed my eyes at him.

He smiled, which made me smile.

My mom came around the corner, prancing like Doris Day in her checkered apron splattered with her world-famous spaghetti sauce, which filled the house with the most tantalizing aromas: oregano and garlic, along with her homemade french bread. Ilene Jenkins is the patron saint of comfort food and the best mom around.

"Cami." Mom threw her tiny arms around me, her head coming to my shoulder. All her children towered over her, as we'd inherited my dad's tall genes. "You look so cute in your sweats." That was her trying reverse psychology. I had a news flash for her: I wasn't falling for it.

"Thanks, Mom. I bought a set in every color they have."

"That's so nice," she struggled to say.

I held back my laugh and returned her hug. There was something so comforting about her. I wasn't sure if it was the way she smelled like gardenias or how she always kept her curly gray hair in some type of cute headband. It was probably the way she held on to me like she planned on never letting go. I needed her stabilizing presence more than she would ever know.

"I hope you don't mind, but I ran into Noah yesterday and invited him to dinner."

I shrugged. "It's fine."

Mom looked up at me with her all-knowing green eyes, in the same shade I'd inherited. "I know that tone. Ignoring Noah is like tossing the baby out with the bathwater." She tapped my nose. "He's not guilty by association, you know."

I knew that but having him here felt like old times. Good times I didn't want to remember. Noah and Ben used to come here all the time. A basketball game always happened, unless the court was full of snow. Add in hot tubbing, s'mores at the firepit, laughing and talking all night long, snowball fights in the winter, and swimming at the lake in the summer. It was, in a word, perfect. We were like the three musketeers. Back when Ben thought I was everything he ever wanted. That all changed after we got married. And for some reason, my relationship with Noah changed too. He became more distant, until the end. It was almost as if he knew it was over for Ben and me. I had even accused him of knowing about Ben's affair and covering for him. I'll never forget the look he'd given me. It was as if I'd sucker punched him. He couldn't believe I would accuse him of such a thing. To this day, I still felt bad about it.

Speaking of the nonguilty party, he walked over with two of my minions wrapped around his legs, squealing like they were on a ride at Disneyland. He'd always had a way with kids. In fact, my nieces and nephews had always gravitated toward him more than Ben. His own nephews, Jaxon and Liam, worshipped the ground he walked on.

"Hello, Mrs. J." Noah kissed my mom's cheek, and I'm pretty sure her laugh-lined face blushed.

"You have always been a charmer." She pinched his cheek before swooping down like a woman much younger than her age and retrieving Aubrey and Melody. "Come help Nana frost some cupcakes."

Their little eyes lit up. Mom did make the best cupcakes. She believed there was no such thing as too much butter. It had served us all well.

"Wait, I want to give them the T-shirts I bought them." I grabbed my bag and pulled out all seventeen shirts.

Noah, without asking, grabbed one and held it up. "I love my BAE." He raised his brows at me before smirking.

I snatched it back from him. "Don't make fun of them."

"I wasn't. I was just wondering where I could get one."

"Sure, you were. Why would you want one?"

"Well, I think that's obvious," Mom whispered to herself before flitting off with a little kick in her heels.

I stared after my mom. "What is that supposed to mean?"

Noah sighed. "Someday I'll explain it to you."

"What is there to explain?" I was getting more and more confused.

He grimaced and walked off toward the kitchen.

I watched him go, feeling as if I were missing something important. Story of my life.

Four

HEY, EX-FILERS, I should have mentioned this in my earlier post, but October is a great time to start booking your travel plans to escape the holidays. I know you will have family and friends who may look down on this and tell you that running away isn't the answer. Just tell them that you aren't running away, you're making a tactical withdrawal for your mental health. That's pretty hard to argue with. Just be warned that your mother will probably put up some pretty tough arguments. Also, a word of caution: Being on vacation lowers inhibitions, and you may find yourself faced with a beautiful stranger who is only looking for a fling. But pseudo relationships are just that: fake. If anything, relationships should be the most real thing we ever have. And no matter what anyone ever tells you, there is nothing casual about sex. Don't be someone's convenient hookup. You deserve better.

Lots of love,

Cami

P.S. Check out my pinned post for the best online places to book your travel plans. If you can't travel this year, see my highlights for one hundred excuses to skip holiday gatherings. You can thank me later.

Between bites, I scripted out my post under the table while the chaos of the Jenkins family dinner swirled around me like a hurricane. I had gotten good at texting without looking. It had helped me over the last few years while my family would discuss the holidays and use the C-word, like they were now. (My family, unlike my best friend, would not cater to my sick game.) My brothers and sisters-in-law were all talking over each other around the massive, rustic-wood table that sat sixteen in my parents' large eat-in kitchen with an island the size of Manhattan. Most of my nieces and nephews were seated around the island, arguing, and telling potty-mouthed jokes that their parents were conveniently ignoring.

It all worked in my favor. Between the chaos and my family basically ignoring me, knowing I would only say no to being included in all their plans, I could pretend to listen, all while tuning them out. It was rude, I will admit to it, but it was torture to hear them talk about all the things I used to do with Ben. Things I used to love to do. Pumpkin picking at Peterson's Pumpkin Patch, the Apple Festival, where we would eat apple pie until we were sick, the corn maze we loved to get lost and make out in until I couldn't catch my breath. That was just in October. In November there were all the craft fairs where I would get a jump on my C shopping, the Aspen Lake Thanksgiving parade, and the Turkey Trot 5K we would run every year. Then came December in all its majesty. Sleigh rides in Holly Park, the lighting of the tree in town square, the winter wine walk, ice skating, drives down Candy Cane Lane to look at the lights, and riding the Polar Express. Not to mention picking out the perfect tree at the Aspen Lake Tree Farm the day after Thanksgiving. I was getting hives and shortness of breath thinking of it all. Too many good memories that were all a lie.

I closed my eyes and tried to think happy thoughts. I thought of the great pictures I had captured on my phone of all my minions wearing their shirts, which most of them had already gotten spaghetti sauce on. My heart rate started coming down thinking of their silly faces. But then Noah, who had insisted on sitting next to me during dinner, squeezed my knee. My eyes popped open. I was so startled that I fumbled my phone, but caught it before it dropped on the hardwood floor. I wasn't used to a man's touch, even a friendly one.

"Are you okay? You're shaking."

I hadn't noticed that. I took a deep breath in and let a cleansing one out. "I'm good." I slid my phone into my hoodie pocket. I would publish my post later.

"Why don't I believe you?" He began rubbing my knee.

I wasn't sure how to feel about that. I mean, it felt nice, but it was weird. He was getting touchy-feely in his old age. I thought of him more as a high-five kind of guy. Perhaps this woman he wanted to marry was helping him get in touch with his feminine side. This wasn't a good time for me to have him try to be so in tune. Didn't he know that I was trying to avoid my feelings? At least most of the big ones. And admittedly, he was stoking some strange long-repressed urges. Urges I swore to never have again.

I placed my hand over his and cleared my throat, nonverbally communicating that he needed to stop. I was on a no-womanly-urges kind of diet. Besides, Noah and I were strictly friends. Hardly even that lately. It felt almost dirty that his touch was making me feel a little tingly. "Really, I'm fine." I popped my hand off his, which I noticed was quite smooth considering he worked in construction.

He didn't get the hint and his hand stayed firmly in place.

I leaned toward him and whispered, "Why are you touching me?"

His baby blues danced with amusement. "Someone recently told me that when you touch someone, it tells them they're safe and they can trust you."

For a second, I thought that was super sweet. Noah had always had this safe presence to him. But … "Let me guess—you got this advice from the poor woman you recently dumped? By the way, I'm done editing your recent photos. If I'd known you were going to be here today, I would have saved you a trip and brought your flash drive." He refused to just let me email his pictures to him.

He slapped a hand across his chest. "Why do you assume I broke up with her?"

"Uh, because you're wearing your photo shoot outfit. Were you having your pictures taken with a new girlfriend today?"

The uptick of the corners of his lips said it all.

I turned from him. "I can't believe you have a new girlfriend already and you're taking pictures with her. Is this your new hobby or something?"

He grabbed a piece of french bread from his plate. "Why does it bother you so much?"

I reached for my grape juice, because my mom wouldn't let us drink wine in front of the kids, while I thought about why it bothered me. I guess it boiled down to . . . "I thought you were better than that."

His face fell and a piece of bread came tumbling out of his mouth.

My brother Seth, sitting on Noah's other side, patted his back. "You all right there, man? Even my three-year-old can keep her food in her mouth."

"It's your sister's fault."

Before I could defend myself, my mom, with her bat ears, who sat at the head of the table near Dad, wagged her finger at me. "Be nice to our guest."

"Yeah, be nice to me." Noah nudged me, laughing.

I ignored him and reached for my phone, keeping it hidden under the table. I lowered my head and read through my post one more time before clicking publish.

Noah's phone dinged and he gave me an impish grin. "Posting at the dinner table?"

"How do you know?"

He pulled his phone out of his pocket. "I get a notification every time you post."

"Why did you sign up for my notifications?"

"Because you're hilarious." He paused. "And kind. The way you personally respond to some of your followers makes me proud to be your friend."

I blushed and bit my lip, so surprised he followed me so closely online. More surprised he still wanted to be my friend. "I'm not that kind anymore." I used to be—like, so nice people hated me for it. So nice I had even fangirled over Claudia Cann the first time I met her, before I knew she was sleeping with my husband. But Ben broke something in me. I vowed never to be blindsided like that again. And that meant no more Miss Nice Girl. Sure, I tried to be there for my Ex-Filers, giving them a virtual shoulder to cry on, and I wanted to be a good aunt, sister, and daughter. And I would give Mara a kidney if she needed one. But I didn't go out of my way for people like I used to. I was pretty dang snarky in real life and online.

He leaned in close. His breath smelled too good for just having eaten garlic. How did he get it to smell like spearmint? I swore, ridiculously gorgeous people knew some kind of magic us normal people of the world had been denied access to.

"There are seventeen kids here wearing *I LOVE MY BAE* shirts, and a million people online who would disagree with you. I disagree with you." He flashed me his charming grin.

Unfortunately, not even I was completely immune to his charm. His kindness warmed my frozen heart just a degree or two. "You might think differently after you read what I just posted."

"I won't. But . . . I do want to know if you really burp songs on demand."

"Of course, you had to read that post." I laughed. "The answer is no, unless you're a potential suitor my mom has sprung on me, which you're not."

He pressed his lips together for a moment. "Let's pretend I am. I want to request a song."

"I don't think so. It makes the minions go crazy, and my mom says she loses a bit of her soul when she hears me do that. Besides, you already know I can burp just about any song. In fact, you once tried to out burp me." A thought popped into my head about a summer night long ago when a huge group of us went camping. Every guy at that campout had tried to outdo me. I was all of twenty and so proud of myself. And happy. Ridiculously happy. Ben and I had just started dating. He and Noah had told me I was the coolest girl they had ever known after they got a taste of my disgusting skill. Obviously, Ben changed his mind.

Yeah, that still hurt.

I scooted my chair back and grabbed my plate and glass before heading toward the kitchen, doing my best to run away from my memories. I hated when they caught me so off guard like that. It was why I had stayed away from Noah. Hot shame consumed me. I hated myself for being so stupid and taken in by his best friend. I rushed to the kitchen to rinse my dirty dishes in the sink.

My minions started chanting my name, "Aunt Cami! Aunt Cami!"

Normally I would have done something irreverent like made

them sing a loud chorus of "Who Let the Dogs Out" to annoy their parents. Instead, I gave them all a weak smile while trying to calm myself. It didn't help when I got to the sink and turned to see Noah looking between me and my dad, like he was torn about what to do. He didn't need to do anything. Yet, Dad waved him down and mouthed something to him that I couldn't make out. Next thing I knew, Dad was on his way over to me. The minions' eyes all lit up. To them Grandpa meant pockets full of cash and candy that he loved to dole out. To the minions' utmost dismay, he only gave a few pats on the head before nodding his head to the side, indicating he wanted me to follow him.

It made me feel even more pathetic. It didn't help that all eyes now seemed to be on me. I knew what they were all thinking—she's finally going to crack. She isn't as happy as she pretends to be. News flash—they were right. But I could never be so wrong again.

Dad wrapped an arm around my shoulder and led me to his office, which had the perfect view of Aspen Lake. When we entered, the evening sun was filtering into the large windows, making the white walls shine more brightly. Dad veered us toward the wall covered in family pictures in an artsy sort of way. Mom loved the rustic look, and each frame was in a different hue of her beloved wood. The large wall was a history of the Jenkins family from weddings, births, graduations, and all the things in between. Dad planted us firmly in front of my college graduation picture. Dad had caught the perfect moment of me jumping in the air in my blue gown, tossing my cap up. The photo screamed elation.

I reached out to touch that girl. That girl believed the world was her oyster and she was going to eat it up. I had everything planned: engagement, marriage, becoming a world-renowned photographer, all while having four kids and running my own photography business. And of course, I was going to be a super wife and mom, just like my own mother. My children were all going to be adorable and have the best of Ben and me. I dropped my hand and rubbed my flat stomach. There was an emptiness there that never seemed to go away.

Dad rested his hands on my shoulders. His hands always brought comfort—even in my darkest days. Most people would find him quite distinguished, with his silver hair and athletic build, including my mother, who loved to call him her hunk, a hunk of burning love—Kellan got his Elvis obsession from Mom. Yet, no matter how handsome or successful my father was, the best part about him was that he was a family man first. We all knew it and loved him for it. "This is my favorite picture of you."

"You always liked my shorter hair." I ran my fingers through my long beachy waves. Ben wanted it long. Said it was more attractive that way. After we were married, he'd made me question so much about myself.

Dad kissed my head. "Honey, it has nothing to do with your hair."

"Proud of how much air I got," I teased.

Dad chuckled. "That was impressive. I've always said you have the best jump shot in the family. But that's not what I'm talking about either. That young woman"—dad pointed at the photo—"never let anything or anyone get in the way of her dreams."

I squirmed inside, knowing what he was getting at. "Maybe she got new dreams."

"Perhaps. Which would be fine, if that's what she really wanted."

I swallowed hard. "What if she just learned they never come true?"

Dad spun me so I came face-to-face with his kind but concerned brown eyes. "Honey, you know that's not true. You are a real live dream come to life for your mom and me."

Wow. That was the most beautiful thing anyone had ever said to me. My eyes welled with tears. Of course, I had to add some humor to the moment. "Well, after all those boys—"

"It had nothing to do with you being a girl," he interrupted. "It has everything to do with the kind of person you've become. You added the sparkle."

"I don't feel very sparkly."

"What are you going to do about that?" Dad asked matter-of-factly.

"Uh . . ." Well, I didn't know. I wasn't sure if it was wise for me to do anything. Sparks could catch fire and I had already been burned.

"Let me give you some advice," Dad jumped in to save me from my stupor of thought. “Those who are fearless aren’t that way because they’ve never been scared. It’s because they’ve stood in the face of fear and didn’t back down. I’ve never known you to back down. I would hate to see you start now.”

I took a step back. “I’m not,” I stuttered, not really enjoying this heart-to-heart. Holly Black was once quoted as saying, *“The truth is messy. It’s raw and uncomfortable. You can’t blame people for preferring lies.”* I wouldn’t mind a lie or two right now. One like, “Cami, you handled your divorce like a rock star. And your avoidance of the holidays is simply amazing.”

Dad sighed and tapped my nose. “Don’t let Ben,” he growled his name, “steal another thing from you. Find your sparkle again.”

I didn’t know what to say, and thankfully, I didn’t have to respond.

Noah popped his head in. “Sorry to interrupt.”

Dad gave him the widest of smiles. “You’re not. In fact, this is perfect timing. Cami’s looking for something, and maybe you can help her find it.”

“I’d love to,” Noah said without any hesitation, not knowing that what was lost might never be found—and even if it could be found, he probably wasn’t the right person for the job, seeing as his best friend stole my sparkle in the first place.

“Don’t worry about it,” I was quick to say.

Dad waved Noah in anyway. “I’ll leave you two alone. You can start planning your recovery efforts.” He gave me a wink before walking off.

I opened my mouth to stop him, but it was of no use. He was out of the room in a flash, and Noah zipped in. They high-fived each other in passing. Weird.

Noah came to stand next to me, and he gave me a good once-over in my sweats. I looked like a slob compared to him. Yet, I didn’t see any signs of disgust in his features. “What do you need help finding?”

“Nothing. My dad misspoke.”

“Are you sure?”

“No,” I whispered the messy truth, but recovered quickly. “I mean, yes.”

He tilted his head. "Cams, I'm sorry if I did or said something at dinner that upset you. I didn't realize burping a song was such a sensitive topic, especially after your post today."

I turned and stared at the picture of me. That girl with her edgy layered haircut, that fell just below her chin, wouldn't have been bothered. She would have taken it in stride. But that girl didn't know the heartache that I knew. I thought of my dad's words about how fearless people had been scared but overcome the scary stuff. I wasn't sure if I wanted to. I mostly enjoyed my nice, safe cocoon of sarcasm and obliterating exes in photos. But there were things I missed—Noah's friendship included.

"It's just, well . . . it's hard to be around you, Noah, and not think about him." I was honest.

He let out a heavy sigh. "How do we change that?"

I shrugged; not sure it was possible.

"Maybe if you burped me a song, that would help." He nudged me.

I couldn't help but smile. "I doubt it; besides, your favorite song, if I remember correctly, is that country ballad "Stealing Cinderella" that's not exactly easy to burp." I had always wondered why he loved that song so much. Especially for a man I thought was never going to settle down with his own Cinderella.

His enigmatic blue eyes twinkled. "I've had a new favorite for a while now."

"What's that?" I was always curious about his taste in music and had even teased him about it. While he loved classic rock, he also had this sweet spot for sappy country songs.

He stepped closer until we were inches apart as if he were going to share some top-secret government intel with me.

My head drifted up and caught his intense gaze. For the last ten years I'd heard women say that Noah Cullen, with one look, could steal your heart and soul. I had never believed it, but for half a second, I understood what they meant. It freaked me out so much, I stepped back, blinking a million times a minute. I shouldn't have thoughts like that about Noah. About any man for that matter. I was living my best single life with Neville. Besides, Noah had his bride all picked out. I brushed it off as my mind playing tricks on me.

"You okay there?"

"Yeah. Yeah," I said, flustered. "Tell me which song." I needed a change of subject.

He leaned in. Apparently, he was bent on having this be a private conversation. He paused as if he were doing it for dramatic effect, before saying slowly and succinctly, "Can't Help Falling in Love with You."

"Of course it's some cheesy Elvis song," I laughed. "Kellan will be thrilled. By the way, you said it wrong. It's 'Can't Help Falling in Love.'"

His shoulders rose and fell dramatically. "No, Cams, I said it right."

"No, you didn't. Regardless, I think it's sweet—but don't tell anyone I said that, especially Mara." I shoved my hands in my hoodie pocket. "This mystery woman must have some hold on you."

He ran a hand through his hair. "You have no idea."

"Well, not that I'm a relationship expert, obviously, but maybe you should stop doing photo shoots with your flavor of the month—or are we up to a week now?" I admonished him.

He gave me a crooked smile. "I'm going to do as many photo shoots as I need to."

"Need?"

"Yep, each photo shoot brings me closer to the woman I love."

I rolled my eyes. "Whatever you say." I started to walk off in search of those cupcakes my mom had made.

Noah unexpectedly grabbed my hand. "Cami, wait."

I looked down at our hands. That strange comfort filled me again.

He pulled me closer before pointing at my graduation picture. "If you need help finding that woman, just let me know." He dropped my hand and strode off like he hadn't just blown my mind. How did he know that's what I had lost? I took another long look at the woman I was seven years ago. I loved her. Not to say I didn't love myself now, but I felt as if part of me were missing. The parts of me I loved the most but made me the most vulnerable. And vulnerability wasn't something I was sure I could ever afford again.

Five

GOOD MORNING, EX-FILERS, I hope you made it through another weekend. Make sure to mark yourself safe and single in the comments. For all of you who succumbed to coupledom, I'll never judge. Believe me, I get it. We seem hardwired with the desire to cuddle. Just remember cuddling is a gateway drug. It starts out all innocent and then the next thing you know, BAM! You're wedding cake tasting. And while some may pass through the gates unharmed or even better for it, there are just as many, or more, who need a twelve-step program to recover. Or worse, their souls die a painful death. It's why I can't caution you enough to stay safe out there. Please. Just say no.

If you do ever find yourself trapped behind that gate, please don't be afraid to reach out for help. I'm here for you.

Lots of love,

Cami

I internally sighed, wishing so badly I would have been brave enough to even acknowledge that all wasn't well in my marriage. Ben had confused me so much, but I'd kept plowing through. Convincing myself over and over again that he was just having a bad day or he was stressed. Or worse, I really just needed to be better, then I would be worthy of his love. If ever I did bring up my concerns to him, he would turn on the charm with expensive nights out and weekend getaways. He would say things like, *You're the best thing that has ever happened to me.* Or, *From the first moment I saw you, I knew my life would never be the same.* He really got me with, *Make a baby with me. I want a girl just like you.*

But that same mouth would criticize my choice of clothes and carefree attitude, even my overexuberance for the holidays. Some days I could never please him, no matter how hard I'd tried. That's because someone else was pleasing him. Judging by the scene I'd come across of them under the tree, she was really, really pleasing him. Let's just say, Claudia can and Claudia did. I didn't even know a body could bend like that. Some vomit rose in my throat just thinking about it. If I could have sprayed Lysol in my eyes that night, I would have.

It was the past. And I had survived. I clicked publish and sat back in the waiting room chair of the fancy schmancy hair salon I'd been going to since high school. My mom said there were three things in life you should never skimp on: shoes, hair, and toilet paper. We were a Charmin family, all the way, baby. No one-ply for us. We were also an Andrew family. Andrew Hanson, that is. He's the best stylist around and does all our hair, even my dad's. There were so many of us now that Andrew had dedicated his retirement account to us.

The thing about Andrew is, he's cut and dry, no pun intended. You got the style he thought worked best for you and your hair. It was his way or the highway. Well, he'd made one exception—me. I knew he didn't like my hair long. But it was like he knew why I had grown it out. And that I hadn't needed another man to tell me I wasn't enough.

Amid the calming atmosphere that smelled of peppermint and citrus, I thought a lot about that girl in the photo on my dad's wall. That girl didn't need anyone to tell her she was worth something. She didn't care what people thought about her hair because she was happy and comfortable with herself. It had never dawned on her that she would ever be anything else. Just like it had never crossed her mind or her heart that Ben would ever be anything but happy and comfortable with her. It was sad how much I had let him wreck my self-esteem. Even sadder was that I was still letting him affect me.

My phone buzzed, letting me know I had a message. I was grateful for the distraction. As much as I missed that girl, I got anxious when I thought about trying to find her. I was afraid that girl would want to succumb to snuggling, and we all knew what snuggling led to. How could I ever trust another man after being so blindsided? I began hyperventilating just thinking about endangering myself in such a way again. I could almost hear my old self laugh at me for being such a scaredy-cat. And taunt me with what I was missing out on. Believe me, I knew. Unfortunately, my body still craved the touch of a man. Kisses to curl my toes and tingle my spine. Gentle caresses and fevered touches. But what I missed most was a hand to hold. Not just any hand—a hand that said, "I have you and I'll never let you go." I wasn't sure there was such a hand. At least not for me.

Phone. I needed to look at my phone. I pressed the home button and noticed the scrapes on my hands. Last night my brothers wanted to get in a basketball game before we all went home, a little three-on-three action. Except Kellan declined, citing that the cold air was bad for his singing voice. Noah had stepped in, and though we were on opposite teams, he got onto my brother Ashton for knocking me down. My brothers had never gone easy on me because I was a girl. Sure, they'd beat up any boy who had tried to mess with me, but they never treated me like a princess. Which I appreciated. It made me a better ballplayer, and once upon a time I thought it made me good at reading boys and men. That was a critical error on my part. Just like me going up against Ashton last night, the biggest and by far the strongest of my brothers. I had tried faking to the right hoping he would go for it, giving me time to make a jump shot, but he was, admittedly, the best player out of all the siblings. He'd blocked my shot and used too much force, knocking my butt to the cement. My hands had tried their best to lessen the impact. They were rewarded with searing pain for their effort.

While nursing my pride and looking at my scraped and bloodied hands, Noah had gotten in Ashton's face, poking his chest and telling him to be more careful. We all stood, shocked by how worked up he was about it, accusing Ashton of being a Neanderthal and making him apologize. This woman of Noah's was having some impact on him. I'd only ever seen him get that worked up once before. It was a memory I didn't wish to remember, but it was emblazoned on my brain like a cattle brand, painful and permanent. I'd had to run into the office a couple of months after *the incident*. Ben and I were already well into divorce proceedings. I had done everything I could at the time to stay away from him. But unbeknownst to me, Ben was at the office, and Noah too, filing some invoices for some contracting work he had done. I'd tried to slip out without Ben noticing me, but he'd cornered me. He'd had the audacity to tell me that I had blown things out of proportion, and I was only embarrassing myself by helping other people remove exes from their photos. He'd said it made me look bitter and desperate. He was right—I was bitter, and desperate to know why he'd broken his promise to love me forever in the most humiliating way possible. I had no words for him that day. I was only able to stand there and blink back the tears, trying to see any trace of the man I loved. He was nowhere to be found, and that killed me more than anything. Noah came to the rescue that day. I'd never seen him so furious. He'd yelled at Ben and told him to shut the hell up and leave me alone. Ben didn't take too kindly to it—and it had almost come to blows. My dad had to intervene.

I never did tell Noah how much that meant to me. I knew that had caused a rift between him and Ben that took a long while to repair, per Mara's intel. But Ben and Noah were more than friends. They were brothers from another mother, as they would say. It was why I had to let Noah go. Except apparently, Noah had other plans for our friendship. Even though I knew it was only a matter of time before he gave up on it. As soon as that woman of his gave into him, and I knew she would, because I'd never known Noah not to get the girl. As soon as she did, Noah would forget about me. It would be a relief and hurt at the same time. Despite my rebuffs, it meant a lot to me that he wasn't willing to let go. For now, that was.

I looked at my achy hands one more time. Noah was sure getting weird.

I focused on the message I received. It was from a client, Rachelle, who had turned into a friend. Poor woman was a glutton for punishment. She was a repeat client, not willing to give up on finding love. She believed her man was out there and that if you wanted the right results, you had to put in the effort, even if that meant dating all the yahoos. Not that she thought they were yahoos to begin with, but they all ended up in that category.

Rachelle: *Hey girl, Dave and I broke up over the weekend. I know what you're going to say and maybe you're right. I just need to give up on men. But I thought he was the one. I don't even have the heart to have you crop him out of any of the pictures we had taken together. Will it ever be my turn?*

My eyes began to water. I felt the heartbreak in each word. So much so, my snarky first instinct to tell her I told her so was obliterated. I bit my lip, trying to think how to respond. Thoughts of how sparkly old Cami would respond started popping up in my head. I rubbed my temples, trying to massage away her perkiness and cheerful outlook on life. Wow, was she a peppy optimist. Thankfully, Andrew saved me from myself when he appeared. Bless him.

"Hello, Cami. Are you ready?"

I popped up like a burning piece of toast. I was one step away from my brain catching on fire. Old Cami had me on overload.

Tell her love is worth waiting for, Miss Sparkly yelled in my head. *Maybe it will still work out. Don't give up hope.*

Oh, no, no, no. It would be best for her to give up hope. The poor girl had been through enough already.

I zoomed toward Andrew like that would help turn Miss Sparkly off. That was wishful thinking.

Your turn is just around the corner, I can feel it. Hang on, she continued.

You are not a psychic, Sparkles. Don't say things like that.

Hey, missy, I was here first. Why don't you let me drive for a while? I don't like the direction you've been going. We aren't any happier, now are we?

Great, the voices in my head were making it sound like I had multiple personality disorder.

Ladies, could we do this another time? I begged. *I just want to get my hair done. Thank you.*

Andrew tilted his head. He was sporting a new skater look, long on top, shaved on the sides. It worked for him. "Do you need a moment? You look bewildered."

That was one way to put it.

I plastered on a fake Cami smile. "I'm great."

He pressed his lips together as if he meant to disagree, but like always when it came to me as of late, he kept his correct opinions to himself. I kind of wished he wouldn't. I didn't want to be handled with kid gloves. I was fine. Really, I was. Maybe I wasn't all sparkles and sunshine, but I was a functioning, successful adult, making my own way in the world. That had to count for something.

Andrew turned and headed to his station toward the back of the salon. I quietly followed him, garnering a few stares, with one woman pointing me out to her stylist. I was semi-famous, or more like infamous, in Aspen Lake. Everyone knew of my situation. I'd made sure of it when I'd posted those pictures almost three years ago. I didn't regret it. But sometimes I wondered if perhaps I'd called Mara first, or gone to my parents' place and let the grief sink in before I'd acted, if I'd be here now. But those first few hours, I was filled with such rage, I didn't even cry. Because I feared once the tears came, they would never stop. I knew I would have to think about things I didn't want to face. I would have to tell Ben why I had come home early. That was too much for me to bear at the time, so I did the only thing I could think of in the moment, that is after I kicked him out. He'd never even said sorry. Instead, he'd blamed me for coming home early. I'd figured since it was so easy for him to discard me, I would return the favor and erase him from my life. If only removing him in photos would have translated into real life.

Without a word, I took a seat in Andrew's chair. We took a moment to stare at one another in the mirror before we commenced with our usual song and dance.

"How's your family?" he started.

"Good. How's Erin?"

His big, goofy, I-love-my-wife grin came out. It was one of the only times he smiled. "Perfect as usual."

"I'm glad to hear that. Tell her I said hello."

He nodded and asked, "How's Neville?"

"As neurotic as ever." I'd left him in his plush bed with his security blanket and favorite stuffed pineapple toy, and with his favorite show—*Beverly Hills, 90210*—playing in the background. I'm pretty sure he's team Dylan and Kelly, as he seemed more agitated when episodes of Dylan and Brenda together came on. Who knew my dog would be a hopeless romantic and love old reruns of the once-popular teen drama?

Andrew chuckled before giving me another hard stare in the mirror. We had come to the time of reckoning. Andrew gripped the back of the chair as if trying to keep his mouth shut. Not that many years ago, this scene would have never played out. He would have already gone to work or scooted off to mix color. Instead, he was searching my eyes, as if he were looking for me.

I took a good look at myself in the mirror, trying to find that woman too. Staring back at me, I saw who Ben wanted me to be. Long hair in waves, too skinny, afraid to be myself. It dawned on me how much I was still letting him control my life. His words and actions had made me doubt and doubt until I didn't even question their validity anymore.

Miss Sparkly started popping up in my head again. *I'm still here, please don't be afraid of me. I just want to help you.*

My eyes, now with a sheeny mist, drifted up and met Andrew's imploring eyes in the mirror. I bit my lip and internally warred with myself. Holding on to who I had become was a safe place where no one could hurt me . . . well, except myself. I realized that was exactly what I was doing by holding on to this version of me who Ben had created. I had cropped him out of my photos, but I needed to crop him out of the rest of my life. With a big, deep, courageous breath, I smiled at Andrew. "I was thinking that maybe you could work your magic today."

A smile a mile wide appeared on his bearded face. "It's about time." He patted my shoulders. "I'll be right back." He headed for the color room.

I fidgeted a bit in my seat, knowing I had taken a monumental step and was scared out of my mind. I caught a glimpse of myself in the mirror. Miss Sparkly said, *You got this.*

I pulled out my phone and clicked on Rachelle's message.

Me: *I'm so sorry. The only thing I can tell you is to trust yourself right now. Even if that means not giving up on Dave.*

I almost choked on my pride typing those words.

Rachelle must have been waiting for my reply, as she responded right back.

Rachelle: *Who are you, and what have you done with Cami?*

That was a good question. I was trying to figure that out.

Six

GOOD MORNING, EX-FILERS, are you looking to lose some weight? Let go of the dead weight of your exes' thoughts, manipulations, and expectations. It's the best weight you will ever lose. I promise. Use your past as a learning tool, not something you keep sabotaging your future with. I know it's easier said than done and it's a process, not a onetime event, but pick one thing today and like Elsa says, "Let it go."

Hit me up in the comments and let me know the weight you're losing today.

Lots of love,

Cami

I flipped down the visor in my car and looked at my new 'do. My hair was the best weight I had lost in a long time. I'd been obsessed with looking at it the last few days. Andrew had outdone himself with the textured, choppy bob he'd given me. He'd even added a few highlights around my face to brighten it up. I felt like a whole new person—a little like old Miss Sparkly. She was super giddy, to the point I had to temper her a bit, but that said, I'd teared up when Andrew had done his big reveal. He must have taken a hundred pictures of me to put on his social media pages. He was so happy I'd let him have his way, he didn't charge me for it. Of course, I had to swear that I wouldn't tell anyone about that. He didn't want it getting around that he was a nice guy. His secret was safe with me.

I ran my fingers through my shorter beach waves one more time before I had to do my job. I was on the California side of the lake today to take pictures for an upcoming listing. I didn't typically do anything on this side of the lake for obvious reasons—as in, Ben. Admittedly, I was getting a little rashy knowing this was Ben's turf. But the listing agent begged me to do the photos. Her famous clients loved my work, and they would only sign with our agency if I was part of the package. It was flattering, but they were friends of the friends of Penelope and Jackson Devan, a professional hockey player. I had done a lifestyle shoot for them back East. It was the shoot I had come home early from to surprise Ben with the best news. News that never got shared.

I had to stop thinking about it. Lose that weight once and for all. For now, I took some deep breaths in and out before grabbing my equipment bag. Miss Sparkly shouted in my head, *Go team go!* I smiled to myself thinking how dang perky I used to be. With that, I exited my vehicle and stood in front of the grand home that was made to look like a quaint cottage right out of a picturesque storybook. It was charming with its board-and-batten and gabled roof. Though it was large, it looked cozy. I was excited to get a peek inside. Meredith, the listing agent, was supposed to meet me there but hadn't arrived yet. I waited by my car, thinking she would show up any second so she could introduce me to the owners.

It was a bit nippy outside, and my denim jacket did a poor job of keeping me warm. Yet I didn't mind breathing in the crisp, clean autumn air. With it came memories of bonfires, homecoming, and the promise of hoodie and jeans weather. All things I relished while growing up.

My little reverie was obliterated when an Audi plastered with Claudia Cann's face all over it pulled up next to me. Suddenly, there was no air. I fell back against my car and held on to the door handle for support, not even able to revel in the fact that Ben's precious car looked absolutely ridiculous. Ben wasn't allowed to appear without my permission. If ever I had to see him, I needed at least three days of prep time to mentally prepare myself.

Miss Sparkly started chanting cheers the crowd used to shout during my high school basketball games. *Cam, Cam, bam, if she can't do it, no one can!* That cheer had led me to some magnificent shots. We are talking nothing but net. I began to picture Ben as my opponent, my biggest opponent—he and I had missed the biggest shot of our lives and he didn't even know it. He'd made me miss a lot of shots. *Why are you still letting him?* Miss Sparkly asked.

When he got out of his car looking like a fashion model, all debonair in his tailored charcoal suit and dress shirt with no tie, I was reminded exactly why. The first time I saw him and his pretty-boy face, with deep hazel eyes and perfectly styled, always clean cut hair, my world changed. Suddenly, there was this person, my person. I knew instantly I would marry him someday. He'd said he felt the same way too. But that changed for him, and for me it never had. I hadn't been able to reconcile how something so seemingly right could go so wrong. So, I had walked off the court, figuratively speaking. If you don't play the game, you can't lose. The problem was never being able to feel the triumph of conquering and winning.

You're not a loser, I was reminded by good old reliable snarky me. I was right. I'd kept myself safe. The thing about safe was that it didn't leave a lot of room for taking risks and nailing those beautiful shots. But it also didn't allow anyone to knock me down and steal the ball.

I really needed to quit having these existential-type conversations with myself. It was giving me a headache and Ben was headed my way. Oh, how I loathed him.

I made myself stand tall and let go of the door handle, even though I wanted nothing more than to crawl back into my 4Runner and run him over before leaving the scene of the crime.

Ben's eyes widened more and more the closer he got. He stopped dead in his tracks with this bewildered look, as if he didn't recognize me.

"What are you doing here?" I snapped, doing my best not to shake in my leather booties.

He shook his head as if coming out of a trance. "You cut your hair."

"Yeah." My insides squirmed while his voice echoed in my head about how I looked better with longer hair. How I needed to care more about my appearance. I ended up caring so much, I didn't even recognize myself. "What are you doing here?" I put some more force behind it this time. I was tired of carrying the weight of his expectations.

"You look—" He paused, rubbing the back of his neck. He always did that when he was nervous. What was he nervous about? Surely not criticizing me. He'd proven to be adept at that. "Meredith's daughter came down sick at school and she had to pick her up," he said, instead of finishing what I was sure was a critique.

I turned toward the car. I didn't sign up for this today. "Well, tell her to call me for a time we can reschedule." Why she hadn't called in the first place, I didn't know, but I was beyond annoyed.

"No can do, this needs to be done today. And I realize I'm not your favorite person, but I was the only one available to come."

I gripped the car handle like a vise. "'Favorite' assumes I have some preference for you, and I don't. You can call Will to do the photos for you." I opened the door with gusto.

He zoomed my way and had the audacity to shut it with his hand that I had memorized, right down to the scar that ran the length of his index finger. I closed my eyes, begging myself not to think about what a comfort it used to be to hold.

"Cami, please, you know this contract will fall through without you. Do you want to do that to Meredith? The company?" he appealed to my sense of honor. "Listings like this are gold for the firm."

My father would say the same thing, but he would never throw me in the path of my ex, whose cologne was making me want to retch. I stepped away from him. He used to smell like a dance in the rain. Now he smelled like rancid moss. It was so bad, I had to put my hand over my mouth.

"What's wrong?" he asked.

I had a long list of what was wrong with him, but I stated the most pressing one at that moment. "Your cologne."

His angular cheeks burned bright red before he cleared his throat. "It's from one of Claudia's sponsors."

My hands clenched at the mention of her name, but old Cami appeared and quipped, "Eau de Outhouse?"

He looked stunned before blowing out a heavy breath. "Do you feel better now?" He used the condescending tone he'd picked up from Claudia. It was a familiar tune. I'd had to learn how to change the station. Life was better when I marched to the beat of my own drum. Sadly, I used to think he wanted to be in my band. Or even to be a sexy groupie. But I didn't need him cheering for me. I didn't need him at all.

"No, but I'm working on it." I threw open my car door. "Goodbye."

"Cams." He sounded like the old Ben I knew, and it startled me.

"You don't get to call me that anymore," I whispered, still shook.

He hung his head. "Cami, please. I apologize," he said, quite strangled as if he hadn't uttered those words in years. "This deal is a game changer for Meredith."

"Right," I scoffed. "It has nothing to do with your office and name."

His hazel eyes hit me like a sucker punch. "You know how it works, but Meredith needs this win." He sounded sincere. Not that I trusted his sincerity.

When I said nothing in return he added, "Her husband lost his job."

I pinched the bridge of my nose. Miss Sparkly wouldn't have had to think twice. She'd do it in a second to help someone out. Not only would she take the pictures, but she'd host a bake sale or something to benefit the family. She was already making a list of contacts in my head. Meanwhile, I had to think about it while I contemplated slamming Ben's hand in the car door. I didn't like that it didn't come naturally for me to want to help. Too many thoughts of how this would make Ben look bad were consuming me. I admit that the desire to nail him to the wall was almost overpowering. Almost . . . Somewhere inside, the real me still lived and breathed even though I had done my best to smother her. That woman with a fabulous new haircut reminded me that not doing it made this about Ben, and that only gave him more power over me. That was a no go.

I let out a cleansing breath. "Fine. I'll do it, but don't ever show up to another appointment again. I don't care if it's for the Queen of

England. Scratch that—if Queen Elizabeth wants me to take pictures of her castle, I would put up with you for a few hours."

Ben smiled his dashing smile that used to do all sorts of things to me—like convincing me to change my last name—but now it only made me grimace.

"The point is that I don't want to see you." I made sure to drive that home.

That wiped the smile off his face. "Fine," he growled as if I were depriving him of something he wanted, when everyone knew he didn't want me. I still had the images of how much he didn't want me burned into my brain. I shuddered from those thoughts and slammed the car door. Sadly, he had moved his hand before I could injure him.

I marched toward the house but had to stop and gawk at his Audi as if it were an accident on the highway. His once-pristine black car was now screaming with not one, but several headshots of Claudia and her slogan in big red letters—*If Claudia Cann, You Can.* As beautiful as she was, the car had gone from classy to cheap and cheesy. Almost as if she'd pranked him. But it was just like her to make every bit of Ben's life about her.

Ben stood nearby, and for a brief second I saw the fumes in his eyes. He obviously wasn't a happy camper about the car. So, I took the time to rub it in a bit. Miss Sparkly even agreed I should.

"How precious is this. I bet it's like the gift that just keeps on giving. She's a keeper." I almost gagged saying it, but I got so much satisfaction out of seeing his mouth drop and ears burn, like Andrew had taken a flat iron to them.

Ben shoved his hands in his pockets. "You, of all people, should know I hate it."

"Funny how that is. I knew everything about you, but it was never good enough." My stupid voice hitched. I stomped off. Mad at myself for showing how much his betrayal still hurt.

Ben followed, jogging to keep up with my long, swift legs. "Cami, wait."

I picked up the pace.

"Cami, please." He tugged on my sleeve.

I stopped and glowered, telling him with my eyes to not touch me. Ever.

He let go, but his eyes held me in place, searching and searching my own. "I forgot how beautiful you are," he blurted.

For a moment I was stunned into silence. He had no right to talk to me like that, especially after making me believe I was anything but beautiful. "You also forgot we were married."

If only I could forget that.

Seven

Hey, Ex-Filers, I wanted to thank you for all your "Letting Go" posts today. I'm not sure I've ever seen so many pictures of clothes on fire. I know I don't say this enough, but thank you. You have no idea how much I needed you all today. I should probably also mention that some of you should invest in a fire extinguisher. Stay safe out there.

Lots of love,

Cami

I clicked publish, a half-smile playing on my lips. Normally, it would be a wide grin thinking of all the pyrotechnics I was treated to today, but my run-in with Ben was still getting to me like a chigger that had burrowed deep in my skin, irritating me to no end. I purposefully didn't mention him by name in any of my posts. He would never have the satisfaction of knowing how much he could still vex me.

I trudged up the stairs of the private entrance to my condo, pretending I was stepping on Ben's big head each time my foot landed. He had no right to call me beautiful, or to tell the family whose home I had photographed today how talented I was. He talked about me like a proud husband. Like he used to. It didn't sit well with me. At. All. I let him know when we left to never talk about me like that again. He had no right to. He had the gall to throw this zinger at me: "I'm only trying to do the right thing."

What? I had no words. I still had none. I didn't even know what he meant, and I didn't bother to ask him. My only hope was to drown myself in cheesecake and forget about our encounter. But like the chiggers that needed major suffocation, I knew it wasn't going away anytime soon. Thankfully, Mara always knew how to make me feel better. I'd vented to her earlier. Before I could unlock my door, she texted.

Mara: *Big brother is now signed up for the newsletters for Cat Faeries and ten new politicians up for reelection. He'll be spammed for eternity. Bahahaha. Love you.*

Mara had me full-on smiling. Her revenge specialty was being able to find the worst email list possible for her victim and sign them up. She'd added Claudia to AARP's and at least a dozen cosmetic surgeons' lists. Claudia was incensed that people would think she was over fifty-five and would ever even think about surgically enhancing herself. If ever Mara heard her complain about it, she signed her up for another one. As Mara would say, *Not all heroes wear capes; some of us just have swift fingers and a wicked sense of humor.* She was a hero in my book.

Me: *You're the best. Love you, girl.*

I unlocked my door and walked in to find Neville waiting at the door for me, looking up at me as if I'd betrayed him, yet again, for leaving him behind. I would actually take him with me if he didn't require a sedative just to travel to the vet's office.

I knelt and he quickly forgave me when he scrambled to jump into my arms. I carried Neville and all my gear to the living room to dump my bag and laptop case on the couch before I took him out to do his business. Once I unloaded my stuff, I squeezed Neville and kissed his furry head. "Oh, buddy, I had a day today. Not only did I have a run-in with my ex, but I've been talking to myself more."

Neville burrowed into my chest as if I'd told him a scary story. It wasn't far from the truth. Admittedly, it frightened me that Ben could still get to me so much. It even had Miss Sparkly silenced for the moment. He'd hurt her the most. Ugh. There I went again talking as if I were two people. I was Cami. Just Cami.

I turned off *Beverly Hills, 90210* before I headed back toward the front door and grabbed Neville's leash from one of the hooks installed by the previous owner. They were convenient but an eyesore. I really needed to think about renovating this place.

Neville began to shake, knowing we were leaving the comfort of his sanctuary. I loved him, but I didn't love him enough to let him do his business on puppy pads and clean up after him. I made exceptions for blizzard conditions. This evening, though, it was clear and just a little nippy.

In the glow of twilight, we made our way down to the designated dog area of the complex. By we, I mean I carried Neville. While strolling across the parking lot, Noah pulled up in his big black truck that advertised his company on the doors—Cullen's Construction. I would add that it was tastefully done with no one's head or ridiculous slogans. Just contact info.

I stood on the sidewalk and watched him park. On Sunday he'd said he would let me know when he was available to pick up his flash drive. I hadn't heard a peep from him all week. Now wasn't the best time. After dealing with Ben, I was done for the day.

Before he turned his truck off, I swore I heard, "Can't Help Falling in Love." Wow. He must have it bad for this mystery woman. *That's adorable,* Miss Sparkly thought. Great. I thought she'd skedaddled for the day.

He hopped out of his truck, all smiles in his signature tight T-shirt and jeans to match. For a guy who worked as a general contractor and liked to do a lot of the work himself, he always seemed to be cleaned up when I saw him. He looked me up and down, landing on what I assumed was my hair. His smile grew even wider.

Have you ever noticed how attractive Noah is? Miss Sparkly asked.

"No," I responded to myself out loud. Then to make it more awkward, I disagreed with myself. "I mean, yes." Oh. My. Gosh. I was an idiot. Of course I noticed how attractive he was. Every woman did.

Noah paused and tilted his head. "Are you okay?"

The obvious answer was no. I was beginning to think I needed to seek help. "I'm fine. Uh, my dog needs to potty." Wow. Just wow. That made me sound even more intelligent. What was wrong with me?

Noah stepped on the sidewalk, chuckling. "Potty? I didn't think people started using that word until they had children."

"Yeah," I whispered. I almost did. Did that count? I walked off toward the dog area.

Noah followed. "Cams." He tugged on my hair. "I was just teasing. You can say *potty* if you want to. I won't judge you. Okay, I might just a little."

I nudged him with my hip. "Don't worry. I'm already judging myself."

"You seem out of sorts. What's wrong?"

I sighed and kept on walking. Annoyed with myself, and impressed with him that he could read me so well. "It's nothing," I lied.

"Cams," he said so sweetly. "It's not nothing. You can talk to me."

I stopped and looked into his entreating blue eyes. Not knowing what to say, or even if I should say it. He was Ben's best friend after all. And more than anything, I didn't want Ben to know he could still affect me. It was bad enough I had to know.

When I didn't say anything, Noah flipped some of my hair. "I love the hair. It's you."

I shrugged. "I don't know who I am anymore," fell out of my mouth before I could stop it. I blinked a hundred times. "Whoa. Just forget I said that. Please." I hustled off. Noah didn't need to know I was going through a mini crisis and hearing voices. My own voices, but still.

"No, ma'am. I think that needs to be addressed."

My brow quirked. "Who are you now? Oprah?"

"I was thinking more late-night talk show host, like Jimmy Fallon," he teased.

"Funny." I smiled. "Well, Jimmy, if you must know . . ." I paused for dramatic effect. "I've been thinking about getting a tattoo of Neville."

Without missing a beat, he responded, "Inquiring minds must know where."

"Wouldn't you like to know?" I wagged my brows, playing along. The comedic relief was doing wonders for my mood.

"I think we all would," he said sexily.

Wait. Did I just think sexily? *Well duh, darling, Noah is sexy. How come you're just noticing that?* Miss Sparkly was getting way too comfortable in my head. And not to be nitpicky but she had never really noticed either. She was too obsessed with Ben. Gah, there I went again thinking like I'm two different people. Okay, playtime was over. I couldn't think of Noah like that. No man really, but definitely not my ex-husband's best friend. The man whose exes I was constantly removing from pictures.

My face flushed and I got all flustered. "Um, you can wait in your truck and I'll bring your flash drive to you after Neville does his thing. You can Venmo me your payment."

Noah shook his head like I had given him whiplash with the change of subject. "I'm in no rush."

Well, I was. I began speed walking, jostling poor Neville.

"Why do I get the feeling you're trying to get rid of me?" Noah kept pace quite easily. His legs were longer than mine.

"Neville is very private. He won't even pee in front of other dogs."

Noah snort laughed.

"It's true. You wouldn't want to be the reason Neville embarrasses himself further when he has an accident, now would you?" Plus, I needed him to leave. Miss Sparkly was too observant of him and it was unnerving.

Noah rubbed Neville's head. "I don't think you give Neville . . . or yourself enough credit," he added poignantly.

I faltered and had to steady myself, not loving where this was going.

Noah unceremoniously took Neville out of my arms and held him up. "Come here, buddy, let's show Cams what you're made of."

"Excuse me, I think I know what my dog is made of." Anxiety meds and a carefully crafted routine.

"I beg to differ." Noah marched my dog over to the dedicated grassy area in the middle of the complex. It was a nice area, with big trees and even a few benches. Not that I ever sat on them. Neville was a get-in-and-get-out kind of dog. If he were a man, he would not be the type to take his phone into the bathroom and stay to watch a show or play a game. My brothers were notorious for this. It drove each one of my sisters-in-law nuts. Meanwhile they were holding toddlers on their laps and helping with math homework all while sitting on the toilet.

I stood stunned, not sure what to think about Noah's brazen ways. And I was getting ready to gloat when Neville proved me right. I only hoped my poor pooch didn't go into cardiac arrest. There was a big German shepherd near one of the large quaking aspen trees with leaves of gold. The kind of dog that would make Neville just roll over and play dead if he came near.

Noah whispered into Neville's ear before he set him down. I clasped my hands, anxious for my dog. I never thought I would be one of those dog parents, but there I was acting like my kindergartner was going off to school for the first time, waiting for him to run back to me and cling to my leg. I even squeaked a bit when the German shepherd made a move in Neville's direction. I went to rescue my baby, but Noah held up his hand as if to say, "Stand down, momma bear."

I bit my lip, uncomfortable on so many levels. I didn't want my baby to have an aneurysm, and Noah's take-charge attitude was attractive. Both of me recognized that. Not sure which was more uncomfortable—the fact I recognized it or that I was referring to myself as two people now.

Neville strayed a few inches from Noah, only to come right back to him and rub against his legs. Noah knelt and gently petted his head while telling him, "You got this, boy. The first steps are always the hardest. Maybe if you can show your mommy how grown up you are, she'll let you finally meet your girlfriend, Luna." Noah winked at me, and I rolled my eyes, albeit with a grin on my face.

Noah pointed at a big pine tree a few yards from them. "Go mark your territory, man."

"He doesn't pee with his leg up," I informed Noah.

Noah's brow raised. "Really? Maybe he needs to see how it's done." He started walking my baby over to the German shepherd, who was peeing on everything.

I put my hands up to my mouth, knowing this probably wasn't going to end well. "Noah." I scrunched my face.

"He's got this." Noah proceeded with confidence. I had always admired his sense of self. I mean, the man was in short sleeves and it was forty degrees outside. Meanwhile I stood shivering in my jacket.

As I predicted, Neville yelped and darted right back to Noah when the German shepherd and his owner began to approach them. I should mention that the owner was a beautiful siren with flowing red hair. It dawned on me that Noah was using my dog as bait to catch his next photo shoot victim. Ugh. Men.

I almost made a move to rescue my dog from unknowingly playing a part in Noah's scheme. Instead, I crossed my arms, annoyed, as I watched the scene in front of me unfold—hoping when my poor pup got the living daylights scared out of him, he'd bite Noah.

The gorgeous woman sized Noah up and dramatically flipped her gorgeous hair. It was like watching a cheesy Hallmark scene. Man, did I miss those shows. Mara would be appalled if she knew.

They were far enough away now that I couldn't hear what they were saying, so I made up my own conversation based on their body language.

Beautiful Woman: "Is that your dog?"

Noah: "No. See that psychotic lady over there who has conversations with herself? He belongs to her."

Beautiful Woman: "Oh, so is she your girlfriend?" She batted her eyes.

Noah: Laughed out loud. "Cami? We're friends. Hardly even that anymore. I just like to annoy her. In fact, it's becoming a new hobby of mine. But I have plenty of time to take you out and break your heart. Do you like photo shoots? I have the perfect spot and outfit already picked out."

Beautiful Woman: "Oh. My. Gosh. You're hilarious. I'm like photo shoot ready. Just name the time and place. And we'll see about you breaking my heart." She giggled loudly and pawed at him. "I have a good feeling about us."

Noah: Shrugged and knelt with my dog, making my poor Neville come face-to-face with the German shepherd, who was just as beautiful as his owner.

I tensed, knowing this probably wasn't going to end well. Though

I had to give props to Neville for even going to Noah. He'd never let anyone besides me hold him, much less venture off with him.

The beautiful woman knelt, too, and tried to pet my dog, but to Noah's credit, he seemed to let her know it wasn't a good idea. Yet, when it came to her dog, Noah inched my little guy forward and let the big dog sniff him all over. Poor Neville froze. I waited for him to have a heart attack and keel over. But . . . to my ever-loving surprise, Neville cautiously started to sniff him back. After a few minutes, Noah set Neville down, and Neville did his business female-dog style in front of an audience while the gorgeous redhead and Noah flirted. Or at least that's what I assumed, given how many times she touched him.

I kept waiting for Noah to pull out his phone and get her number. He never did, but I bet he just memorized it. Show-off. I wanted to yell out that he was already in love with someone else and to save her breath, but I knew it would do no good. Noah Cullen had a way with women, and this stranger would risk the heartbreak. Little did she know that she would soon become a victim to Photoshop.

After several minutes the beautiful people parted ways, but not before she glared at me like I was Satan or something. What had I done? I had no idea, so I just smiled and waved. That seemed to irk her more, judging by her curled lip. I shrugged it off. The redhead had nothing on Claudia's condescending treatment of me.

Meanwhile, a smug Noah walked my way while Neville pranced on his leash toward me, acting like a whole new dog. That was until someone slammed their car door nearby. Neville immediately hit the ground and played dead. That was my boy.

Noah chuckled and scooped him up. "Hey, boy, you did real good. We'll keep working on your issues. Before you know it, you'll be brave, just like your mommy *used* to be." Then Noah gave me a poignant look.

My jaw dropped. How dare he be so right. "I am brave," I whispered.

He stepped closer. "Prove it."

I blinked several times, not knowing what he wanted.

"Tell me what's wrong. Maybe I can help you fix it."

"I don't understand why you would want to."

He squeezed Neville tighter. "You're one of the best friends I've ever had, Cams. I miss you," he sheepishly admitted.

Oh. Wow. That was sweet. Honestly, I missed him too, but it was complicated.

"I know it's hard for you to be around me because of Ben," he growled his name, "but the woman I used to know wouldn't let that get in her way."

Yeah, well, Miss Sparkly wasn't as brave as he thought she was. "I saw Ben today," I admitted.

Noah's jaw tightened while he cleared his throat. "Did he do something to you?" He got all protective like my big brothers.

I shoved my hands into my pockets. "Other than telling me I'm beautiful and amazingly talented, no."

"Damn him," Noah snarled. "He has no right to talk to you like that."

I didn't expect Noah to be so incensed by his best friend's actions, but I couldn't agree more. "Right? Can you believe him?" I was still fired up about it.

His ears pinked. "Honestly, it doesn't surprise me."

I tilted my head. "Why?"

He pressed his lips together as if he didn't want to say, but eventually relented. "I don't think he's exactly happy."

"Please, Claudia can do anything. And I mean anything. I saw her in action." I grabbed my stomach while it roiled.

"Claudia," he hissed her name, "is a fake. I think Ben is beginning to see that."

I wasn't sure if I believed that. "I don't care what Ben does, as long as he leaves me alone." My voice went way too pitchy.

Noah carefully held Neville in one arm while using his free hand to rub my arm. "Cams, I didn't mean to upset you."

"You didn't."

"You're a liar." He grinned. "Let me make amends by taking you to dinner. To make you feel better, you can bare your soul to me over barbecue chicken pizza and red cream soda."

Two of my favorites. I was touched he still remembered, but . . . "You don't have to do that."

"What are friends for?" He gave me his most charming smile.

"Noah, it's . . . I mean, you—"

"Cams," he cut me off, "I know what you're going to say. It's hard to be around me because of Ben. But the only way to get over hard things is to face them, just like Neville did today. Maybe . . . and this is just a guess, but perhaps you've been the one holding Neville—and yourself—back."

My brow hit my hairline while I shifted uncomfortably. He really was turning into Oprah. I didn't like it. The truth cut like a knife.

When I didn't answer, he said, "Sometimes you have to fight for what you want. Like I said on Sunday, if you want to find the woman in the picture, I'll jump in the ring and go as many rounds as it takes."

I blinked back the tears stinging my eyes. He had no idea what that meant to me, but the truth was, I was afraid of stepping into the ring. Fighting meant I could get hurt. *You never really stopped hurting*, Miss Sparkly reminded me. *Myself* was really getting on my nerves with all her truth bombs. But she was right. I mean, I was right.

Noah stepped closer; his eyes dared me to take him up on his offer. He held up Neville. "Do it for your dog." He made me laugh.

"Well . . . I am hungry."

"I can fix that."

Miss Sparkly popped into my head with an unexpected question. *What else do you think he could fix?*

How would I know?

I think maybe we should find out.

I think you should quit talking now.

I think you're afraid to find out.

I think you're right.

Eight

HEY, EX-FILERS, SORRY for all the posts today, but I have a serious question: What's everyone wearing to the Halloween Bash? I still need to pick out my costume. I'm feeling some witchy vibes. Drop me some ideas.

Lots of love,

Cami

I paced the floor with Neville, waiting for Noah to return. We couldn't go out to eat because Neville had apparently had too much excitement for one day and when I tried to leave him, he'd made the most gut-wrenching sound I'd ever heard and tried to scramble up my legs. It would appear we both had some major issues. Trusting in ourselves being one of them. Or maybe Neville heard voices too.

Noah was kind enough to go get the food. Actually, Noah was being more than kind. I was trying not to be suspicious about it, but you know, trust issues. Seeing your husband fornicating under your beloved tree kind of does that to you. I wasn't sure what Noah would want from me, other than free ex-cropping services. That was a no go, though I should probably give him a frequent flier discount or something for as often as he used me. Or I should up my prices to deter him. Seriously, he was getting ridiculous about it. But I couldn't think too ill of him. He was being awfully kind. Even if he was calling me out.

Believe me, plenty before him had tried to point out the error of my ways, but no one had ever said they would fight the battle with me. Not even Mara. But that was because Mara championed this new me. Which was exactly what I needed after the divorce. Only she truly knew what I had lost. It was more than just me. Her acceptance of who emerged out of the ashes was a lifeline, and I adored her for it. However, I wasn't exactly feeling comfortable in this new skin anymore. Yet I was afraid to shed it. I didn't know what that meant for me. I mean, I built a brand around this tough girl. I had people counting on my snark. Could you be snarky and sparkly at the same time? I didn't know. And I was absolutely terrified of what would be on the other side if I peeled the layers back. Exposed skin could get burned.

Noah knocked, forcing me out of my head.

I headed toward the door, thinking it had been a long time since I'd had anyone but Mara over. You know, other than Noah, but I never invited him, he just showed up. I used to be such a social butterfly, as my mom would call it. When I was growing up, I think I had a slumber party every weekend. And in college if I'd heard about a party, I was there. Even when I was with Ben, we did a lot of entertaining. That was until he started making me feel so self-conscious.

I opened the door to find a smiling Noah, with pizza and a six-pack of my favorite soda in hand.

"Look at that, I only had to knock once. See how easy it was to answer," he taunted me.

"You are bearing my dinner."

"So, food is the key?"

"It couldn't hurt," I teased.

"I'll keep that in mind." He walked in. My place instantly smelled like heaven with a side of garlic bread.

I carefully set Neville down and relieved Noah of the soda. "Thanks for picking up the food. I can Venmo you for half."

Noah's brow scrunched as if I'd offended him. "It's my treat."

"Okay. Next time, though, it's my treat," I said before I thought about what I was saying.

Noah's eyes danced. "So, what I'm hearing is this is going to be a regular thing between us from now on."

I set the soda on my counter. "Uh, I don't remember agreeing to that."

"Why don't we agree on it now." He set the pizza next to the soda.

"Why don't we see how tonight goes."

"Then it's a sure thing. You're going to see I'm the best friend you've ever had."

"Mara will fight you for saying that, and just so you know, she fights dirty."

Noah waved his hand in the air. "I can take her."

I walked around him and opened the cupboard near the stove to get some plates. "That won't be necessary. Mara's place as my best friend is secure. Besides, we all know how busy you are with your photo shoots." I smirked. "Is the redhead with the German shepherd going to be your new victim, I mean girlfriend?"

Noah took the plates from me, wearing a look of consternation. "You know, someday you're going to feel bad for teasing me about my so-called photo shoots."

"And why is that?"

"Because I have noble intentions."

I busted out laughing. "Right. I'm sure this mystery woman you're in love with will really appreciate you dating every woman in Nevada for her. That's so romantic."

"It is, actually." He pulled no punches.

I narrowed my skeptical eyes at him. "How do you figure?"

"If you want to know my secrets, we'll have to become best friends first."

I rolled my eyes. "Would you like a glass with some ice?"

"You're avoiding my offer."

"Noah," I whispered. "You're Ben's best friend."

He set down the plates and placed his hands on my shoulders, making sure to squarely look me in the eye. "Cams, once upon a time, I was one of your best friends too. Don't you remember?"

At least a dozen good memories popped in my head. From fun camping and beach trips to tender moments, like when he and Ben drove all day and all night to see me play in the final basketball game of my college career. They even made signs that said, *Cami J., Shoot Three for Me* and *Cami's Number One Fans.* I kept those posters for a long time. I burned them in my fireplace not long after moving into my condo.

"Sometimes I wish I could forget. It was the best time of my life, but I don't even know if it was real."

His eyes widened.

Miss Sparkly interjected, *I don't think we have properly admired his ice-blue peepers. A girl could get lost in them.*

Not us, I had to remind her. I mean me. Oy vey, I was giving myself a headache.

His masculine hands gently squeezed my shoulders. "I promise you, every bit of it was real."

"Then why did Ben cheat and leave?" I extricated myself before Miss Sparkly had any more unhelpful insights. And I didn't want to hear the reasons why out loud. Believe me, all you had to do was look at Claudia to know why. Sometimes I wondered if their affair was going on for much longer than the couple of months he'd owned up to. Honestly, I hoped it was true. It would explain so much. Especially why I wasn't good enough for him anymore.

"Ben," he groaned, "lost his way."

"Right." I threw open my dishwasher to grab some glasses. "That's a good spin on it."

"Cams." Noah skimmed his finger along my jaw to turn my head in his direction. He was really getting touchy-feely in his old age. It was weird, but not a bad weird. Except it awoke cravings in me I had long buried and hoped to keep that way. But there was something about a man's touch that my soul longed for. Not from Noah, of course. He was a friend. My ex-husband's best friend. And he was taken.

"I know you think it was you, but don't you dare think like that," his gravelly voice begged me.

"You don't know that." My voice betrayed me and cracked. "Ben ended up hating everything about me."

Noah's face burned hotter than the Vegas strip in July. "No. He hates himself. As he should. He's a prick for what he did to you. But this I can promise you," his tone softened, "when Ben met you, he said, you're *the girl. The girl* we each get. The one you change your life for. The one who makes you forget about all the other girls."

A stupid tear leaked out of my eyes. I wanted to believe him, but how could I? "Apparently, I'm a short-term memory kind of girl."

"Cams, you are a make-a-man-lose-his-mind, think-about-you-day-and-night kind of woman."

I rolled my eyes. "You don't have to say that."

"You're right, I don't. I'm telling the truth. Ben knows it too," he seemed reluctant to say.

"I don't care what Ben thinks," I spewed.

"Are you sure about that?"

I stood tall. "I'm one hundred and ten percent sure."

"Do you still love him?" Noah seemed to hold his breath.

I spat out a maniacal laugh. "Not even an ounce."

Noah went from a pensive stance to a much more relaxed one. "Good for you," he said hastily. "We should eat the pizza before it gets cold."

"Good idea." We broke apart. I took a moment to watch Noah dish up two plates of ooey gooey goodness. He caught me staring at him and smiled. The kind of smile that said, "I see you."

Hey, Me, please don't let this friendship go. Please and thank you. Sincerely, Miss Sparkly.

I'll see what I can do. Yours truly, Me.

Nine

My dearest Ex-Filers, you never cease to amaze me. I'm loving all the costumes and suggestions. I can't wait to see so many of you at the Halloween Bash. Don't forget to purchase your tickets online. There are only a few spots left. If you can't make it in person, you can still donate online to the women and children's shelter.

Lots of love,

Cami

P.S. I promise this is my last post today. Have a good night. And make good choices. There's nothing wrong with being alone on a Friday night. Or any night for that matter.

I heard Noah's phone buzz as soon as I clicked publish.

"Am I boring you?" He set his empty plate on my coffee table and grabbed his phone out of his pocket.

I still couldn't believe he signed up for my notifications.

"Not at all. I'm enthralled with your caulking tips and tricks." I grinned. "But I need to choose a costume stat, and my people are helping."

"Is that what you call all your worshippers."

"They don't worship me."

"Please. I read the comments. Or at least some of them. You have thousands for almost every post. There are a lot of bitter people out there."

"Hey." I tossed a pink Mongolian long-hair throw pillow at him. "We prefer the term *indignant*."

He caught the pillow and chuckled. "That's much better."

"A lot of my followers have been through a lot of heartache," I added.

"I don't doubt that," he said sincerely.

"Unlike you,"—I looked down my nose at him—"who makes a mockery of my services."

He pretended to stab his heart. "Believe me, I take your services very seriously. In fact, I would be lost without them."

"Uh-huh."

"You'll see." He wagged his brows and tossed the pillow to the side so he could read my post. His brows furrowed more and more, the longer he stared at his phone.

"Something bothering you?"

He hemmed and hawed before scrubbing a hand over his face, which was covered in his signature five-o'clock shadow that all the women went gaga for, like he wasn't sure what he should say. "I'm just surprised by how anti-relationship you've become."

My cheeks started to burn. I don't know why it embarrassed me that he would call me out about it. "I'm anti–bad relationship," I tried to defend myself.

He perked up. "So, you're open to being in a relationship?"

I shuddered at the thought. "No."

Meanwhile Miss Sparkly was saying, *Not so fast. I could really do with a good make out session.*

Ooh. That did sound nice, but that was beside the point.

"What do you mean, no?" He was clearly agitated. "You just said you were against bad relationships. What about good ones?"

I rubbed my chest. Those kinds of thoughts gave me a serious case of heartburn. The hives would come next. "The thing is, any relationship can go bad. Believe me, I have firsthand experience."

Noah scooted toward me on the couch with a sympathetic look. He picked up Neville on his way, making it so our legs were practically touching. His snickerdoodle-scented cologne hit me.

Who wants some cookies? Miss Sparkly interjected.

Are you saying you want to taste Noah?

Hmm. I just thought cookies sounded good, but that's an interesting thought. I mean, look at those eyes and his lips. I bet he's a good kisser.

Oh. My. Gosh. Be quiet.

Now I couldn't help but stare at his eyes and lips. They were quite nice. It was also nice that in his baby blues I saw genuine concern.

"Cams," he said softly, "what would the woman in your graduation picture say to you about your outlook on relationships?"

I know! I know! Miss Sparkly was practically jumping up and down in my head.

I rubbed my head, she was so loud. At the same time, I was trying to ignore her.

"That bad, huh?" Noah guessed when I didn't answer.

I let out a huge breath. "That woman didn't know better."

Ugh. Excuse me. Apparently, I'd offended myself. Seriously, I needed help.

"That woman would have gotten back up on the horse after being knocked off," Noah stated.

I scowled at him. "You don't know that."

He's right, Miss Sparkly sang.

"Yeah, I do." He tapped my nose. "Deep down, you know it too."

I like him.

That was debatable. I didn't like how he was making my insides squirm with uncomfortable truths. All defenses went up. "Why do you care how I feel about relationships?"

"I care about you, Cami," he sounded wounded. "I would hate to see you have any regrets," he half snarled while moving away from me with my dog.

I felt terrible. I had gotten too used to being snarky. "Noah." I placed my hand on his thigh. Ooh. Wow. He was a muscular specimen. I didn't even need Miss Sparkly to tell me that. I probably should have popped my hand right off, but when he smiled and placed his hand over mine, there was something so comforting about it all. It was as if he were saying that he accepted me where I was at.

"I appreciate your concern. Really, I do. But I don't know if I can risk another Ben." The thought had me internally hyperventilating.

Noah enveloped my hand and squeezed it. He had no idea how much that brought my anxiety down. Maybe he was right. Holding someone's hand does tell you that you're safe. "I would be happy to choose the next one for you." He sounded awfully serious.

"No thanks." I laughed. "You obviously have your hands full picking your own dates. I think I'll stick with Neville." I removed my hand from Noah's and scratched my pooch's head. He was quite at home on Noah's lap.

"I don't know. His breath stinks and he doesn't know how to pee like a man," Noah teased.

"Hey, don't diss on my man. At least he's loyal," I whispered.

"Cams," his tone took a more solemn tone. "There are good, loyal men out there."

I rolled my eyes. Sure, my dad and brothers were good men. But outside the Jenkins gene pool, I wasn't too sure. Even Noah, as good as he seemed, was dating half the women in the state. I didn't mention it because he would just say it was for a noble purpose. Not sure how he figured that.

"Are you happy?" He threw out that question without any warning or pretense.

I sat back, feeling like he had sucker punched me. I needed to catch my breath before I could answer. "I'm not unhappy," I responded honestly.

"That's not the same thing as being happy." He looked around my condo. "Where are all your Halloween decorations? You have to be missing your pumpkin-shaped pillows."

I totally am. I can't believe you threw those away. Miss Sparkly was about to cry.

"Have you even watched *Hocus Pocus* or *Practical Magic*? Had a *Harry Potter* marathon? What about *It's the Great Pumpkin, Charlie Brown*?" He taunted me, knowing exactly how much that one would get to me. It was a beloved classic of my family's.

I glared at him for daring to go so low.

My withering glance did nothing to faze him. In fact, he grinned when he leaned over and went in for the kill. "How could you miss *The Nightmare Before Christmas*?"

I hurried to place my finger on his warm lips before he could say it, but I was too late. He had me shaking where I sat. "We do not say the C-word in this house. Ever." Especially in regard to the movie I loved as a child. A totally genius movie that combined my two favorite holidays.

He looked pleased with himself and didn't even try to remove my finger. Instead, he held my gaze.

I felt like he was trying to tell me something with the mesmerizing ocean of blue that swirled in his eyes, but I didn't understand. What I did know was that I liked the feel of his lips; they were the perfect amount of supple. That was enough to pop my finger right off them. I chalked it up to my dry spell of manly affection. Seriously, this was Noah. My ex's Noah. The man who dated every other woman on the planet, Noah. I felt like I had to keep reminding myself of that.

Besides, I was like a dating camel. I had gone a long time between watering holes in the desert, so to speak. I meant to keep it that way, but sometimes it was hard not to get thirsty.

"Christmas," he taunted me.

I clucked my tongue while clutching my heart. "Excuse me. My house. My rules."

"As far as I can tell, you need some new ones. For you and your dog's sake."

I slumped against the couch. "Maybe," I squeaked. "But don't say that word."

"We'll ease into it." He grinned.

I groaned, knowing how childish it was. But honestly, if you wanted to talk about a nightmare before the C-word, I felt like I kind of took the cake.

"Hey." He scooted closer. "I have a plan."

I raised my brows.

"Don't look so skeptical. This plan is foolproof."

"Uh-huh." I was totally skeptical.

He handed Neville over to me so he could pull something up on his phone. When he held it up, I saw what looked like a spreadsheet. "What's that?"

"My overly organized sister made this. I don't know if you remember me mentioning she's pregnant with twin girls. She just got put on bed rest."

I snuggled Neville tight. I did remember him telling me that Shanna was pregnant, but I'd glossed over it. Not because I begrudged anyone such a beautiful gift. It's just that longing for something you've lost and will probably never have, always takes your breath away. When I finally caught it, I responded. "I didn't know she was on bed rest. Is everything okay?"

"Babies are healthy, they just want to make an appearance before it's showtime."

It was sweet how tenderly Noah spoke about his nieces.

"When is she due?"

"The end of the year."

"That's a long time to be on bed rest."

"The doctors are hoping to at least get her to the first week in December. Which is why I've been helping with the boys. A lot actually. I would have been by earlier this week, but with my mom gone now," he choked up a bit, "I've been trying to do what I can."

Oh. Oh. Oh. My insides squirmed with hot shame. When I'd heard last year that his sweet mom, Penny, had passed suddenly from a pulmonary embolism after a routine gall bladder surgery, I was shocked and saddened. But I couldn't bring myself to contact Noah. Even when he first messaged me at the beginning of this year about cropping an ex out of a photo for him, I didn't offer my condolences. I was too busy worrying about myself and him trying to reinsert himself into my life. Who had I become?

You should have called him or at least sent a card, Miss Sparkly berated me.

I know. I know. I feel terrible.

"Noah." I bit my lip. My eyes even got a sheen over them. "I'm so sorry about your mom. I should have said that earlier. I should have done a lot of things. You shouldn't even want to be friends with me."

The tears started to trickle down my cheeks. That set off a chain reaction as if my body were saying, "Finally." I had held back my emotions for so long, biology took over. We are talking the floodgates burst open and I was ugly crying with a capital *U*.

Noah didn't even flinch. Instead, he took Neville and placed him on the couch next to me before enveloping me in his arms. My head landed on his shoulder and I sobbed. I mourned for all I had lost, especially the loss of myself. I cried because I was scared. I clung to Noah because for the first time in a long time, I felt safe to be me, even if it was only for a few minutes.

Noah did all the right things by not speaking and trying to make it better. He only stroked my hair and held on just enough. Enough that I didn't feel suffocated, yet I knew I was being sheltered from the storm that raged inside of me. I had been here once before with him. It was after I posted all my cropped wedding photos online. Noah was the first one to me. And even though I had accused him of covering for Ben, he still took me in his arms and comforted me. After that, he helped me take down the last tree I ever had. Something he'd said to me that night came to memory. It was something I had tried to forget because I had needed to forget him. "I'll always be a safe landing place for you. Even if it's a crash landing."

I was crashing all right.

I cried harder.

Noah was a true friend and a good person, even if I didn't approve of his dating habits.

"I'm sorry, Noah. I've been awful to you," I stuttered out between sobs, the weight of my behavior the last few years bearing down on me.

"Cams, you can totally make it up to me." He chuckled, making me laugh.

I wasn't expecting that response. I lifted my head and met his penetrating gaze. His eyes told me that he was still willing to be a safe landing place and that he would even help me clean up the wreckage.

Noah tucked some of my hair behind my ear. "Do you feel better now?"

I had to think for a moment. "Kind of." I still felt pretty jerky about not contacting him about his mother, among other things.

Especially since he was so close to his mother, given his father had left them all when he was only five.

"Don't worry, I can help fix the rest."

"You sound like Sam from the movie *Holes*."

"Great character. Great movie."

I nodded.

"So, back to my plan. Not only will it help you feel better, it will also make up for your ill treatment of me." He grinned.

"Is that so? How?" I shuddered through the last of my tears and sniffled loudly. It was really attractive. Good thing Noah and I never saw each other in a romantic way.

Not so fast. Look at those eyes and that stubbled jawline. Mmm. Miss Sparkly butted in again.

Seriously, stop. This is Noah.

I see that.

I had to stop egging her on by responding to myself. Listen to me. I was a nutjob.

With a glint in his beautiful eyes, he said, "Well, my sister with her type-A oldest child syndrome has designated me for all Jaxon's and Liam's entertainment needs. Which, I'm not afraid to admit, is a bit overwhelming. This is where you come in."

My brows popped.

"I need help."

"Babysitting?"

"Not just babysitting. Keeping two boys alive and entertained is not for the faint of heart."

I giggled.

"This is serious. Do you know how fast kids are? Don't even get me going on all the questions they ask. I mean, how do I answer questions like, 'How come God can't kill ghosts?' Or 'Why is the moon called the moon?'"

"It comes from the medieval word *mōna*," I easily answered.

His jaw dropped. "How did you know that?"

"Google." I laughed. One of my nieces had asked me that a while ago. "You should try it."

"See, this is why I need your help."

"Okay. I could set up a few playdates with them and some of my nieces and nephews."

He wagged his finger at me. "While that's nice, my sister has their entire lives mapped out for the next two months. I just need a partner in crime and someone good with Google." He winked.

"Um . . . I don't know if I'm the right person. Why don't you ask your girlfriends or the woman you're in love with? Knowing you, I bet she loves kids."

"You are correct. She's amazing with kids."

"Great. You're all set."

He let out a meaningful sigh. "Cams, I really would love your help. Besides, you owe me." He gave me a crooked grin. "And I want you to feel better for being such an awful friend to me."

"Way to shove the knife in my heart."

"I don't want to hurt your heart any more than it's been injured already," he said tenderly.

His words had some rogue tears leaking out. No wonder women adored him.

"Honestly, I think some of the activities my sister has planned will help you."

"How?"

"Well . . ." He paused. "Let's just say they have a holiday bent to them."

I clutched my throat.

Noah removed my hand from my throat and held on to it. "Cams, you gotta start living your life again. You need pumpkin throw pillows and pumpkin-spice candles. That's you."

Oh man. I did love a good pumpkin-spice candle. I could smell it now. But . . . "It's not that simple." Candles, like snuggling, were gateway drugs. I wasn't sure I was ready to go through any gates. Who knew what was on the other side?

Noah squeezed my hand. "What are you afraid of?"

"So much," I whispered.

Noah held up my hand and gently traced the scrapes, from falling on the court, that were mostly healed. I'm not going to lie, Miss

Sparkly and I felt the tingles it was causing. One of us was more pleased than the other about the long-repressed sensation a man could invoke.

"I'm happy to see these are healing nicely." His eyes bored into mine. "Would you let the fear of getting injured keep you from playing basketball again?"

"Of course not."

He placed my hand in my lap. "Because you love the game, right?"

I bit my lip. "I know what you're getting at."

"You used to love life, Cams," he said plainly. "I don't get that vibe from you anymore."

I wrung my hands together. "I don't hate it."

"Not the same thing."

"I know," I said quietly.

He grabbed his drink and leaned back. "Let's change that, starting tomorrow."

"What are we going to do?"

"You'll see." He wagged his brows. "Get your Han Solo outfit primed, and I'll take care of the rest."

"Han Solo outfit?"

"You know, the high boots, jeans, vest."

I laughed for a second before I said, "I don't know about this."

He shrugged. "Fine, but you're going to keep beating yourself up about being a terrible friend."

He was right, but I was still wary. "I'll think about it."

"Great. While you think, I'll pop some popcorn, and you pick a movie."

"You're staying?"

"Yeah. That's what friends do." He stood and walked toward the kitchen.

I turned and watched him, so at ease in my kitchen, like he owned the place.

He's good for you. Miss Sparkly had to have her say.

I had some things to say to her too. After all, she disappeared for a reason. *Are you sure you want him to open the doors you've been hiding behind?*

I'm ready to let him in. Are you?

I'll let you know.

Ten

DEAR EX-FILERS, HAPPY Saturday. I know the weekends are hard for so many of you. Here's some food for thought. Think of starting a relationship like getting a variable rate mortgage. At first everything is great. You get a beautiful home for a low monthly payment. It all feels like a dream that's too good to be true. That new-love feeling is so intoxicating, you brush over the fine print, thinking the rate will never change, or if it does, you'll be able to afford it. So, you sign on the dotted line. But then, sneakily, the costs begin to rise. Your partner starts nitpicking you or spending more time with his buddies or on business trips he never had to go on before. You think, okay, I can still afford it, it's no big deal. He's right, I could lose a little weight, or he has to do what's right for his career. Then little increases start to add up and deplete your self-worth. He's gaslighting you, making you think it's all in your head. You're the crazy one. Then one day, BAM! The rate gets so high you're underwater and unable to make any more payments because all your savings have been sucked dry like your soul. You're upside down on your loan and in your life. He's made you lose your sense of self until you don't know who you are or if you even want to be who you were. The only closure you get is foreclosure—no house, no money, and the lingering debt.

Wow, so that was cheery. With that said, have a great weekend!

And always read the fine print. If you do end up signing on the dotted line, I'll be here winter, spring, summer, and fall to remove them all.

Lots of love,

Cami

I clicked publish before looking in my bathroom mirror and swiping on my favorite pink lip gloss. I smiled at my *Han Solo* outfit, complete with a white long-sleeved shirt, black puffy vest, tight jeans, and leather boots. It hit me that I looked like me. I bit my lip and stared a bit longer. "Hi," I whispered while flipping my new do. "Are you ready for this?"

Outside of my Ex-Filers chapter events, Mara, monthly family dinners, and work, I didn't brave going out into the world. Sometimes I even had my groceries delivered so I didn't have to be around people. It was a far cry from who I used to be. To think, I used to go to the store hoping I would see someone I knew. I'd even had ice cream melt in my cart from talking so long to strangers.

Let's do this, Miss Sparkly shouted. She was such a social butterfly.

I, on the other hand, was a bit nervous. I wasn't even sure what Noah had planned—or what his sister had planned, I guess. Noah thought it would be better if it was a surprise. He said he didn't want me to overthink it. I still thought about it all night. I questioned my sanity for saying yes. But it's kind of hard to say no to a man who brings you pizza and your favorite soda and lets you stain his shirt with mascara. You should have seen my eyes. So embarrassing, but Noah never mentioned it.

He also promised to never mention that we watched *Cosmetics and Crimes* together. Mara would kill me if she knew I was cheating on her like that. Even though Noah and I only watched old episodes. Noah was intrigued with my latest pastime. Or more like disturbed. He kept scooting away from me on the couch like he was afraid I was taking mental notes on how to dissolve a body in acid. Soooo . . . I may have googled what acids dissolve what. I'm probably on some NSA watch list now. But good news, Coke will not dissolve your teeth. It's an urban myth. Too bad, since Ben used to streamline the stuff. I would pay money to see him toothless. Except Claudia Cann can't do Coke. Something about empty calories or some nonsense. The best-tasting calories are the empty ones.

I shook each part of my body and jumped up and down a few times, trying to get Claudia and Ben out of my head. I could be friends with Noah and not have it wreck my mental state, right? After all, last night was one of the best nights I'd had in a long time. Don't tell Mara.

I looked in the mirror one more time. "Okay, self. I'm talking to you, Miss Sparkly. We are going to keep our eyes and, yes, our hands to ourselves today. Don't think that I didn't notice how your hand inched a little too close to Noah's last night in the popcorn bowl. That is a hard no. I don't care how long it's been since we have held hands with a man." I blew out a deep breath. "Let's do this."

Go us! Miss Sparkly cheered in my head. *I hope he's taking us to a pumpkin patch.* She practically squealed.

No. No. No. We weren't ready for that. That could go one of two ways. I could either end up in the fetal position or I could go pumpkin crazy. We are talking filling the back of Noah's truck with every pumpkin in the patch and then going on a carving extravaganza. But that would mean I would have to pull out all the Halloween movies, because you can't carve pumpkins unless you are watching one of those. And if I watched my favorite Halloween movies, I would want someone to snuggle with while watching them, and you know what snuggling leads to. Let me tell you, it's not the Virgin Islands. So, no pumpkin patches.

Maybe this was a bad idea.

I pulled my phone out of my pocket to text Noah that I needed to cancel. But my phone buzzed with a text from him. Weird.

Noah: *Don't even think about backing out. You'll only feel guilty. By the way, I'm here and willing to knock on your door for however long it takes for you to answer it.*

That wasn't just weird. It was freaky weird. Could Noah read my mind?

He knocked on the door.

I gripped my counter. "You can do this, Cami," I said to myself.

Yeah, you can. Get out there, sister. We have a lot of making up to do. You should still send a card of condolence. You should probably make his sister dinner too.

That wasn't a bad idea. But, whoa, was Miss Sparkly getting bossy. Was I that bossy before?

I needed to quit talking to myself—Noah was now shouting, "Free Cami!"

I laughed all the way to my door, where Neville was already perched as if waiting for Noah. I knelt and scratched his head. "Hey, don't get any ideas of ditching me for Noah. I don't care if he does let you run free at the dog park. Remember when you played dead yesterday after that car door slammed? That's what a life with Noah will get you."

"Cams, are you trying to turn your dog against me?" Noah yelled through the door.

"I'm just reminding him who loves him the most," I yelled back before kissing Neville's head and standing up to open the door.

When I flung the door open, I found Noah leaning against the doorframe on one arm like he was a Luke Perry knockoff, except even more attractive. He was in his signature tight blue jeans and black T-shirt, his tattoos proudly on display. His hair was mussed perfectly with his curls dancing above his ears.

Dang, Miss Sparkly purred.

I did my best to ignore her, but she was right. Noah Cullen was a hottie, like my sixteen-year-old self used to say. Just thinking it made me smile.

Noah didn't smile back. Instead, his baby blues widened and I was pretty sure his jaw dropped before he quickly recovered.

I looked down at myself and Neville, who was traitorously jumping up on Noah's legs, begging to be picked up by him.

Noah shook his head and picked up my dog.

"Is everything okay? Did I not nail the Han Solo look?"

He cleared his throat. "No, you nailed it. It's just you look like . . . you."

I bit my lip. "Is that a bad thing?"

"No, Cams. It's the best thing I've seen in a long time."

"No need to lie," I teased him. "We both know that honor goes to your mystery woman."

"She is beautiful," he said all dreamily.

"I have no doubt." I rolled my eyes. I'd cropped enough of his photos this past year to know that he only dated women who, if you saw them on the street, would make you stop and stare and wonder if they were real or not.

"Don't roll your eyes. You're going to feel bad when you find out who she is."

"Is it Mara?" I was dying to know.

He coughed as if he had choked on some foul-tasting medicine. "Absolutely not. Why would you think that? She's like a little sister to me."

"She's gorgeous and intimidating."

"She's more than intimidating—she downright scares the hell out of me. Don't tell her I said that." He genuinely sounded frightened of her.

I laughed at him. She was a little scary at times. Don't tell her I thought that either. But she was the best friend a girl could ask for. She would totally bury a body for you—or sign them up for the most annoying email list of all time.

"So, it's not Mara."

"No."

"Who is it?"

He stepped closer and leaned in, his snickerdoodle scent making Miss Sparkly take a huge whiff and giggle. Thankfully, silently to herself. Or you know, myself.

"You really want to know?" he sang.

I nodded—the suspense killing me. Meanwhile, Miss Sparkly was thinking things like, *It's kind of a shame we will never get to kiss him. Seriously, look at those lips. Why didn't we ever make a play for him?*

Uh, hello, we were married to his best friend.

I'm not taking the fall for that.

Oh, yes you are. You were all over Ben.

You were too, Miss Handsy.

Okay, so she kind of had me there. He used to be very touchable, but that was neither here nor there. *Seriously, stop talking to me. I need to find out who Noah's mystery woman is.*

It's weird, I kind of want to claw her eyes out, Miss Sparkly mused.

That was the end of that conversation. We could never, ever, think like that. I rubbed my chest. I was having some strange sensations there.

Meanwhile Noah was taunting me with his enigmatic smile. His lips parted as if the name were on the tip of his tongue.

I held my breath.

"Her name is . . . ," he held the last syllable like it was clinging to life support. "You'll find out when we're best friends again."

I let out a huge rush of air and snarled at him. "How old are you anyway?"

"Old enough to know better."

"What does that mean?"

"It means when the time is right, you will know her and love her."

I don't think so. I still want to claw her eyes out.

I ignored Miss Sparkly. "I'm sure she's great."

"She's the best," he said so wistfully, I was a little jealous. I'm not sure a man, not even Ben, had ever spoken so in awe of me. Not that I wanted a relationship, but there were things I missed. I could at least admit that.

"I'm happy for you," I said hastily. "Let me grab my bag and turn on the TV for Neville."

Noah narrowed his eyes and looked between me and Neville. "Your dog watches TV?"

"He loves *Beverly Hills, 90210.*"

Noah busted out laughing. "Are you serious? This explains so much." He held up Neville. "Listen, buddy, you are going to watch a man's show today. How about *SEAL Team*?"

"That's too violent. You'll give him nightmares."

Noah chuckled. "You think *Beverly Hills, 90210* doesn't? I think I would poke my eyes out if I had to watch that every day."

"Neville has a sensitive soul," I retorted.

"I think she's brainwashing you," Noah spoke to my pooch before addressing me. "Can he at least watch something like *How I Met Your Mother*? That's somewhat respectable. We'll move on to the hard-core stuff later."

I thought back to the many nights of watching the reruns of that show with Ben and Noah. We had laughed and laughed. Ben loved the character Barney, who was a major player. I probably should have taken note of that. Instead, I used to tease Noah that he was the player. Come to think of it, he never appreciated it. "I don't know. I'm not sure he'll get the humor."

Noah's brows knitted together. "I think you need to get out more. Go get your bag and I'll take care of Neville. I might have to sue for custody at this rate," he teased me. "Luna needs a manly dog."

"Neville is neutered by the way."

"Perfect. Luna is spayed."

"I still don't think she's Neville's type."

"Are you saying he has something against big-boned women?" He smirked.

"I'm saying he's a gentle soul who needs his safe place."

"Cams, I promise to keep you and your dog safe," he said without a hint of sarcasm.

There was that word *safe* again. Could Noah keep me safe? Even from myself?

My vote is yes, Miss Sparkly sang in my head.

Of course, she thought that.

Eleven

OKAY, EX-FILERS, I think I finally picked my costume. What do you think of this? Too gothic? Too sexy? Thanks again for all your suggestions.

Lots of love,

Cami

Before I clicked publish, I attached a photo of the witch costume I planned to order.

"Posting again for all your worshippers?" Noah glanced my way while he carefully drove us to his sister's house to pick up his nephews.

I was more than nervous about it. I hadn't seen Shanna or her kids in a long time. And there was the whole 'I never even paid my respects to their dearly departed mother' issue. *Not even a card,* I lamented to myself before Miss Sparkly could berate me again. It was the reason I hadn't jumped out of the truck screaming. Guilt does weird things. Like getting me out of the bubble I had created to keep myself protected at all times. The thing about bubbles were that they eventually popped. I was already feeling mine starting to burst. I mean, I was in a truck with Noah going to do who knew what today. And I was in Carson City, a place I tried to avoid as much as possible, even though Jenkins & Scott Realty's headquarters resided there. Carson City was the place Ben and I had called home. These were all major breeches to the bubble.

I worried where I was going to land when the bubble popped. Would I get major road rash from the asphalt, or would I find a soft, safe place to land? Was there any such thing as safe? That was probably the better question.

"Everyone wants to know what I'm going to be for Halloween." I threw my phone in my bag. It was probably rude to post when I should have been engaging Noah in conversation. Sometimes I forgot things like that. It was easier to be in my world. Or to avoid the world.

"What did you decide?"

"A witch. It seems fitting, don't you think?" I whispered.

He stopped at a red light in the heart of Carson City and immediately turned my way, his brow scrunching. "No, Cams. Maybe you haven't been yourself lately, but you're no witch. Unless it's like Glinda the Good Witch." He smiled.

I fished for my phone and pulled up the costume before the light turned green. I held it up to show him. It was definitely not Glinda worthy.

Noah's eyes widened and he swallowed hard. "Hello. That's some witch costume. Maybe you should be a witch." He winked.

"It is kind of trampy."

"I was thinking more like sexy. But it's not really you." He faced the road and sailed through the green light.

"You don't think I can be sexy?" I was highly affronted.

"No," he spluttered. "That's not what I meant. You're totally sexy."

"You think I'm sexy?" I teased.

His face turned bright red.

I wasn't sure I'd ever seen him embarrassed. It made me giggle.

"You're enjoying this, aren't you?"

"Well, yeah. Except for the part when you said the sexy witch costume wasn't me," I fake grumbled.

"Cams." He reached out and placed his hand on my thigh.

He has a nice grip. Miss Sparkly decided to butt in.

I looked down at his masculine hand. She wasn't wrong.

"I only meant that," he interrupted my thoughts, which was a good thing, "you are more than you think you are." He patted my thigh before his hand popped off.

I tilted my head. "What does that mean?"

"It means you're not a witch."

I'm glad he thought so, but . . . "Who am I?" I asked more to myself.

"Like I said, hang around with me and follow my plan and you'll figure it out."

I looked down at my phone, wanting so badly to believe he could help me figure it all out.

My phone exploded with notifications. I half smiled. "I think you've been overruled. Everyone is loving the witch costume."

Noah shrugged. "They don't know the real you, Cams."

I wasn't sure I did either. I turned my phone off and sighed.

Noah gave me a sympathetic smile as if he knew I was a lost little puppy trying to find her way home. "Hey, if it makes you feel any better, I'm going to be there."

"What? You bought a ticket for the Ex-Filers' Halloween Bash?"

"Don't sound so surprised. I'm a big fan of your work."

"Uh-huh." I wasn't buying it. "You know, there are no couples allowed."

"You made that perfectly clear." He chuckled. "But . . . how do you enforce that? Or what if people hook up there?"

"Are you going so you can find your next victim?"

He slapped a hand against his chest. "That hurts. For all you know, the woman I love could be there."

I grabbed my midsection. It felt a little squirmy all of a sudden. "The woman you love is a member of my Ex-Filers chapter?"

Noah flashed me a wicked grin. "Could be," he taunted me.

I bet it's Annika, Miss Sparkly fumed. *I never liked her. She's so fake. Her boobs are way too perky to be real. And please, she has hair extensions. And let's not forget about her using a tanning bed. She's going to die of cancer. Do you want that for Noah?*

Hey, you're supposed to be the sweet one out of the two of us. Annika is nice. She worked a deal and got us the civic center for free, I argued with myself, which was so sick and wrong. *And her ex-husband was truly awful to her. We are talking prostitutes and clearing out their bank account awful.*

I had gone above and beyond cropping and photoshopping her wedding photos. Let's just say it looks like Annika is stabbing him in a very sensitive area. She had that baby framed and kept it on her nightstand as far as I knew.

That is sad, Miss Sparkly agreed. *But do you really see her with Noah? She's so short, and I think she might cry if someone threw a basketball at her. Have you seen those acrylic nails of hers? You know how much Noah loves the game.*

I think they could be cute together. You know, besides the whole her keeping a picture of herself impaling her ex-husband by her bed. That is a little crazy.

Exactly! Miss Sparkly shouted.

But . . . it's none of our business who Noah dates and loves. Besides, they dated in high school. Remember? They were like the junior homecoming prince and princess.

Ugh. Miss Sparkly wasn't so sparkly anymore and gave me the silent treatment.

The more I thought about it, the more Annika made sense. Maybe Noah had been pining for her all these years.

"Well, okay," I said in an octave well above my normal range. I really needed to get out of my head. "Just no coupling up at the event. It's supposed to be a safe space for singles."

"I think you need to get out of your comfort zone," he grumbled. "And a lot of your sycophants probably do too." Was he talking about Annika there?

"Wow. Why are you so salty?"

He loves Annika, Miss Sparkly growled.

I think she was right.

He didn't answer right away, so I added in, "By the way, the only sycophants I have are my nieces and nephews."

Noah's lip twitched. "Perhaps *sycophants* was the wrong word. It's just, don't you think you take this whole singles thing too far sometimes? I mean, what if you're hurting people more than helping them?" He launched that out there like a missile to my heart.

I rubbed my chest. "I'm not hurting anyone," I defended myself. "Not everyone gets to be so lucky in love like you," I tossed back at him.

His face turned redder than when I'd embarrassed him earlier. But this was a different kind of red. It was an angry-bull red. Noah gripped the steering wheel as if he might bend it. "You're not the only person, Cami, who knows what it's like to lose the love of your life." His words cut deeply—so much so, I teared up.

He rendered me speechless. I didn't know he was carrying around that kind of heartbreak. Of course not, because all I'd cared about the last few years was myself. I looked out the window at all the storefronts dressed for fall and wiped my eyes. "I'm sorry, Noah," I whispered. "I think you should just take me home." I had no business being around people. I wasn't Miss Sparkly anymore.

You could be, she whispered. *Please don't lose me.*

Noah pulled over near an old eatery. He threw his truck in park before reaching over the console for my hand. "Cams, I'm sorry. I shouldn't have snapped at you like that."

I squeezed his hand like a lifeline, though I couldn't face him. "It's okay. I'll call an Uber."

He tugged on my hand. "Cams, come on, look at me. Please."

I wiped my eyes with my free hand before turning toward him. I found Noah wearing a pensive expression.

"No one's calling an Uber. You got this. We got this," he amended. "Besides, I have it on good authority that the day is going to end with your favorite dark chocolate caramel apples. And I know you would kick yourself for missing out on one or two." He tucked some hair behind my ear.

Do not miss out on those apples, Miss Sparkly begged. *Or the day with Noah. Look at him all concerned. Don't screw this up.*

I was afraid I already had. But I did love a good caramel apple. "Are the apples from the The Chocolate?" It was the best place in town. I hadn't been there in over three years.

Noah's face broke into a huge grin. "Where else?"

"I can't believe you remembered that place is my favorite."

"Well, you did make *us* drive through a blizzard once to get you an apple there."

By *us*, I knew he meant Ben and him.

"It was more like a moderate snowstorm. Besides, I didn't force you. I just mentioned I could go for one."

" *We* had a hard time saying no to you."

That seemed like forever ago. It was hard to believe Ben was willing to do anything for me once upon a time. Even Noah seemed happy to tag along to fulfill my whims, whether it was caramel apples on a snowy night or polar bear plunges in the lake on New Year's Day. That was ancient history though. "Ben got over that," I said flatly.

Noah cleared his throat. "Let's not talk about him."

"Fine by me." I had to remind myself not to go into a tailspin about it. Ben didn't deserve the honor.

Noah inched closer and smiled. "Cams, I am sorry."

"I am too. I had no idea you lost someone you loved. Who was she?" I dared to ask.

"I'd rather not tell you right now." He wasn't curt, but his tone said not to push him about it.

It had to be Annika. He'd really kept that close to the vest. I didn't even know about her until she'd moved back a couple of years ago. She'd left Nevada after high school and went to college in the Midwest. She'd lived there with her husband until their divorce. The only reason I even knew she'd dated Noah was because I'd posted one of his photoshopped pics on my website in the "My Work" section and she mentioned they dated for a while in high school. Come to think of it, she did swoon a bit talking about how he was even better looking now. However, she did go into a tirade after about how all men were the spawn of Satan.

"Anyway," I said. "I'm sorry. I know how much it hurts."

"It hurts like hell, but I'm better now." He brushed his thumb over my hand.

Oh baby, that feels nice. Seriously, so surprised by his soft skin. Miss Sparkly was about to lose all self-control.

I get it. It had been a long time since we'd had any male affection. And we used to be a super fan of affection. Like number one fan.

Regardless, I pulled my hand away before Miss Sparkly did something I would regret, and Noah too. "I'm glad you're better."

He stared down at his empty hand and curled it into a fist. "We better get to my sister's house before she sentences me to death for being late. The only thing she can control right now is her precious schedule. Believe me, it's ugly when all doesn't go as planned."

Oh, did I know all about how ugly things got when life didn't go as planned. Which reminded me. "What are we doing today?"

He flipped on his blinker. "Don't worry, it's nothing too Cami-esque. We're going to start off slow."

At this rate, it was going to need to be snail-paced.

Twelve

HEY, EX-FILERS, SCRATCH the witch costume. There has been a new development. I'm still searching.

Boy, wasn't that the truth.

In other news, here's another pro tip to make your bed feel less empty. Stop folding your clothes. Let those babies pile up next to you. And as a bonus, fresh, clean laundry smells way better than morning breath. You're welcome.

Lots of love,

Cami

I probably should have added a word of caution in there that if you have a skittish dog, he wouldn't take too kindly to a pile falling over on him. Poor Neville was still trying to recover. Weren't we all?

Like right now, I was trying to get my heart rate to calm the heck down. We were on Shanna's street. The cab of the truck had been awfully quiet since Noah pulled over earlier. For the last several minutes my mind was spinning with thoughts of him and Annika. She was painfully beautiful, even with a boob job and extensions, which I had no solid evidence of. But I had a feeling Miss Sparkly would be checking her out more carefully when we saw her in a couple of days, for the final committee meeting for the Halloween Bash. I just hoped she wouldn't want to claw her eyes out. She had no right to be jealous.

Hello. I can hear you thinking about me. Miss Sparkly was apparently offended.

I smiled to myself. I was pretty hilarious. Deranged, but funny.

You won't be smiling when you finally wake up and realize what we could be missing out on, she scolded me.

I took a peek at Noah, who also seemed lost in his thoughts, as he drove slowly down his sister's very suburban street, filled with upper-middle-class homes and large SUVs and a smattering of foreign luxury cars. There was no denying how attractive Noah was. But he was clearly in love with his mystery woman, a.k.a. Annika. And I obviously had no business being in a relationship. I mean, I was talking to myself. Even arguing with myself. That had to be like next-level crazy. Besides, I would never be the other woman. I hated that woman. We all know her as Claudia. Not to say it was all her fault. Ben could have honored our marriage vows.

I scratched my neck. These thoughts were giving me hives. See? I was better suited for single life. It was hive-free.

Noah glanced my way and caught me staring at him. He flashed me that brilliant smile of his. His dentist deserved an award.

"Shanna's really looking forward to seeing you."

I bit my lip. "Really? I'm surprised she doesn't hate me." Not only had I not even sent a condolence card, but she'd also been begging me to take her family pictures for the last few years. But I'd turned her down every time, even though she'd offered me a lot of money and flattered me with the sentiment of no one being as good as I was. I had done several photo shoots for her beautiful family in my previous life. Oh, what a life that was.

I miss it. Miss Sparkly sighed.

Me too.

"No one hates you, Cams." Noah pulled in front of Shanna and Adonis Diaz's house. Adonis, the professional ex–baseball player, now highly sought-after trainer, was from the Dominican Republic—and his first name was fitting, as he was quite gorgeous, along with the rest of his family. Their boys got Adonis's beautiful dark skin and those Cullen blue eyes. The women of the future had no chance once the Diaz boys were older and set loose on the world.

I wrung my hands together and blew out a deep breath. "If you say so."

"I know so." He threw his truck in park and turned it off.

I hoped he was right.

"I'll get your door."

I smiled at him. "You don't have to. Remember the awkward moment we just had at my condo?"

I thought back to how he'd followed me to the passenger side to open my door for me, like we were on a date. I'd teased him about how he was on autopilot and he must date a lot to make that kind of mistake. We had both reached for the door at the same time, and our hands did this weird dance. I had finally just let him open the door. It was apparently his thing, which was endearing. It was good to know there were still polite men out there.

"I like awkward moments." He hustled out of the truck and around the front to grab my door.

I watched him, not sure what to think. But, hey, whatever floated his boat. Maybe he didn't want to get out of practice for Annika.

He was to my door in no time and opening it like a proper gentleman, except he looked like a rogue.

A sexy rogue, Miss Sparkly purred.

I needed to see if there was some sort of medication to shut her up. She wasn't helping the situation any. I was already nervous, and thoughts of how sexy Noah was weren't helping any.

I think it's you who needs some medication.

She might be onto something, but I didn't have time to think about it or her. I was mentally trying to prepare myself for a day of who knew exactly what. All I knew was that it involved some part of my former life, and that frightened me. The bubble was about to burst a little more.

"You ready?" He wagged his brows.

"Nope." I jumped out into the cool fall air. I swore it smelled like a cinnamon-and-spice latte. Oh wait, that was Noah. Dang him and his yummy cologne.

I took some deep cleansing breaths as I stared at the gorgeous home. The stone-and-wood beauty was worthy of the neighborhood. I noticed the large, covered porch looked bare. In the past, during this time of year, that porch would have been decked out in a Pinterest-worthy fall scene. We are talking mums and pumpkins galore, placed perfectly on bales of hay with darling scarecrows to match. I had taken their family photos four years ago in front of the happy scene. I bet Shanna was sad to miss out on one of her favorite times of year. She loved Halloween almost as much as I used to.

Hello? I still do love Halloween. And I'm just throwing this out there, but you should really offer to decorate her porch for her.

Oh. Oh. Oh. That was like giving a vampire a taste of blood. It would result in an unadulterated feeding frenzy. By feeding frenzy, I meant buying out Hobby Lobby and the local nursery. It wouldn't be pretty. Total gateway drug.

All I'm going to say is condolence card.

Wow. Miss Sparkly was getting vicious. I thought she was the perky, cute one. I gripped the door handle of the truck, trying to ground myself before I went running into the house, begging Shanna to let me do what was probably the right thing. Three years ago, this wouldn't have been a question. That porch would have already been decorated by yours truly.

Come on, you know you want to, Miss Sparkly taunted me. *It's the right thing to do. You're a good person.*

Well, I used to be.

"You okay?" Noah tilted his head.

I probably looked like I was having a mental episode. Which I was. "Yep," I said, again reaching that octave well out of my range.

"You're going to be fine, Cams," Noah tried to reassure me. What he didn't know was that he wasn't the only person talking to me, and that was beyond disturbing.

"Come on." He grabbed my free hand and wrenched me away from his truck.

Miss Sparkly took advantage of it and gripped his hand tightly. I swear I could hear her giggling and trying to figure how to make me go offline, so she could have Noah all to herself. Every time I thought of letting go of his hand, she gripped tighter. She was only in for some major disappointment, but she didn't care. She wanted a taste of my ex-husband's best friend. Admittedly, it did feel nice. Okay, more than nice. There was something about Noah. Something I had never taken the time to see or appreciate. He was—in a word—comfortable. Like your favorite pair of jeans. That's what Miss Sparkly was feeling. She could be herself around him. She'd always been able to. That's where my discomfort came in. I wasn't comfortable in my own skin right now.

Numbly, I proceeded and let Miss Sparkly have her way for a minute or two. She felt alive and like herself. Meanwhile, I was trying to process and remind her that he was our friend and it was best for her to keep her hand to herself. But she persisted and clung to the familiarity I had been denying her for months on end. I could hardly blame her. Noah was a connection to the happiest time in our life. A time I had done everything to shun, even the good parts.

When we walked up the stone steps together, I couldn't tell if it was Miss Sparkly or me who clung to Noah. Either way, part of me didn't want to let go.

"Thanks for being my friend," I whispered into the light breeze.

Noah stopped on the top step and smiled the warmest of smiles. "I like being your friend." He squeezed my hand and let it go.

I think Miss Sparkly was a tad disappointed he reminded her that we are only friends, but I realized it was something I didn't want to take for granted. I obviously had this need inside of me to connect to my past. And Noah had been a big part of it.

Feeling more settled, I walked toward the door, staying a step behind Noah. Unfortunately, that gave Miss Sparkly the go-ahead to check out his butt.

Yowzers! Those jeans should be on fire.

I averted my eyes. I needed help. Lots and lots of help. I was grateful Adonis opened the door.

"Hola. Qué lo qué?" Adonis came straight at me and wrapped me up in his big, bulging arms.

I almost teared up. I wasn't expecting such a warm reception from someone I hadn't seen—okay, someone I'd avoided—for almost three years.

"El cielo," I responded cheekily, which, if I remembered correctly, meant *the sky.*

"Very good." Adonis laughed his hearty laugh. He gave me another squeeze before releasing me.

"It's nice to see you." I smiled at the tall, lean man who was all muscle. He and Noah were deadlocked for who had the best layer of stubble.

"It's good to be seen. It's been a long time, friend." He waved his arms toward the door. "Come in. My bride is anxious to see you."

I loved how after ten years of marriage he still called Shanna his bride. Maybe Noah was right, there were still good men out there, outside of the Jenkins gene pool. It still didn't mean I needed to date them.

Don't be too hasty, Miss Sparkly had to throw in her two cents.

While Noah and Adonis did some handshake ritual, two of the cutest little boys came running down the circular staircase yelling, "Uncle Noah!" They had grown so much since the last time I'd seen them. Jaxon had been three and Liam one, and barely toddling around.

Noah's eyes lit up while he knelt down, allowing his nephews to tackle him to the floor. That had to hurt, considering the floor was made of hardwood. Noah didn't seem to mind. He hugged the boys fiercely. "You got me." He pretended to be under their complete control, letting them pin him to the floor.

It was adorable.

While Noah got attacked, I looked around their grand, high-ceiling entryway at some of the canvas photos hanging on the wall. Photos I had taken of the beautiful family that used to be showcased on my old website—Candids with Cami. I was quite proud of them, especially the ones taken near Lake Aspen. The evening light was perfect and they all glowed, especially Shanna, who was holding newborn Liam. I held my stomach. I glowed once, too, when I looked at two pink lines telling me a life was growing inside of me.

I had to force my eyes not to water. It was frightening how fast life could change.

Adonis shook me out of my head by easily picking up each son with one hand. "Don't beat him up too badly yet. We need him." Adonis sounded super grateful for Noah. Noah was seemingly trying to play the hero for everyone. That used to be me.

You could decorate that porch, Miss Sparkly reminded me. *Or a freezer meal wouldn't hurt.*

I shifted uncomfortably from my own thoughts. I was ashamed I was so hesitant to help. It's not that I didn't want to. But opening the door to the old me meant being willing to be vulnerable.

"Come on back here," Shanna shouted from their family room.

Noah jumped up and we followed Adonis back. He was still holding his children upside down, but they were laughing hysterically, so I assumed they enjoyed it. It was something my minions would certainly love to have done to them.

We walked back to find Shanna all propped up on a leather couch, a bag of chips in one hand and a remote in the other. It wasn't a bad life. Basically, it was my life, minus the bulging pregnancy belly and gorgeous husband and kids. *Tomato, Tamato.*

Shanna's beautiful Cullen blue eyes landed squarely on me. At first, she pursed her lips, making me pause, but then she broke out into a huge smile. "Get over here." She waved me over. "It's been forever since I've seen you. You look as gorgeous as ever." She was such a liar, but what the heck, I went with it.

Noah gave me a little nudge and I tiptoed over.

Shanna carefully scooted over on the couch and patted the empty space.

I cautiously sat next to her, admiring her long, braided blonde hair and fabulous skin. She didn't even have a lick of makeup on and still looked like she could model for COVERGIRL.

"Hi," I said almost inaudibly.

She didn't hesitate to wrap her arms around me. "Hi, friend."

I clung to her, soaking up her familiarity and warmth. I realized how much I had missed her and missed out on by staying away. "How are you?" my voice cracked.

"Oh, you know, just being a human incubator and couch potato. It's the life." Her tone said she wouldn't have it any other way.

I leaned away and looked down at her swollen belly—covered in a hot-pink blouse—which was moving. What a miracle.

"She's amazing," Adonis chimed in, while lowering his boys to the floor.

Shanna grinned at her husband. "He says that now, but when I said I was craving a cheeseburger at six o'clock this morning, he was singing a different tune."

I had noticed it smelled faintly like grilled hamburgers when we walked in.

Adonis lowered his chin to his chest. "But who got a cheeseburger?"

He was getting the best husband award in my book. My brothers were going to hear about this.

Shanna laughed and rubbed her belly. "The girls and I thank you." Shanna then looked between me and Noah. "It's good to see you two together again. Feels like old times. Good times," she added.

I couldn't disagree with that, so I nodded.

Noah gave his sister a meaningful look before clapping his hands. "We should probably get going."

Shanna looked at the large wall clock near their rustic fireplace. "Oh yes, you're going to be late. Come here, boys."

Late for what, I had no idea. I went to stand but Shanna kept ahold of me.

Jaxon and Liam gathered around us, looking as cute as could be in their designer-brand jeans and matching camo shirts. They probably hated that they matched. I knew my nieces and nephews never appreciated it when their parents or I subjected them to such torture.

"Boys," Shanna said, "this is Cami. She's the lady I told you about. I want you to be good for her and your uncle today. She's the nicest, most fun person I know."

Oh, direct blow to the heart. I wanted to be that woman again.

Let's do it! Miss Sparkly shouted before she took over my mouth and we said, "I can decorate your porch for you."

I covered my mouth, but it was too late. Miss Sparkly had made her debut, and she made it clear she wasn't going down without a fight.

Thirteen

DEAR EX-FILERS, I just saw the best shirt. In bold letters it said, I THINK, THEREFORE I'M SINGLE —LIZZ WINSTEAD. I don't know who this Lizz is, but she's a genius. Like, I think we could be best friends. If anyone knows where I can get one of these shirts, give a sister a shout-out in the comments.

Lots of love,

Cami

I published my quick post while taking a bathroom break in the tiniest restroom of all time. We were at Jaxon's school carnival, and I had to say, I could have used a mini toilet back in the day. I'd fallen in once, back in second grade. I still have nightmares over it. Nothing like having to call your mom with soaking-wet pants and your classmates thinking you peed yourself. Good times.

Thankfully, I came out of the bathroom as dry as could be to find three handsome men waiting for me. Waiting for me to obliterate them, that was. I took ring toss and balloon darts seriously. I had just kicked all their butts, and they were looking for revenge. We were on to bobbing for apples and the football toss next. I had my arm and my pearly whites ready to take on the Cullen and Diaz boys.

Jaxon and Liam were shoving their faces full of cotton candy, which I was pretty sure was on Shanna's no fly list, but as a trouble-making aunt, I would give Noah a pass. If he wanted to defy his sister and spoil his nephews, I would support him.

Noah stood with his hip cocked, holding all my recently won tickets.

It wasn't lost on me how many women's gazes landed on the gorgeous man. Even some of the married women. Noah didn't seem to pay them any attention. Instead, he smirked at me and handed me my tickets when I landed by his side.

"Thank you. I hope you didn't steal any because I counted them."

"Count away if you're worried." He grinned.

"Don't mind if I do." I plucked the tickets out of his hands.

He laughed at me.

"You boys ready to go back into the gym?" I asked between counting.

"Yeah!" they both shouted with their mouths full of colored sugar. With blue mouths, there was going to be no hiding Noah's treachery.

Noah and I each took a boy's hand and weaved through the crowded halls of the private school. They were filled not only with people, but several glass cases full of awards and pictures of days gone by.

Little Liam, whose hand I held, looked up at me with his big blue eyes and asked, "Are you Uncle Noah's girlfriend?"

I stopped, stunned, as did Noah.

"Uh, no," I spluttered. "We're just friends." I looked to Noah to emphasize that fact, but all he did was press his mouth together while his ears pinked.

"Okay." Liam sounded depressed.

"I think my mom will be mad," Jaxon jumped into the awkward conversation.

"Why?"

Jaxon took a big bite of his cotton candy before saying with a full mouth, "Because my mom says she wants Uncle Noah to date nice girls and quit bringing home skanks." His brow furrowed. "What's a skank?"

I certainly didn't need to google that definition. That was an easy answer—Claudia Cann. But before either a shocked Noah or I could answer, Liam yelled, "Skank!" Then laughed like a mad scientist.

I think every head turned our way amid deafening silence.

Noah held up his arms as if he were going to preach a sermon. "Nothing to see here, ladies and gentlemen, boys and girls. He said *skunk*."

"I said *SKANK*!" Liam shouted.

I had to throw a hand over my mouth before I busted out laughing. This was seriously the best time I'd had in a long time. Kids were the best entertainment around. And watching Noah squirm was worth the price of admission. The price being that Miss Sparkly was totally in her fall-loving element here. She was desperately trying to take over and hit the pumpkin decorating station and buy the fundraising booth out of all the pumpkin-spice candles, but for now I was holding her back. It was one of the reasons I had gone to the bathroom to post. That shirt I'd seen was like a link to reality, and I'd seized it.

I felt obligated to help Noah. And that's when I remembered: I had googled *skank* once upon a time, sure that Claudia's picture would pop up. Google had severely disappointed me, but I had learned something new.

I stood on my tiptoes and smiled at all the onlookers. "Everyone, I'm taking a dance class, and we are learning how to dance the skank. It's a dance you do to reggae music. My little friends here are just excited to see my performance. Thank you for your attention. Please carry on." I bowed deeply to the chuckles of several people.

When I came up, I was met with Noah's eyes. Deep gratitude swelled within them. "You are still the coolest girl I know."

That was the best compliment I had received in a long time. Oh, and Miss Sparkly was all aflutter about it. I tucked some hair behind my ear. "We better get these two back in the gym."

"So, a skank is a dance?" Jaxon was highly disappointed.

"Yes, it is."

Jaxon's button nose scrunched. "How can you bring home a dance?"

"I'll show you later." I laughed.

We herded the boys toward the gym, where all the action was taking place.

Noah sidled up to me. "I want to see how you do the skank," he whispered.

I nudged him with my shoulder. "I might be so inclined after I learn how to do it, and if you tell me which skanks you've been bringing home," I teased him.

Get those names and see if Annika is one of them. Miss Sparkly was still a little salty.

Noah ran a hand through his gorgeous locks. "Shanna has her opinions."

"I'm sure she does. Does she like your mystery woman?" I wondered out loud, mostly for Miss Sparkly's benefit.

"Loves her," Noah said without missing a beat.

Miss Sparkly wasn't thrilled, but I was happy for my friend. "You're all set, then."

"I have to win the girl first." Noah wagged his brows.

"I suppose there's that, but first I need to win some more tickets. Come on, boys, let's go bob for some apples."

Miss Sparkly was super excited about that. We all raced to the large metal tubs. I totally planned to go for the gold even if it meant dunking my entire head in. While we stood in line and listened to the boys chattering about how they were going to score the biggest apple the fastest, I looked at the world around me. I allowed my blinders to come off, and for the first time in a long time, everything came into focus. It was as if I was actually living, instead of getting by. I noticed harried carnival organizers and dads chasing unruly toddlers. I smiled at how bougie the PTA had made the gym. They must have had a big budget. All the booth workers wore matching black-and-white striped aprons, and they had a quality DJ emceeing the thing. Not to mention each booth was a handcrafted masterpiece. The most important part was that it was a happy place. Most importantly, I felt happy.

I smiled at Noah, who was already staring at me. "Thank you," I whispered.

"For what?"

"For helping me to find a piece of the woman in the photo."

I'd never seen him smiler wider.

"Now get ready to lose." I winked.

We sat at the back of The Chocolate, waiting for our order to arrive. I looked like a drowned rat, but it was totally worth it. I was the champ of apple bobbing. Noah sat across from me at the tiny circular table, holding Liam, whose eyes kept drifting closed. We had apparently tuckered the kid out.

Someone who wasn't tired was Miss Sparkly. She was enjoying her view. *Is there anything more attractive than a man holding a child so tenderly? Noah is going to make such an amazing dad someday. By the way, I think one of our ovaries just popped an egg.*

She was ridiculous. I wrenched our gaze from our attractive friend and focused on Jaxon, who was still curious about the skank. I pulled up a YouTube tutorial. It was of some hilarious kid from several years ago. Jaxon and I watched him, laughing as we went. When it was over, Jaxon gave me a toothy grin—well as toothy as he could; his bottom two teeth had recently fallen out.

"I want to try." Jaxon pushed his chair back.

"Let's see what you got." I smiled at him.

"I think Cami wants to dance too." Noah flashed me an impish grin.

I looked around the crowded dessert shop, then thought it wouldn't be the most embarrassing thing I had ever done. This coming from the woman who made her husband's affair public and did some pretty outlandish things to their wedding photos. And in my college days, I was all for making a fool of myself in front of crowds. I once stood up in the student union building and sang "Don't Stop Believin'" by Journey on a dare, to give my fellow students some inspiration while we were all studying for finals. I wasn't sure I had helped anyone with their grades, but it turned into a great musical battle as several more people got up and serenaded us. If anything, it had been a welcomed stress release.

We were so cool. Let's be cool again. Miss Sparkly relished in the chance.

I think saying we're cool means we're not.

"Please," Jaxon begged.

That was all it took for Miss Sparkly to seize the moment. I swear my body, of its own accord, popped out of the seat.

"Fine." I gave Noah a faux evil eye.

I took Jaxon's hand and we scooted around to the front of the table. We didn't have a lot of room to work with in the cute shop that was once a house.

"All right, DJ Noah, find us a good beat."

Noah chuckled while reaching for his phone on the table, careful not to jostle Liam too much. He really was going to be a great dad someday. Annika was a lucky woman. I had this fleeting thought—maybe I should help him win her over.

Are you insane? You hate relationships. Don't start getting soft on me now. You tell Annika, single life is the best life.

That was a great motto, but she could have said it more quietly. I had to rub my head, Miss Sparkly was so loud.

I thought you wanted us to be more like you? I fired back at myself.

Not for this. Look at the man.

You realize he loves someone else?

I don't see a ring on his finger.

You need to be quiet now.

Meanwhile, back in reality, Noah found a suitable song with a great beat.

"Show me what you got," Noah said with a little too much sexiness in his voice, as he clicked play. Or was that Miss Sparkly's wishful thinking?

Anyway, I was going to live up to my coolest girl title. "All right, Jaxon, let's show your uncle our moves."

Jaxon and I high-fived before we started.

"Feel the beat." I clapped in time with the music so Jaxon could get a better feel for it.

He followed along with me. The kid already had great rhythm.

I showed him the first move by standing on one leg, my weight slightly forward. Then I bent my raised leg toward my butt before kicking it forward in time with the thumping song.

Jaxon mimicked me well.

We then hopped onto our kicking leg, adding in our swinging arms.

By this time, we had a crowd. I was afraid we might get kicked out for making such a scene.

We had also woken up Liam, who decided he wanted to try the funny dance too. He joined Jaxon and me. This only hyped the crowd up. People were now cheering us on and clapping to the music. I felt like a break-dancer in an eighties movie as people circled around. My inner sparkly self was coming out to shine. I had forgotten what it felt like to dance like no one was watching, even though everyone was watching. But I only cared about one person who looked on, cheering the loudest. His look said, "Hey, cool girl."

Miss Sparkly channeled *Grease* and said, *Tell me about it, stud.*

I, on the other hand, grabbed my friend's hand and together we danced. Miss Sparkly liked that much better than her plan, especially because we were no longer doing the skank. No, Noah twirled me and then he pulled me close. Like flush against his body close. I thought it had been awkward when he opened my door. This had nothing on that moment. We both stared at each other as the heat rose between us, but I was too stunned to do anything about it. I mean, Miss Sparkly had some suggestions, but I wasn't kissing him or grabbing his butt. Though his lips did look inviting. And I had to admit, being in his arms wasn't bad at all. There may have been some goose bumps. There were definite heart palpitations. In fact, my heart wasn't sure what to do; it hadn't felt like this in a long time.

Thankfully, Noah came to his senses and let go of me, putting plenty of distance between us. He picked up Liam and spun him around, all but ignoring me.

Oddly enough, I couldn't move at all, but felt as if I were spinning. Where I was going to land was anyone's guess. I had a feeling, though, if I kept this up, I was in for some serious road rash.

Fourteen

DEAR EX-FILERS, THANKS for all the shirt links. I think I bought one in every color I could find. I'll be giving some of them away at the Halloween Bash. Tickets are sold out, but you can still donate online for the women and children's shelter. I can't thank you all enough for your support. Here's a little wisdom for the day: "Remember that sometimes not getting what you want is a wonderful stroke of luck." —Dalai Lama

And yes, that goes for relationships too.

Lots of love,

Cami

I clicked publish and shoved my phone into my jeans pocket. I was still a little shaken from my day with Noah yesterday. There was some serious weirdness between us on the ride home. He hardly said a word to me, like he knew what Miss Sparkly had been thinking when we'd danced, and he wanted to make sure I knew we were on a strict friends-only basis. Of course, I knew that but I made sure to remind good old Sparkles about what kind of damage relationships do. Last night I cropped exes for hours, reminding her and myself of the terrible heartache that coupling brings about. I forced Miss Sparkly to read all the gut-wrenching details people had sent me. Everything from spousal abuse and neglect to cheating with the spouse's best friend.

I honestly thought I had silenced the urge to date. I wished there were a twelve-step program for recovering hopeless romantics. I needed a hotline.

Mara walked in from the kitchen, where she'd been talking on the phone. We were at a client's home that was ready to go on the market. I was there to take the pictures for the listing. Mara was going to play my assistant.

"Sorry, I had to take that call. The house I listed on Elm is in a bidding war." Mara smiled, ever so pleased.

"No worries." I unzipped the case where I kept my reflector discs.

Mara tilted her head. "Hey, are you okay? You seem bummed."

Oh man, I wanted so badly to talk to her about my weekend. Tell her how ridiculous my sparkly half had behaved. She would help me to just laugh it off. But in a way, I felt as if I had cheated on her. Not only had I shown Noah *Cosmetics and Crimes*, but I'd agreed to decorate Shanna's porch, and I had gone to a fall carnival and danced in public. I was totally falling off the wagon.

The guilt bubbled up inside me. "So, I did a bad thing."

Mara gripped her chest. "Did you succumb to watching a Hallmark movie?"

"No, no, nothing that bad." I grinned.

"Whew." Mara faux-wiped her brow. "So, what did you do?"

"Okay, so it's not necessarily a bad thing—actually it's a good thing, but I feel like it might lead to bad things."

Mara scrunched her brow.

"You know how Shanna Diaz is pregnant with twins."

Mara nodded.

"Well, she's on bed rest until the babies come, which will hopefully be in December. Soooo . . ." I twirled my hair. "Noah has been helping out a lot with his nephews, and he asked me to help because I'm way cooler than him and know how to use Google."

"What?" Mara wasn't following.

"That's neither here nor there," I rambled. "You see, I did help him on Saturday, and before I knew it, I was offering to decorate Shanna's porch for fall and now I can't back out, but I haven't been in a Hobby Lobby for almost three years, and you know how I get in that place. More importantly, you know they already have the holiday-that-shall-not-be-named decorations up. But what if I can't resist and I go crazy and eat all the candy canes and rearrange all the decorations on the trees, because, you know, sometimes they don't do them right? Worse, what if the manager shows up and hauls me out of the store while I'm clinging to garland, but he's super gorgeous and since I've already lost my head and I'm high on sugar, I tell him that we should meet for drinks, and he agrees. And then we cuddle and get married, and I bear his children and then he leaves me for one of his checkout girls." I took a deep breath in and let it out. I'd obviously left out the most important part—that I'd danced with Noah and liked it. A lot. But I couldn't own up to that. That was really crazy. Oh, and I didn't dare mention I was talking to myself. That was certifiable. But maybe some time at a "facility" with locks would be good for me.

Mara pressed her lips together but was shaking from holding back her laugh. "Wow." She giggled. "Are you sure you aren't high on sugar now?" She reached out to feel my forehead.

"Sugar highs don't cause fevers." Not to say I hadn't felt a tad feverish yesterday. "This is serious."

"Okay." She wrapped an arm around me. "First of all, if you want, I will go to Hobby Lobby with you and keep you away from the Christm—I mean the holly jolly aisles."

We both laughed.

"Secondly, I've never seen a gorgeous man work at Hobby Lobby, so I think you're safe."

"You don't really shop at Hobby Lobby," I reminded her. Mara was a crocheter, but she was a yarn snob and Hobby Lobby didn't do it for her.

"I've been in there with you plenty of times, and it's mostly been pimply teenagers wearing blue vests."

This was true.

"Thirdly, you don't like the bar and club scene, so you would never ask a man out for a drink. You're more of a 'let's stuff your face with bread or pasta' girl."

"Good point."

She gave me a good squeeze. "And lastly, you are way too smart to get married again."

"Yeah. Totally smart. Genius-level smart."

Liar, Miss Sparkly was calling me out.

Mara patted my arm. "See, you're okay."

I let out another deep breath. "Thank you."

"That's what best friends are for. Now let's snap some photos. Mama needs some commission and a new wardrobe."

I handed her one of the reflector discs before reaching for my camera bag.

You know, Miss Sparkly whispered, *she only says that about marriage because she's just as scared as you are and she doesn't want you to get hurt again. You've both had some terrible luck when it's come to men. But is it really smart to write them all off? Think about it.*

Well, of course I was going to think about it now. She was in my head. And maybe she was right. Not about writing men off per se, but definitely about Mara.

"So how was it, hanging out with Noah?" Mara asked, shaking me out of my head.

I pulled out my camera. "Oh, you know, he was Noah."

"Annoying, then?"

"He can be," I sort of lied. "He's really good with his nephews."

"Did you find out who he's in love with yet?"

"I think so."

Mara's eyes flashed with excitement, waiting for the juicy reveal. "Do tell."

"He wouldn't tell me, but I think it's Annika."

Mara tapped her finger against her lip, thinking. "That makes sense. She's definitely intimidating. She's the one that keeps the picture of her impaling her ex on her nightstand, right?"

I nodded.

"And didn't they go to homecoming or something together in high school?"

"Yep."

"You might want to warn Noah to hide the knives around her."

Or just warn him altogether. I don't think she'll make him happy.

That's not our call, I had to remind the Miss.

"Good idea," I responded to Mara.

Mara looked around the cozy living room in the single-story modern bungalow. "I want to make sure we showcase the wood beam ceilings and window seat in this room."

"You got it, boss."

"I do love it when you call me that," she teased.

Honestly, I didn't think she was teasing. She wasn't being rude at all, but I think deep down she longed to be the boss. To find her place in the company. She lived in Ben's shadow. Ben had been given his own office to run when Mara was every bit as qualified as he was, albeit younger. But that was Jay, their dad, for you. I wouldn't say he was a sexist pig, but . . . he was. However, I couldn't say that to Mara's face. She loved her father, despite their complicated relationship.

I got my camera primed to go and walked over to the corner of the room where I could get the best angle. I took a few practice shots for fun, and to check the hotspots, so I could properly utilize Mara's reflector disc–holding skills.

"So why did you change your mind about the witch costume?" Mara asked offhandedly.

I bit my lip, not sure what to say. It was an easy answer, yet I felt like I couldn't tell her about that conversation with Noah. Which was crazy. Mara was my best friend. We didn't keep secrets from each other. She even knew my biggest, most heart-wrenching secret. Yet, I couldn't tell her because the way Noah saw me was different. Not that Mara thought I was a witch. It's just that, for now, I needed both Mara's and Noah's points of view, unfiltered from each other. And maybe, just maybe—if I was being honest with myself—that conversation I'd had with Noah felt intimate to me and I was embarrassed for thinking that way. No need to bring it up.

"Dressing up as a witch is kind of cliché," I told a half-truth. It really was cliché. I felt like a terrible friend. "I was kind of thinking of being a Gallagher Girl. Remember those books?" Books about a group of girls attending a very exclusive high school for spies. The main character's name was Cammie or Cameron, just like me. Though hardly anyone ever called her, or me, Cameron.

"Yes! I loved them in high school."

"Me too. But do you think anyone would get the whole prep school outfit?"

"Uh, who cares? You'd look totally hot."

"Like that matters. We are going to be at an event with a bunch of people who would rather lick the bottoms of their shoes than date again."

Mara laughed. "I would totally lick the bottom of my shoe before entertaining another relationship."

That's just so sad. Miss Sparkly sighed.

A few years ago, that's what I would have told Mara; today, though, I responded, "I'd lick two pairs."

That is disgusting. Our tongue was not meant for licking shoes. Now Noah, on the other hand. Miss Sparkly dreamily oohed and aahed.

Wow. She had it worse for him than I thought. This was a problem. I was going to have to help him win Annika over so Miss Sparkly would let it go.

By the way, I heard your plan, and you can't help them because that's not you anymore, remember? Or are you really me? You can't be both of us. Sooner or later, you're going to have to choose. The fact you're hearing me says something.

I was getting a headache . . . again. That was happening a lot lately.

"Thankfully, we are two intelligent women, so no need to lick any shoes. And I love the Gallagher Girls idea. So fun," Mara said.

Yeah, we were so smart. Why, then, was I feeling a little dumb?

I was just about ready to place Mara for the photos when her phone rang.

Her brow crinkled. "It's my dad. I better get it."

She never let a call go from him. I think she hoped the next call would be the one where he would finally give her his stamp of approval, and deem her worthy of following in his and Ben's footsteps.

I lowered my camera and patiently waited for her.

"Hey, Dad." She sounded cool and confident. But then her face dropped, and her eyes welled with tears.

I rushed toward her.

"I'll be right there." She hung up with a look of horror on her face.

"What's wrong?"

"It's my mom," her voice hitched. "She collapsed at the gym after complaining about chest pains. They're rushing her to the hospital now. I have to go."

My hand flew to my mouth. I loved Kellie Scott. Though I had done a poor job of showing it to her, like everyone else in my life the last few years. I knew she understood the distance I had put between us. I think she even welcomed it, as it was just as painful for her to be reminded of how good it all used to be. The promise that was once held in my marriage to Ben. We'd often talk of the little ones she'd hoped we'd have. We'd planned their nurseries and what she would be called: Gigi. Then poof, it was all gone, and she was left with Claudia Cann, who could do anything; but there was one thing Claudia was adamant she couldn't do and that was have children. Not that she couldn't, she just didn't want to. They would ruin her figure and cramp her lifestyle. Hey, no judgment if kids weren't for her. I was thankful she wasn't releasing any of her genes out into the human pool. But . . . her husband, once upon a time, wanted children more than anything. And her mother-in-law longed to have grandchildren.

"Go. Go. I'll lock up here. Please keep me posted."

She gripped my shoulders. "Cams, I need you to come with me."

My heart stilled. Oh. I knew that. What kind of friend was I? I should have offered to take her. It's just that, well. It would mean seeing Ben. And that was never easy.

Cams, don't let him rule us anymore. Please. You're stronger than this. Than him.

It was probably the smartest thing Miss Sparkly had said since she'd popped back up. She was right. Don't tell her I said that.

Oh, I heard it.

I grabbed Mara's hand. "Let's go. I'll drive."

Fifteen

Dear Ex-Filers, "To fall in love with yourself is the first secret to happiness." —Robert Morley. Please be happy.

Lots of love,

Cami

It was the thought that kept coming to me as I sat in the waiting room, while Mara was in with her mother and father. It felt like I had been there forever, but it had only been a few hours. Kellie had an electrolyte imbalance due to working out too hard and not eating and drinking enough. It was all I could do to hold back the tears. Tears of relief that it wasn't worse, and tears that it was worse than I feared. Kellie was such a beautiful woman, but she never felt good enough because Jay always found something to criticize about her. And his philandering ways hadn't helped any. So here this poor woman was, almost killing herself trying to stay thin and perfectly in shape. She'd had plastic surgery and fillers. Yet Jay was never satisfied.

A shudder went through me, thinking that was the life I would have had, had I not caught Ben cheating on me. Ben, who was thankfully at some couples retreat in the desert. I was praying that Claudia Cann would do a sunrise yoga livestream and get bitten by a rattlesnake. But I knew I wouldn't be that lucky. And I wouldn't wish that upon the poor snake. I should probably be thanking Claudia for saving me from a lifetime of hell. For as much as Ben swore he would never be his father, that was exactly who he had become. I hoped he saw what it was doing to his mother.

I leaned back in the uncomfortable waiting room chair and clasped my hands together. I was beginning to realize that I needed to make some changes. Big changes. I wanted to love myself again. To be happy. Happy like I was yesterday, dancing in a crowd of strangers and dunking my head to bob for apples. But the scary part was, that woman wanted more than that. She wanted love. And I wasn't sure I could give her that. All love had taught me was that I was never good enough, just like poor Kellie.

That's not real love, Miss Sparkly obviously needed to chime in.

Then how would I ever know what was? Ben was a seemingly wonderful person for a long time. He seemed to love me for who I was. I assumed Jay was like that once upon a time too. How could you tell if the person is going to stay good or not?

Miss Sparkly was silent.

My phone buzzed.

Noah: *Hey, I just read your post. I want you to be happy.*

I smiled at my phone. I was surprised he was contacting me, after how weird we'd left things yesterday. When he'd dropped me off, he'd basically just said, *Thanks for helping me today, bye.*

Cami: *Are you saying I should fall in love with myself?*

Noah: *Yes. Do you want some help?*

Cami: *I'll let you know. By the way, can you say a prayer for Kellie? She's in the hospital. She passed out from an electrolyte imbalance. They're going to keep her overnight to monitor her. I'm here with Mara.*

I thought he should know. Kellie was like a second mom to him.

Noah: *Which hospital?*

Cami: *Regional Medical Center.*

Noah: *I'll be right there.*

I wasn't expecting that, but I suppose I should have. Like I said, he loved Kellie as much as any of us.

The next thing I wasn't expecting walked through the automatic doors, looking harried and a bit sunburned from his time in the desert.

I almost dropped my phone, but caught it in the fumble. My next move was to pretend I hadn't seen him. I set my sights on the TV that hung in the corner. A football game was on. I had no brainpower to focus on who was playing, but it didn't matter. I just needed something to stare at. All while I berated myself for still letting Ben have so much control over me. I should be able to face him with confidence. But it dawned on me, I had buried the strongest part of me, thinking it was what had made me weak. These epiphanies were hurting my brain.

While avoiding my ex and having an existential crisis, Mara appeared, and I heard her say to Ben, "Oh, look who showed up. I thought you were too busy chanting around a fire, naked."

"We weren't naked," Ben defended himself.

But they were chanting around a fire? Who had he turned into?

Mara snorted. "I'm glad you draw the line somewhere."

"Just give it a rest. I'm here." Then he shocked the heck out of me when his tone softened and he asked, "How is Mom?" He sounded worried. I didn't know he had any decency left in him.

"She'll be fine. They have her in her own room now. I was just coming down here to get Cami." Mara outed me. Dang her.

I slowly turned to face the siblings as they inched toward me. Sometimes I forgot how much they looked alike. It was their noses and eye shape. They were both gorgeous in their own rights, though Ben wasn't attractive to me anymore. Even more unattractive was the way his jaw hung open while he stared at me.

"He can go first." I pointed at Ben. I hated to call him by his name. It humanized him too much.

Mara gave me a sympathetic look. She, more than anyone, knew how much it pained me to be around her brother. "Mom really wants to see you, Cami."

I grabbed my heart. I loved that, but it also kind of killed me. I would be brave, though, and see the woman I used to call *Mom*. Except . . . "Uh, Noah is on his way. Maybe I should wait for him."

Both sets of siblings' brows raised.

"I thought he should know about your mom, so I texted him."

"You're still in contact with Noah?" Ben asked like it was any of his business.

It caused Mara's eyes to get all glinty with devious wonder. "Of course she is. They're like BFFs," she highly exaggerated. Although that's exactly what Noah wanted us to be. At least I thought so. I wasn't sure after yesterday.

"What did you guys do yesterday? School carnival with his nephews, right?" Mara really was driving it home.

The way Ben's face erupted in fire, I knew exactly why Mara was doing what she was doing. She loved to get to Ben anytime she could.

Before I could even answer, Ben growled, "He's never said anything."

"You're not his babysitter. He can hang out with Cami anytime he wants to," Mara taunted him further.

Ben's jaw and hands clenched.

I wasn't sure why it bothered him so much. Noah and I used to hang out all the time together. Besides, Ben no longer had any say in my life.

"You guys can go up and see Mom. I'll wait for Noah." Ben marched toward the entrance he had barely just come through.

I stood, not sure what had just happened.

Mara looked absolutely delighted with herself as she watched her brother stomp away.

I linked arms with her. "You are a troublemaker. Even if I don't understand why he's upset."

She spun us back toward the elevators. "Don't you see the regret in his eyes when he looks at you?"

I shook my head. "All I see are eyes that used to judge everything about me."

Mara pulled me closer. "I love my brother, but I hate what he did to you. I wish you would have told me earlier."

"Me too," I whispered.

Mara pushed the elevator button. "My dad does the same thing to my mom," her voice swelled with emotion. "But she won't leave him. I'm so glad you found the strength to."

"Well, I had some help from dear old Claudia," I choked on her name. "Where is she anyway?"

"Hopefully my brother left her in the desert, but she's probably livestreaming in front of the hospital."

"Maybe we should go photobomb," I teased.

"Nah, I'll just sign her up for a hemorrhoid cream mailing list or something."

"Even better." I giggled.

We stepped into the elevator; our arms linked together. It was only the two of us. For a moment we said nothing as we rose higher and higher, but I could hear Mara thinking. She pierced the silence by asking, "You're happy, right?"

"I'm not unhappy." I was finally honest with her.

She looked over at me, her beautiful eyes boring into mine. "That's not acceptable."

"I've kind of been thinking that."

"Would it help if you watched a Hallmark movie?" She gagged a little.

I threw my arms around her. Just knowing she would support me in such an endeavor meant the world to me. "I don't know, but I promise I won't make you watch one with me."

"You don't know how much I love you for that." She smiled.

"I love you too. Now let's go face my ex-in-laws, I mean your parents." I let out a deep breath.

"Mom misses you."

"I'm going to change that." I stepped out into what felt like a brave new world for me. Miss Sparkly was anxious to see both Kellie and Noah. And was she ever excited about the prospect of a Hallmark movie. I was trying to temper her expectations, but was failing miserably. She was listing all her favorites, including the holly jolly ones. I tried to tune her out, as we click-clacked our way down the tile hall toward Kellie's room. The smell of hospital food lingered in the air. My guess was beef stroganoff or roadkill—it was a toss-up.

Mara barely tapped on the door before we walked right in. In my line of sight was Jay, sitting in the corner staring at his phone like he was bored. He was decked out in some tapered golf pants and long-sleeved polo shirt. He looked like a man in his mid-forties, instead of late fifties. He for sure dyed his brown hair. The gray in his five-o'clock shadow said it all.

Mara took my hand and pulled me all the way into the room.

Jay barely looked up and glanced our way. He gave me a passing hello before he focused back on his phone. It didn't bother me, other than that he was just plain rude and inattentive to his wife, who was sitting up stick straight in her hospital bed applying a layer of lip stain. Kellie looked painfully perfect with her long, dark hair curled and makeup done just right. She was the master of contouring. She held her head high so that not one crease in her neck would show. Heaven forbid she showed any age.

I wanted to wheel her out of that room and into a place where she felt safe to be herself. But how could I help her when I was afraid of my own self? Mara and Noah were right, I needed to change that.

Kellie's eyes began to water, as I approached her ever so carefully. It had been a long time since we'd seen each other.

"Hi," I whispered. "How are you feeling?"

She placed her lip stain on the bedside table and gave me a small smile, showing off a glimpse of her capped teeth. "Better now that you're here."

That gave me the courage to inch closer to her. She helped me out, by holding out her perfectly manicured hand with nails the color of pink ballet slippers. I grasped for her and let her close the distance between us.

She gave me a good once-over. "You're beautiful. I love the hair."

"Thank you." I almost said she looked beautiful too, but I felt like she needed to see that she was so much more than a gorgeous face. Instead, I said, "I've missed you."

"Darling," her voice hitched. "I've missed you more."

I'd missed me too.

Mara stood on the other side of the bed and took Kellie's free hand. "Ben's here."

Kellie's brown eyes lit up. "I didn't think he would come."

"The bonehead is full of surprises," Mara quipped.

Kellie gave her daughter a disapproving stare.

"What? You know you agree with me." Mara kissed Kellie's head.

Kellie softly laughed. "Where is he?"

"He's waiting for Noah. We're all worried about you."

"All my kids." Kellie sounded like her heart might burst. Judging by how thin she was, that was probably a possibility. Get this woman some of that roadkill, stat.

Mara and I each took a seat on the bed next to her.

"So, tell me what you've been up to?" Kellie asked me. "I mean, Mara tells me everything, but I want to hear it from you."

I didn't even know where to begin. "I bought a little place off the slopes that needs to be updated, but I love it."

"Are you still skiing every chance you get in the winter?"

I nodded. I loved skiing, and as a bonus, it was a sport I could do on my own, and with all the gear, no one even recognized me. Except that wasn't sounding as appealing to me as it did the last couple of seasons.

Noah loves to ski, Sparkles reminded me.

I was well aware of that. I was more aware of how much fun I knew it would be if I invited him to join me, once the resort opened next month. Memories of playing follow the leader and tag with him on the slopes made me smile. I tried to omit the fact that Ben had been there too.

"I've been following you online," Kellie brought me back to reality.

I bit my lip, not sure how she would feel about my antics, especially the one where I outed her son as a cheater.

She squeezed my hand, and with this steel determination, she said, "I admire your strength more than you will ever know." Her gaze drifted toward her inattentive husband.

I so badly wanted to tell her that she didn't need him. That it was okay if she loved herself and left him, but I wasn't sure how Mara would feel about me trying to break up her parents—and we had company.

Noah and Ben showed up. Each of them wore a scowl on his face. And if I wasn't mistaken, they were purposely keeping several feet apart from each other.

Noah's eyes landed directly on me, and my other half couldn't help but stare at him. He looked like he had just come from the gym, in athletic shorts and a tight tee that showed off how ridiculously built he was.

I popped up like an idiot when I realized I was ogling him. Our eyes locked, and the brooding attitude he was sporting slowly dissipated when he smiled at me.

"Hi," my voice squeaked.

"Hi there," Noah's gravelly voice filled the room.

Every set of eyes in the room was ping-ponging between us, especially Ben's. I caught a glimpse of him looking at Noah, like he might throw a punch.

I think Kellie noticed, too, and quickly acted. "Boys, it's so good to see you. Come hug your mother."

I backed out of the way.

Awkwardly, both Noah and Ben came to my side to hug Kellie. When Noah noticed, he backed off and went to Mara's side.

Mara stared with interest between Noah and Ben. Their dynamics were all off. Normally it was all fun and games between them. Or at least it used to be.

Meanwhile, Jay went back to staring at his phone. I was calling him all the bad words in my head. And thanking God, more and more, that I'd caught Ben cheating on me. If not, in thirty years, it could have been me in that hospital bed, with an uninterested husband wishing he were anywhere but there with me. And what about his kids? Did he have nothing to say to them?

My focus switched back to Kellie, who was tenderly patting Noah's stubbled cheeks. "It is so good of you to come."

"There isn't anywhere else I would rather be right now."

Oh my gosh. He is the sweetest. Miss Sparkly was about to explode.

I would give it to her that Noah was sweet. Much sweeter than his best friend, who was throwing daggers at him with his eyes.

Not to be outdone it seemed, Ben kissed his mom's head. "I rushed to get here as soon as I got Dad's call."

Kellie smiled, though she cleared her throat. "How was your retreat?" she forced herself to ask.

Ben waved his hand around. "It's not important."

"And where is Claudia?" Kellie said her name like she was scratching her fingernails against a chalkboard.

"She's outside." Ben rubbed the back of his neck. "She had to update her feed."

"You mean she's livestreaming outside the hospital?" Mara rolled her eyes. "Wow."

Noah caught my eye, the corners of his mouth ticking up. He was obviously amused by Claudia Cann's lack of decorum, and Mara calling her out.

"It's her business," Ben did a poor job of trying to excuse her behavior.

"Well, it's Cami's job too, but we don't see her in here trying to market off our mother's illness."

Ben's head whipped my way. "No, she just used me to catapult herself to fame."

Oh no he didn't! Miss Sparkly roared.

I was so stunned; my first reaction was to run away. It's what I was good at lately. But then Noah grabbed Ben's shirt and pulled him across Kellie's bed. "Don't you ever talk to her like that again."

This had Jay jumping up. "What the hell is going on here?"

So many things. My head swirled as I looked around at everyone in the room. From Mara's wide eyes to Kellie's tear-filled ones. It was then that something in me snapped. It was about time that I did more than just stick up for the lonely and abused online. I should have stuck up for myself a long time ago. Sure, I had left Ben, but I hadn't left him behind, and it was about time I started to.

I stood tall, having an answer to Jay's question. "I'll tell you what's going on." I blasted my ex-father-in-law with a withering stare. "Your wife is practically killing herself because she thinks it will make you happy. And your son, always wanting to follow in your footsteps, tried to do the same thing to me. You know what? It worked. I let go of the best parts of me. But no more." I faced Ben. "Don't think for a minute that you have anything to do with my success. I don't need you." I paused. "I never did."

Drop the mic, sister, and walk out of here. I'm so proud of you.

For once in a long time, I was proud of me too. Now excuse me while I go to Hobby Lobby.

Sixteen

Dear Ex-Filers, to quote Kathie Lee Gifford, "They don't call me spontaneous and irreverent for nothing." Oh man, did I just do the most irreverent and spontaneous thing I've done in a long while. And oh, did it feel so good. Try it out.

Lots of love,

Cami

The doors to the elevator opened and I rushed out, still feeling the adrenaline of what I had just done. My only hope was that Mara and Kellie didn't hate me for it. I had run out of the room before anyone could say anything to me.

My phone buzzed. I looked down and smiled.

Mara: *You're a freaking rock star. I love you.*

That answered that.

Mara: *P.S. You're my ride. Don't leave me here.*

Me: *I would never leave you stranded, unless Ian Somerhalder wanted to whisk me away and make out with me for the night. No strings attached, of course.*

I looked around the hospital lobby.

Me: *You're in luck, Ian isn't here. I'll wait for you in my car. Take your time. I hope I didn't cause too many problems. Love you.*

I pocketed my phone and sailed through the lobby, needing some fresh air. What I had forgotten in all my haste was that perhaps leaving the hospital wasn't the wisest thing. I was smacked in the face with Claudia Cann. She had set herself up near a small patch of trees that were turning shades of red, orange, and gold. The shameless woman even had portable ring lights. I grabbed my phone and snapped a picture for Mara. This was worth her getting on a few more email lists.

I stood just outside the entrance in the cool evening air, staring at the woman who I thought had stolen my life, in her wide-brimmed hat and floral peasant dress. She had to be freezing in that getup. She was posing perfectly to make sure she looked as thin as possible. Her lips pouted just right as she rambled on and on about her time in the desert and how hard it was to be without electricity for two whole days. "I couldn't even bring my makeup cooler," she whined.

I didn't even know they made coolers for makeup. What I did know, was that I was going to stop being jealous of this ridiculous woman. Claudia Cann can do a lot of things, but she can no longer have a hold on me. I even refused to see flashes of her and Ben under the tree.

I rubbed my arms for comfort, and because I was chilly. I was only wearing a long, button-down shirt that could almost pass for a dress with some leggings.

"I have a jacket in my truck," a familiar voice rumbled next to me.

I turned to find Noah standing next to me, grinning from ear to ear.

I tucked some hair behind my ear. "What are you smiling at?"

"You. You were amazing up there."

I let out a deep breath. "I surprised myself, that's for sure."

"And everyone else. I think that whole family needed to hear what you had to say."

"I can't imagine they're too happy about it." I headed toward my car to get warm.

"Half of them are." Noah followed me.

I didn't have to guess which half. "The question is if the other half will listen."

Noah shrugged.

"Were there a lot of fireworks when I left?" I hesitated to ask.

"If you mean a major staring contest, some pacing and then blaming you, sure."

I expected that Ben would blame me. "By the way. Thanks for sticking up for me. But I don't want to come between you and Ben, even though sometimes I can't understand why you stay friends with him."

Noah tugged on my sleeve. "If you have time, I'll tell you."

I stopped, surprised by his response. "Um, I do have to wait for Mara. I'm her ride."

"Excellent. I'll grab us some jackets and we'll walk and talk."

"Okay." I smiled. I could use someone to talk to and a good walk. I had all this nervous energy coursing through me, and Miss Sparkly was anxious to get to Hobby Lobby. It was then that we both remembered that Hobby Lobby isn't even open on Sundays. Oh well. We would drive to Reno tomorrow and get our fix. Our first step forward in rediscovering ourselves. Well, me. I should really stop referring to myself as two people.

We had to pass by Claudia. She stopped mid-livestream and pursed her lips at me with such an evil glare.

I waved and smiled at her. "Don't forget you're live," I sang.

She shook her head, all flustered. I had to admit, it was a beautiful sight.

"As I was saying," she went on. "What was I saying?"

Noah chuckled deeply. Obviously, there was no love lost between the two even though she was his best friend's wife.

Claudia didn't take kindly to us and flipped him off. But she knew right away that was a huge mistake. She started to splutter, "That was just a joke." She sounded as if she might cry, though she was fake laughing. "Anyway, I need to sign off. My dear mother-in-law is in the hospital. Please pray for her. And don't forget, if Claudia Cann, you can. Toodles." She scrambled to turn off her phone.

She was shameless using Kellie there at the end. She was shameless, period.

As soon as she was offline, she gave us a look that could melt iron. She was about ready to unleash on us when two women approached me. "Oh my gosh, are you Cami Jenkins?"

"That's me."

"We love you," one of the women squealed. "Your posts are the best."

"I totally want you to photoshop some pictures of me and my loser ex-fiancé," the other woman said.

"I would be happy to. You can upload them to my site."

"Seriously, this is the best day ever," she responded.

I caught a glimpse of Claudia, and let's just say this wasn't her best day ever. She was furious, judging by her red face. It was like karma had blessed me.

The women noticed my line of sight and looked behind them. When they turned back around, they tried to whisper, "Who livestreams at a hospital?" but epically failed. Not that I was complaining. It had Claudia grabbing all her gear and marching off to probably eat some seaweed or something equally disgusting.

"Some people," I responded with an evil grin. Inside I was saying, *Buh-bye, Claudia.*

It was then the women took notice of the handsome man by my side, who was patiently waiting.

"Is this your boyfriend?" one of them asked. "I thought you swore off men." She sounded disappointed.

"Oh. Uh. Noah and I are just friends. Like platonic with a capital *P*, friends."

The women giggled, but I noticed them eyeing him like he was a piece of candy, and they wouldn't mind a lick.

Tell them to keep their eyes to themselves. We are not done discussing Noah as an option, Miss Sparkly scolded me.

How many times do I have to tell you he's taken? Besides, we aren't even close to thinking about a relationship with anyone. Let's try Hobby Lobby and a few Halloween movies before we get carried away. Okay?

Fine. But don't you back out on me this time. I need some pumpkin spice in my life.

Once I was done arguing with myself, I noticed that Noah wasn't enjoying this. At all.

"I'm sorry, we need to go. It was really nice to meet you."

Noah took the out and gently pushed me forward. When we were out of earshot of the two, he said, "Platonic with a capital *P*? What, are you ashamed of me?" he teased.

"Not at all, but people look up to me."

"Hmm," he sighed. "So, you have to stay single forever to appease people who don't even know you?" He sounded a bit cranky.

"I was thinking more along the lines of, so I don't get my heart broken again." I nudged him with my elbow.

He gave me a sympathetic smile. "I thought the woman in the hospital room might think differently."

"She does about some things."

He tilted his head. "What things are those?"

"Well . . . I mean, she really wants to go to Hobby Lobby, and I think she's up for a *Harry Potter* marathon and maybe a pumpkin pillow or two."

Noah chuckled for a moment before he paused as if he had to think about what to say. "Would she possibly be interested in taking my nephews to Peterson's Pumpkin Patch with me?"

Miss Sparkly got all tingly and was shouting in my head, *Yes! Yes! Yes!*

I did love that place. I could taste their homemade apple cider and pumpkin-spice doughnuts now. But . . . "The last time I went there was with Ben," I whispered, trying not to think how I knew then that something wasn't right between us. I'd felt it in my bones. He had been overly attentive yet distracted.

"Maybe it's time to make some new memories there," Noah stated.

Take this step back to loving us again, Miss Sparkly pleaded. *Don't waste what you just did up in that hospital room. And all I'm going to say is 'condolence card'.*

Sheesh, you are vicious, Sparkles.

Only when I have to be.

"Okay." I grinned. "I'll go with you and your nephews on two conditions. We get to cuddle the bunnies for at least a half hour, and you jump in the corn cribs with us."

"Deal." He beamed, not even having to think about the conditions.

"Great. Now that that's settled, I really could use a jacket." I hugged myself and rubbed my arms.

He grabbed my hand. "This way."

Miss Sparkly was in heaven holding his hand again, not to mention she was giddy thinking about going to the pumpkin patch. I let her have her moment and I took advantage of it too. This was a big day for me, and since I couldn't have Mara right now, I accepted Noah's comforting touch. After all, we were platonic with a capital *P.*

He led us to his truck and retrieved a hoodie for him and his leather jacket for me.

I couldn't get his jacket on fast enough. The sun was setting and I was freezing. Not only did warmth engulf me, but so did that incredible scent of his. It felt as if I were swallowed whole by a snickerdoodle. I breathed in deeply, to Miss Sparkly's delight. I knew I shouldn't tempt her, but she'd shown up for me today in a big way.

"Shall we walk?" Noah asked.

"Yeah."

The hospital campus was lovely, even in the semi dark. I believe they had even won an award for how beautiful the grounds were. It's kind of hard not to be beautiful with the Sierras as your backdrop and the sun setting it all on fire. I looked at the mountains, feeling as if I had climbed them today and come out on top. "So, what was going on with you and Ben today?"

"You can't guess?"

"I gather he doesn't like us being friends. Which I don't understand."

"He doesn't understand, either." Noah shoved his hands in his pockets.

"What does that mean?"

"For once in Ben's life, I have something he can't have. And he knows it's his own fault."

"Ben wants to be friends with me?" I asked incredulously.

"Ben wants his life back, but he knows it's not possible."

I stopped and had to blink a few times to comprehend what he was trying to say. "Ben doesn't want me back. You hear the way he talks to me, about me."

"Yeah, I do, Cams. In private moments when he's not playing the part of prick, he knows he screwed up."

"You guys talk about me?"

He tugged on a strand of my hair. "You are still the coolest girl we know."

The thought of Ben still thinking that was impossible for me to believe. "He has a funny way of showing it," I growled.

"Don't you get it, Cams? He's stuck in his own personal hell where he can see you, but you will always be out of reach. And you were right up there." He pointed at the hospital, now in the distance. "You never needed him, but he needed you."

My eyes welled with tears, not sure Ben ever needed or wanted me the way I had wanted him. "How did it get so messed up, then?"

Noah wrapped an arm around me. I leaned into him, trying not to let Miss Sparkly get too comfortable. But Noah was exactly that, comfortable.

"I don't know." He rubbed his hand down my arm. "But I know you're stronger than the mess."

I wiped my eyes. "I'm working on it."

"That's the difference between Ben and you. He keeps digging himself in deeper because he can't see a way out of the mess he created."

I leaned away from Noah. "Are you trying to help him too?"

"Cams." He hit me with those eyes of his. "Ben has been my best friend since kindergarten. He chose to do another year of first grade when he found out I was being held back."

I used to love that story of how Ben had begged his parents to let him repeat first grade so Noah wouldn't have to do it alone. I thought I was getting such a good person to spend my life with.

"He made me want to try harder," Noah continued, "after giving up a year for me. I keep hoping that maybe I can do the same for him right now—help him try harder."

I was in awe of him. Not only could he still see the good in Ben where I saw none, but he saw the good in me, even when I gave him no reason to. "Noah, I might be the coolest person you know, but you are the best person I know. Don't tell Mara I said that." I giggled.

Noah laughed and pulled me in for a hug. He rested his chin on my head. "All of your secrets are safe with me."

I naturally nestled into his chest and took a moment to breathe him in, believing he really could keep me safe. It wasn't my brightest move. Miss Sparkly was all aflutter. *Don't tell me you don't like this.*

I couldn't lie to myself. But I could keep it a secret, and that's what I planned to do.

Seventeen

DEAR EX-FILERS, MY mother would often say to me in my teen years: "I hope you see your beauty, not in the mirror or in what others may say about you." Find your beauty today.

Lots of love,

Cami

P.S. Check out the volunteer section. My local Ex-Filers chapter is looking for people to help serve dinner on Thanksgiving Day at the Reno homeless shelter. Come hang out with me for a good cause. If you can't volunteer that day but would like to help, see the donation link. Also, check out all the other Ex-Filers chapters across the country for more opportunities to help your community.

I clicked publish and prepared myself mentally for what I was about to do. I looked out my car window at the big orange letters that spelled out Hobby Lobby. It was five minutes until opening and Miss Sparkly was like a racehorse at the gate, chomping at the bit to be released. Meanwhile, I waited for my partner in crime for the day, Mom. Mara had a client meeting she couldn't miss. Mom was almost giddier than Miss Sparkly. She said, and I quote, "It's about damn time." Then she giggled because she swore. She probably washed her mouth out with soap afterward too. I made her promise me, though, not to try and trick me into taking a stroll down the holly jolly aisles.

I may have watched twenty hours' worth of Halloween movies

and specials in the last few days, and lit so many pumpkin-spice candles that it looked like I was holding the world's largest séance, but I wasn't sure I would ever make peace with the supposed "most wonderful time of the year". Which was why I had already booked my trip to the Virgin Islands. What made it even better? Mara was coming with me this year. I could hardly contain my excitement about it. While everyone else would be unwrapping presents, we would be covering ourselves in suntan oil and sipping on piña coladas while soaking in all the virginity the islands had to offer. Not like there was a lot of abstinence going on there. I'd seen some pretty X-rated things on the beach. But most of it was so ridiculously embarrassing, and fueled by alcohol, that it only gave me more resolve to stay a born-again virgin. Hallelujah. Mara was going to love it.

Miss Sparkly, on the other hand, was having second thoughts about our decision—but she and I had come to an agreement: I would do my best to enjoy Halloween, and possibly Thanksgiving, if she left holly jolly day and Noah alone. There would be no more checking out his butt or trying to snuggle up to him while we watched the first three *Harry Potter* movies. You should have seen her inching over on the couch. She was shameless. But she'd had a reality check at the last Ex-Filers meeting to finalize our Halloween Bash plans. Annika was there and when I'd mentioned that Noah was coming, we both saw the flash of excitement in her eyes. And when I'd told Noah that Annika was looking forward to seeing him, he blushed. I didn't even know he could do that.

Regardless, it gave ole Sparkles the shot of reality we both needed her to have. To ease her pain, I'd ordered the cutest pumpkin pillows from Pottery Barn. I even paid for overnight shipping. I had to admit, the cozy pillows in creams and browns made my little heart sing. I might have even slept with one last night. Neville was highly affronted I'd cuddled up to something other than him, but he was a traitor anyway. He was totally sucking up to Noah, sitting on his lap and wanting Noah to take him out. And get this, I think he likes *How I Met Your Mother* more than *Beverly Hills, 90210.* I'd turned on the latter show for him today before I'd left, and he'd barked until I changed it. Men.

The minutes ticked down until the store opened. I admit, I was antsy to get in there and do some damage to my debit card. I had extra cash to spend, as I had been doing a lot of photoshopping exes out. This was the start to my busy season that ran until the end of February. It seemed people were trying to move on before the holidays. Or, you wouldn't believe the number of people who gave the cropped and edited photos to their exes, especially for Christmas and Valentine's Day, or as I liked to call it: Happy Trivial Interpretation of Love Day. (Yes, that sounds totally bitter.) Those gifts were like next-level savage. Not to say I didn't applaud such actions. I'm kind of jealous I hadn't thought of it. But I guess posting my photoshopped wedding pictures online was like the gift that kept on giving to me, so I couldn't complain.

At five after the hour, my mom pulled up in her cherry-red 1966 Mustang that my father had restored for her as a birthday gift last year. Seriously, my parents were too cute. They made marriage look like a dream. Even though I knew Mom would say it was no fairy tale. She still complained about my dad leaving the toilet seat up and plucking his nose hairs in front of her in the bathroom. Believe me, I didn't need to know that. But there was something to be said for being so comfortable around someone, you could shove tweezers up your nose and you knew they would still love you. That was true love right there.

Mom flitted out of her car wearing her *Hello Pumpkin* sweatshirt and a cute pair of mom jeans. Her hair was tied up in an orange bow. She was, in a word, adorable. I always thought I would grow up to be like her. Maybe there was still time; you know, minus the adoring husband and children.

I grabbed my stomach. Was I ever going to get over that loss?

I didn't know, but I put on a smile anyway and got out of the car.

Mom rushed to my side. "Sorry I'm late, I wanted to make a few freezer meals for Shanna and I couldn't find my big cooler to put them in."

See, I told you we should have made some.

Hey, I'm decorating her porch.

Miss Sparkly was still trying to boss me around. And she was right, I should have made some freezer meals.

"That's really nice of you, Mom. I know she'll appreciate it."

"I just hope a dozen is enough," she sighed.

I wrapped my arms around my cute mom. "Mom, you are the best."

She clung to me. "Don't make me cry. I'm already flummoxed that we're going to the holy land today." She was referring to Hobby Lobby.

"Just remember, you promised no holly jolly aisles or talk of the C-word." I had to scratch my neck.

Mom pulled away from me with a knitted brow. "Against my better judgment, I promise."

"Thank you—"

"But . . ." She pointed at my chest. "I just have to say, you will never be you without the song of *Christmas* in your heart." She sounded like Dolly Parton, minus the southern accent, in one of her TV C-word specials.

I tried my best not to cringe when Mom said the word that had become my kryptonite. I tried even harder not to believe her. I failed at both. "I'm trying my best right now." It's all I had to offer.

She patted my cheek with her cold hand. "I know, baby girl. You'll get there."

I didn't verbally disagree with her.

She looped arms with me. "We're off to see the Wizard," she sang.

We followed the yellow brick road all the way to Oz. When we walked in, it was like everything went from black and white to technicolor. There were no munchkins to greet us, but Dorothy was right, there was no place like home. I stood still and looked around the holy land filled with all my favorite things: fall pillows, scarecrows, pumpkins in all colors and shapes and sizes, cutesy Halloween signs, and fake sunflowers as far as the eye could see. I had come home. I breathed in the scent of candles and potpourri. My heart sang a little. Not a full chorus, but a few lines.

I was so overwhelmed; I didn't even know where to begin. But I did check to make sure the manager wasn't gorgeous-slash-single before I went on my feeding frenzy. I was in luck; it was a guy named Chuck with a beer gut and yellow, stained teeth. I think I was safe from asking him out for dinner or even drinks. All I had to do was stay away from the *holly jolly* aisles and I should be fine.

Mom and I each grabbed a cart. We meant business. Shanna was going to have the best porch around. And I had a feeling I was going to have the best day I'd had in a long time.

While I was arranging some of the pumpkins and gourds we'd bought at the nursery around the gorgeous bronze mums we'd picked up, Mom casually tossed out, "So, Kellie called me."

I dropped the green gourd and looked up at Mom, who was setting a darling scarecrow on a bale of hay. I knew Kellie and Mom were still friends, even though it was awkward now. But not as awkward as my dad and Jay still being business partners. I can't stress enough how important it is not to marry your dad's business partner's son. Even so, it wasn't unusual for Kellie and Mom to talk, but I knew what this conversation was about. Mara had given me some of the 411, especially about Claudia Cann's woes. Apparently, some of her fans found it distasteful that she would flip anyone off, especially at a hospital when her mother-in-law was sick. Even better was that someone recorded it, and it was making the rounds on every social media channel. The hashtag #CannClaudia was trending. Was it evil how happy that made me? What was even better? Mara was using her fake accounts to spread that hashtag around. I seriously loved her.

"What did she say?" I asked innocently.

Mom gave me a knowing smile. "Something along the lines that I have a wonderful daughter and you gave her a lot to think about."

"Yeah." I knew I had caused a lot of heartburn for the Scott family. We are talking, Kellie kicked Jay out of their bedroom. And I think she might have binged an entire pizza and skipped Pilates. "I might have broken up a marriage."

"No, my love, that marriage was broken a long time ago."

"In my heart I know she should leave him, but I know it will hurt Mara."

"And you will be there to help her if and when that time comes."

At least I knew I would always show up for Mara. "Why is love so complicated?"

Mom set her scarecrow on the porch and walked down the stone steps to me. We both took a seat and let the autumn sun warm us. I rested my head on Mom's shoulder, contemplating the meaning of life. Well, sort of. I wasn't that deep.

Mom kissed my head. "Honey, just because something is complicated doesn't make it bad."

"For some," I whispered.

She sighed that sigh of hers, the one that said she didn't know what to say to me anymore to change my mind about love, but she wished with all her heart that I would. She had more journals to give to me. Journals she wanted me to pass down to my own daughter.

"Kellie mentioned Noah was there on Sunday too," Mom said out of the blue.

"He was."

"Apparently, there was some trouble between him and Ben," she growled his name.

"Ben had to run his mouth and Noah stuck up for me."

"That's nice," Mom said, all cheery.

"Noah's a nice guy."

"He is," Mom sang. "And I hear you've been spending more time together," she said conspiratorially.

"Who told you that?"

She waved her hand around. "I hear things."

"Okay." I had no idea who would tell her these things. "Noah and I are friends. Friends hang out sometimes."

"And do you have fun together?"

"Yes, Mom. And we share our toys too," I teased her.

"Like sex toys?"

My head popped off her shoulder. "Mom! Why would you say that? Noah and I aren't having sex."

"I saw that movie, *Friends with Benefits,* and thought I should check."

I scrunched my nose. "What other movies are you watching? You know what? I don't want to know."

Mom laughed evilly.

That didn't make me feel better.

Mom took my hand. "Oh, lighten up, buttercup. I've had six kids—you don't think I've seen it all?"

"Regardless of what you see or what you and Dad watch, I don't need to know about it. In my head you only watch Disney movies, and I want to keep it that way. Besides, I'm a proud born-again virgin."

Mom rolled her eyes.

"I thought you would be happy that I wasn't sleeping around."

"Darling, I'm proud that you don't need to find your worth in a man's bed, but don't you ever miss waking up in the arms of the person you love?"

I swallowed hard and rubbed my chest. Of course I did, but . . . "The only man I ever shared a bed with left me alone in the dark." I had to hold back the tears.

Mom let out a heavy breath and gave me a sympathetic look. "For that, he deserves everything he's gotten—but you, my love, you have the power to turn the light back on if you choose to." She stood and walked back up the stairs.

"Being in the light means exposing all of me," I said more to myself than to her.

"Oh, how lucky that person will be."

I turned to find that she was back to busying herself, as if she knew that was all she should say for now. It was a beautiful, but scary sentiment. I wasn't sure how we'd gone from talking about my ex-in-laws to my nonexistent sex life. But I did have a question for her. "Why would you think Noah and I are having sex? Did someone say something to you?" That's all I needed were those kinds of rumors. My Ex-Filers wouldn't be happy about that.

Mom gave me an impish grin. "Honey, I have eyes to see. Hubba, hubba." She wagged her brows.

I have to agree with Mom there. He is yummy, Miss Sparkly entered the conversation. Again.

First of all, she's my *mom. Second, you promised me you'd let the Noah thing go. Do you want me to cancel watching* It's the Great Pumpkin, Charlie Brown*? Because I will.*

Fine, I'm zipping my lips. She pouted.

Now back to my mother. "Mom! We're friends. And if you must know, he's in love with someone."

"Is that so?" Mom held up the scarecrow. "Who is she?"

"I don't know for sure, but—"

"Honey," she cut me off, "let me give you some advice. There are a lot of things you don't know right now, so if I were you, I would stop trying to guess."

I slapped a hand against my chest. "Are you insulting me?"

"No, honey," she used her cutesy voice that said she was totally insulting me. "I'm only trying to save you from looking like a fool."

My eyes widened to the width of a football field while my mouth hung open and I spluttered, not knowing what to think about what she'd just said.

To make matters more interesting, Noah pulled up in front of his sister's house. I wasn't expecting him, especially since it was in the middle of the day and Jaxon was at school and Liam was with Adonis's mom.

"Well, look who's here." Mom was positively giddy.

"Did you know he was coming?"

"I know everything," she said all mysteriously.

For reals, she was starting to freak me out.

Noah was out of his truck in no time and walking our way, a little dustier and dirtier than I normally saw him. It looked like he had come straight from one of his jobsites. Which got me worried. I popped up. "Is Shanna okay?"

He stopped on the lawn and wiped his brow. He glistened in the sun.

Oh wow. That was a cheesy observation. I couldn't even blame Sparkles for it.

"As far as I know," he responded.

"Good," I replied, relieved. "So, what are you doing here?"

"I thought I should come check on your work," he teased. "And I try to stop by every day to see if Shanna needs anything."

Wow. He truly was the best. Before I could respond, though, Mom jumped in.

"Well, that is the sweetest thing. Why don't I check on your sister while you inspect Cami, I mean while you inspect her work."

Oh. My. Gosh.

Mom laughed in evil undertones, knowing that she'd said exactly what she meant to say the first time. It was a lost cause. Noah was in love with Annika, and I, well, I was a hot mess who had no business thinking about a relationship—especially with my ex-husband's best friend. I was barely letting pumpkin pillows back in my life.

"Don't worry, I'll check her out, Mrs. J." Noah winked at my mother before she skedaddled.

I grimaced at him. "Don't encourage her."

"Oh, come on." He approached me. "Let her be happy."

"Fine." I stood. I knew he was only teasing her.

Noah peered at the porch. "Wow, Cams. You outdid yourself. Shanna's going to love it."

I looked at Mom's and my handiwork; I would say it was Pinterest worthy. "We had a lot of fun doing it."

Noah's brows raised. "You had some *holiday* fun?" He was obviously taunting me.

"Yes. Okay. I did have fun. I even survived Hobby Lobby."

"Look at you," he said playfully, before adding sincerely, "I'm proud of you."

"Thanks. How's your day been?"

Noah looked down at his dirty jeans and T-shirt. "I had to fix some duct work in a crawl space today."

"That doesn't sound like fun."

"It's a living."

That actually reminded me of something I had been thinking about, in my pursuit to find me. I thought it would be good if I finally made my condo truly my own place. "I'm thinking about renovating my place. Probably starting with the kitchen. Can you recommend a good contractor?"

He faux-stabbed himself in the heart. "Why wouldn't you ask me to do it?"

"I know how busy the firm keeps you and how much you're helping your sister right now."

He stepped closer; his chin dipped. "And you think I wouldn't make time for you?" he said lowly.

"Um." I gripped the stair railing. Something inside me was stirring. I assumed it was Sparkles. "I don't expect you to." I said, very breathily.

His smile grew, the closer he got to me. "We are friends, are we not?"

I nodded.

He is so sex—

Don't even think it, I begged Miss Sparkly. *Believe me, I know he's sexy.*

I knew it! she cackled.

"Best friends, right?"

I tucked some hair behind my ear and let out a nervous laugh. "We're *good* friends," I stuttered.

His beautiful blue eyes lit up. "I've been promoted to good. I can live with that . . . for now."

"You're going to have to fight Mara for the title of best friend." Not like I would ever give Mara up.

He stepped onto the bottom step, now at eye level with me. His snickerdoodle scent, mixed in with his natural muskiness from working, really worked for him. Or should I say *on* me? I had to grip the railing tighter. Miss Sparkly was purring on the inside.

Noah leaned in. "You're worth fighting for."

Maybe I was worth fighting for, but I lost the fight with Miss Sparkly when she threw our arms around Noah. I was totally canceling *It's the Great Pumpkin, Charlie Brown.* She didn't care.

Noah wrapped me up tight. "What's this for?"

My head rested on his shoulder naturally.

Soak him in, girl, soak him in.

I tried not to, but Miss Sparkly was on a mission. I breathed in deeply and let it out slowly. "It's just you've been so good to me. I don't deserve you."

"True." He chuckled.

I softly laughed on the outside. Inside, I was having a major battle between my two selves. I realized Miss Sparkly wasn't only on a mission—this was war. She planned to battle me for control.

Oh no, she knows my plan, she mocked me.

Yeah, well, I would show her—right after I took another whiff of my friend. Whoa. He should bottle it and sell it. Eau de Noah. It would be a big hit.

I abruptly pulled away. "That was nice," I said all nervously.

"Very nice," he agreed.

"Well," I squeaked, "I should probably clean up and let you get back to your day."

Noah tilted his head. "Everything okay?"

"Super great," I lied. I was having a mini identity crisis. Okay, a humongous one. I was so freaked out that I ran up the steps to do who knew what. I couldn't remember.

"Cams." Noah followed me.

I stopped and turned to face him.

He was observing me, probably wondering if he should take me in for a mental evaluation. "You're safe with me." How did he know to say that?

"I know." And that was a big problem.

Eighteen

Dear Ex-Filers, do I have a funny story for you, and the best comeback of all time, if I do say so myself. Last night at the grocery store, while I was deciding on how many pints of ice cream I should buy (I got four if you must know), some random man slid in front of me as I reached for my precious dairy products and said, "Hello, angel, did you fall from heaven?" Before I gagged on that cheesy line, my brain gifted me with a zinger. "Why yes," I purred. "But remember, so did Satan," I said in my deepest evil voice. The man about wet himself before he fled from my presence. Good times.

Stay safe from cheesy pickup lines this weekend. If you do fall victim to one, just remember I'm here winter, spring, summer, and fall to remove them all.

I'm off to snuggle bunnies now.

Lots of love,

Cami

I published my post and then picked up my pooch to snuggle on the couch. Neville and I had been having a lot of heart-to-heart talks since yesterday. I think he'd come to the conclusion that I probably needed anti-anxiety meds more than he did. He wasn't wrong. I was blaming Miss Sparkly, but she was pinning it all on me, saying if I would just let go, we would be so much happier. I was willing to compromise and let go of a few things. I mean, I'd gone to Hobby

Lobby and bought pumpkin pillows for goodness' sake. And my condo smelled like I was smoking pumpkin spice. Why couldn't that be good enough? Why did she think we needed a man's touch? Didn't she remember how safe we had felt with Ben once upon a time?

I snuggled Neville to my chest, like that would help vanquish the earth-shattering feelings Ben's betrayal invoked. There was no safe anymore.

There never was, you ninny, Miss Sparkly rudely interrupted my thoughts. *At least not in the way you're thinking,* she softened her tone. *There are no safety nets in life; if you want to feel the highs, there is always a risk of falling.*

To our death, I reminded her.

You live like we are dead. What's worse?

Ouch.

I only say these things to you for our own good. Do you think I like that we're talking to ourselves? If you would only come to terms with me, your true self, we wouldn't be having these conversations anymore. The ball is in your court here. Are you going to start playing the game we love again, a.k.a. life? Or are you going to sit here on the couch, talking to me and Neville for eternity?

I like Neville. You, not so much.

You love me. You're just scared.

I let Neville rest on my lap and plugged my ears, as if that would help Miss Sparkly go away.

Still here, she sang.

Ugh.

Now get up, Noah will be here soon to pick you up.

I had planned to call and cancel on Noah after arguing with Miss Sparkly last night for hours about her behavior around him. She was thinking some crazy things, like that maybe Noah thinks about me as more than a friend. My mother obviously thought so, and even Mara had said something when I'd driven her home from visiting her mom in the hospital. She'd found it interesting how quickly Noah had come to my defense, and apparently after I left the room, he'd told Ben he only had himself to blame for letting go of the best thing that will ever happen to him. But Mara only said it was interesting.

Anyway, it was all crazy thinking. Except . . . No. Never mind.

Say it, Miss Sparkly begged. *You know you felt something in his arms.*

Maybe. But it doesn't matter. He loves Annika.

You don't know that.

Not for sure, but it makes sense. Besides, we kind of built a business around the whole being single thing.

That was you, girl. Not me. Though I get why you did. But is that really it for us? No more sleeping on chests and waking up to sleepy smiles and warm kisses? And what about a baby?

I rubbed my abdomen, tears leaking down my cheeks.

Don't even say artificial insemination. You know that's not the way you want to go. You want to create a life with someone you love.

That worked out really well for us last time.

Ben was a hit and a miss. So that means you're never going to try for a home run again?

I thought I had made that clear.

Then Ben wins. Congratulations.

I wiped the tears from my cheeks. It was more complicated than that. But yeah, I heard her message loud and clear.

I held Neville up and kissed his head before setting him back down on the couch. Noah would be here in fifteen minutes, and I didn't need him to see tear-stained cheeks. Part of me was hoping not to see him at all today. But I knew how excited Jaxon and Liam were about me coming. Not only that, but my mom was also getting devious. She'd told all my siblings where I would be today, so several of them were showing up with their kiddos, so happy that Aunt Cami was finally joining in on the holiday fun.

I had no choice now but to show up for the children and be happy. Admittedly, I was excited. I'd missed Peterson's—although I was nervous. A lot of good memories with Ben lived there. And Miss Sparkly might think I was letting Ben win, but going to Peterson's today was proving I may just be the victor. Perhaps not in all the ways she wanted. But I was trying. Truly, I was.

I went to my bathroom and dabbed under my eyes, removing the mascara stains before fixing the damage I had done. I went with a soft, neutral smoky eye to match the warm-brown, off-one-shoulder sweater I was sporting for the occasion. Yes, Miss Sparkly suggested the outfit. It did make me feel pretty. Not gorgeous like Annika or Claudia, but at least I looked like me.

I had barely finished fixing my makeup when Noah knocked on my door. His knock was as distinctive as he was. I'd told him I would just meet him and the boys there, but he didn't trust me to show up. It was probably a good call on his part.

On the walk to the door, I wanted to tell Miss Sparkly to behave herself today, but it was futile. She was in battle mode, and wouldn't be backing down until she'd overtaken us once and for all. Part of me wanted to give in to her. She was happy and a lot of fun. But she had her flaws like everyone else. She was naive, and probably too much of a people pleaser, for starters.

Better that than scared to live my life and unwilling to send condolence cards.

She was never going to let that go.

Neville was by the door when I got there. How he knew it was Noah, I didn't know. Normally when someone came to the door, he hightailed it to my room and hid under the bed.

With a deep breath in and out, I opened the door, and Noah hardly gave me a glance before picking up my dog. He didn't even pay attention to me when he strolled in with my pooch. At least Liam and Jaxon were excited to see me. Jaxon hugged my middle while Liam hugged one of my legs.

I wrapped my arms around them. "Hi, guys, how are you?"

Shouts of "Good!" and exclamations that they couldn't wait to get to the pumpkin patch filled my ears and condo. Meanwhile, Noah was aimlessly walking around my small kitchen with my dog.

I shut the door and the boys ran to Noah, anxious to pet my dog. I wasn't sure how that was going to go. Neville hadn't ever cared for my nieces and nephews.

I walked into the kitchen, not sure what I was more nervous about: my dog being grumpy with the boys or whether Noah would acknowledge my presence. Was he upset with me?

Well, if we're being honest, you are kind of a nutjob. It's exhausting, Miss Sparkly went in for the kill.

Is that how people saw me? I exhausted them? My eyes started to water.

I didn't mean to hurt your feelings. Please don't cry in front of Noah. He already thinks you're crazy.

I thought you didn't want to hurt my feelings? I zinged back at her.

Oops.

I was so done with her. I turned around to get my emotions under control. The last thing I wanted was for Noah to see me cry. I fanned my eyes and took shallow breaths. That was until I heard Liam giggle.

"He's licking me," he squealed.

I turned to find Noah and the boys sitting on my kitchen floor. Noah held Neville carefully out toward Liam and Jaxon. Neville would sniff the boys and then give them a lick. Who knew he had it in him to be so normal? I guess Noah did. Apparently, I was holding my dog back. Or maybe I had screwed him up in the first place.

Noah glanced my way, and he went from smiling to flatlined lips. What could I say? I was good at killing every good thing.

"We should probably get going," Noah finally spoke to me.

I said, "Yeah," all while trying to think how I could get out of this. Noah clearly didn't want to be around me. "You know, I should probably drive myself. It seems silly for you to drive all the way back here when you and the boys live in Carson City. I feel bad you even came out of your way this morning."

Noah pressed his lips together as he stood. I had no idea how to read him. Then he shrugged. "That does make more sense."

I had to grab the counter next to me. I'm not going to lie, I thought for sure he would tell me I was being silly and of course we should go together. "Okay," I whispered. "I'll meet you there. Sorry you drove all the way up here."

"No worries." He gently set Neville down before he reached into his pocket and pulled out a flash drive.

Miss Sparkly stopped breathing.

"I wanted to give you this anyway."

I stared at the flash drive.

"I'm ready for my lecture," he teased.

I was in no mood to give one. I grabbed the flash drive. "No lecture. I'll edit these as soon as I can."

His face dropped as if I'd disappointed him, but he recovered quickly. "Great."

"You guys can head on out. I'll be five minutes behind you. I just need to get Neville settled." And my heart for that matter. Miss Sparkly was in a tailspin and she had my pulse racing. She couldn't believe I was right. But even she recognized that if Noah cared for me as more than just a friend, he wouldn't have brought me another photo shoot to crop his ex out of. Whoever she was. Maybe it was the owner of the German shepherd.

Noah gave me a shrewd look. "Are you trying to fake us out and not show up?"

I shook my head, afraid if I opened my mouth, Miss Sparkly would come out. She wanted to know why he was acting so offish and if I had done anything to him. I knew she blamed me. But the truth was, I was right, and she was wrong.

Bite me, Cami.

Nineteen

DEAR EX-FILERS, THE best advice I can give you today is to keep your expectations low. We are talking subbasement level. Things can only go up from there. Now carry on.

Lots of love,

Cami

I walked down the steps of my private entrance, wishing so badly I could bail. Even Miss Sparkly wasn't too thrilled about going now either. I wasn't sure if she was more upset at me for being right or herself because she was wrong. Or if she was mad at Noah. All I knew was that I had a lot of turmoil brewing in me, and it wasn't pretty. My stomach was even making weird whale sounds for being so upset. I needed to get that under control before I got to the pumpkin patch.

I'm not going to lie, even I was taken aback by Noah's behavior. Where was all his "I'll be a safe landing place for you" attitude this morning? The vibe I'd gotten was "Find a new landing strip to crash into, psycho." He didn't even know I was having major debates with myself. And it was safe to say I was annoyed about the flash drive. It didn't matter how wonderful this mystery woman of his was, she wasn't going to appreciate all the women he not only dated but did photo shoots with. Maybe he had a weird fetish I never knew about. *See, Miss Sparkly, you've been saved from another major mistake.*

It was crickets from her.

I guess that was one good side effect of Noah's behavior.

If only my family weren't going to be there. But I'd promised myself I was going to try and be a better sister, aunt, and daughter. Then there were Jaxon and Liam, who seemed disappointed that I wasn't driving with them. It seemed to give Noah some pause, but he had quickly brushed off their complaints and whisked them off.

Regardless, I'd made a commitment and I was going to go. It might not be half-bad. I mean, there were bunnies and pumpkin-spice doughnuts. And this way, I would have my own car and could leave whenever I wanted to. Huh. This worked out even better than expected.

Liar.

I knew she wouldn't stay quiet for long. Dang her. Unfortunately, she was right. I thought Noah wanted to be best friends. I'll tell you this, Mara would have never treated me in such a way. Ever.

I opened the private entrance door and breathed in the fresh, cool mountain air that sent a little chill down me. I walked out into the bright sun toward my 4Runner. To my surprise, Noah's truck was parked next to it and he was leaning against his door with his arms folded.

Miss Sparkly got a little excited, seeing him in his tight jeans and sexy plaid button-down with his sleeves rolled up. I made sure to tamp down her expectations real quick.

"Didn't think I would show up?" I snarled. Not sure why he cared one way or the other.

Girl, this animosity toward him says I'm not the only one who has some feelings for him.

Shut up, Sparkles.

"Cams," he sighed. "The boys really want you to drive with us."

"The boys?" I veered toward the driver's side of my car.

"Hey." Noah hustled my way, while the boys waved and shouted my name from their booster seats in the back of Noah's cab. I should mention he had his own set of booster seats for his nephews. That's the kind of guy he was, but Miss Sparkly was right, I was feeling animosity toward him.

Noah gently grabbed my arm before I made it to the door of my car. "Cams, please wait."

When I turned and faced him, he dropped my arm and stepped back like I had the plague. Obviously, I had done something to offend him.

He ran a hand through that hair of his that begged to be played with. Not by me of course, but it was tempting to Miss Sparkly.

"I want you to come with us too," he said as if he were exasperated.

My nose crinkled. "I'm not buying it. And it's fine. I'm a big girl and can drive myself."

He inched closer, albeit cautiously.

Did I smell? I was panicked, trying to remember if I'd put on deodorant. Miss Sparkly finally became useful. *Remember when I begged you to use the pillow-talk scented one today and you refused and went with plain old baby-soft scent? Big mistake by the way.*

And, she was done with her usefulness. At least I knew I didn't reek of BO.

"I'm sorry." He blew out a huge breath. "I know I'm out of sorts today."

"Did something happen?"

He ran his hand through his hair again. He must be really stressed.

"I know you hate relationships," he growled as if I'd slapped him, "but I could really use your advice about this woman."

"The woman you love?" I hesitated to ask, or more like Sparkles was putting a stranglehold on my vocal cords. She did not like this woman, whoever she was.

"Yes, her." He was clearly irritated with her too. "She's driving me mad. One minute I think she's finally in a place where we can be together, and then the next minute, BAM! She's pulling away again."

His booming voice made me falter a bit. "What's her reasoning?"

"That's a good question. I thought I knew what it was, and she was working through it, but there's more. There's always more. And it's so damn frustrating. I've waited years for her, and some days I don't know whether it's a lost cause or if I should grab her"—he placed his big man hands on my shoulders—"and look her squarely in the eye and say, 'Are you blind? Can't you see that I'm in love with you? That I would do anything for you?'" He sounded desperate.

Wow. He really had it bad for this woman. I had to admit if Noah looked at me that way and told me he loved me, I think . . . I think . . .

Say it, Cami. You feel something for him. Please admit it, Miss Sparkly pleaded.

It didn't matter what I felt; Noah's eyes begged me to take away his misery. I wish I knew how, but Miss Sparkly was withering inside. Her sparkles were more like a dim light. I felt for her. I felt for Noah. Yes, I might have even felt for myself. But there was a woman out there, probably Annika, that Noah had waited years for. I felt sorry for her too.

"I'm sorry, Noah. I wish I knew how I could help you." I really did. No matter how I felt about relationships or even how unsettled I felt now, Noah deserved happiness. He was a good man who saw the good in others, even when we didn't deserve it.

His hands dropped and he hung his head. "I wish you did, too. More than you know."

"Maybe I could help if you told me a little more about her." You know, like a name?

He laughed a tired laugh. "She's everything I've ever wanted. When she walked into my life, I knew she was the one, but she's never seen me that way."

"Have you ever told her how you feel about her?"

"Yes, but she's not listening," he complained.

She must have an iron will. I didn't know there was a woman alive who wouldn't fall for Noah Cullen if he said he loved her to her face. You know, except me.

That's a lie.

I ignored that comment. "Well,"—I smiled, though Miss Sparkly was not happy about it—"perhaps she's not ready yet, or maybe she's not the one." Miss Sparkly made me say that at the end.

"She's the one, Cams. That, I know."

Don't say it, don't say it.

You would say it. You know you would.

Miss Sparkly sighed. *You're right. I can't be selfish. It's not who we are.* And it wasn't.

"Then she's worth waiting for."

Noah smiled a genuine smile. "She is."

Though my heart pricked, it felt good to help my friend. "So, I'll meet you there?" I needed a moment to decompress. I felt a sense of loss I didn't expect. Like I had lost my best friend.

"Oh no. You're driving with us."

"It's okay. This way you won't have to go out of your way again."

"Cams, I really am sorry. Please come with us."

"I'm not upset with you. How could I be? You've been more than kind to me. But maybe it would be best if we didn't hang out. Perhaps the woman you love is hesitant because she thinks you're not available. I mean, look at all the photo shoots you do. And if I saw the guy I liked with another woman, I would think twice." More like a hundred times over.

He pinched the bridge of his nose. "Hell."

"I'm obviously frustrating you." Though I wasn't sure why. I thought I was being helpful. A good friend even.

"If you only knew, Cams." He gave me a strained smile.

"See, I should drive myself."

The boys had now reached their patience limit and were pounding on the windows and yelling that it was time to go.

Noah unceremoniously took my hand. "You're coming with us." He pulled me toward his truck like a gentlemanly Neanderthal.

I pulled my hand away from his, just as we almost made it around his truck. Miss Sparkly even agreed I should. Hand-holding to some women was sacred. This woman of his might not appreciate "friendly" hand-holding. "Hey, I really think I should drive myself. I know how women think, and this could be bad for you."

He rubbed his temples and groaned. "Cams, please just get in the truck."

"No."

He seemed to take a cleansing breath as if I were trying his patience. When he calmed himself, he explained, "I swear to you on my mother's grave, the woman I love, as infuriating as she can be, doesn't care that we're friends. In fact, she thinks I'm a better person when we hang out."

My brow raised. "You talk to her about me?"

"Of course. I have nothing to hide."

"And she really doesn't mind? I mean, it's not like there's anything going on between us, but I know how women can be."

"Yeah, big pains," he grumbled.

"Hey. I'm trying to do the right thing here. I want you to be happy."

He flashed me his dazzling smile. "If you want to make me happy right now, please get in the truck."

"Fine. You're being so bossy. But first, tell me who this woman is." Miss Sparkly clenched our fists. She wasn't taking this very well. Yet, we both knew it was better to face the truth head-on. We'd let Ben lie to us for so long because at the time the lies were easier to bear than the truth.

He let out a heavy breath. "Cams, when she's ready for me to tell you, you'll be the first to know."

"How long do you think it's going to take?" Inquiring minds needed to know.

"At this rate, forever."

Twenty

Dear Ex-Filers, it is said there is nothing so beautiful as a happy child, and I think that goes for our inner child too. Case in point, look at me with all these bunnies. Listen, if you are looking for something sweet and soft to cuddle up to at night, look no further.

Lots of love,

Cami

Of course, I couldn't bring one home. I already had Neville to cuddle up to at night. Besides, he'd seen a bunny in the wild a few months ago and instead of chasing after it like a real dog, he'd tucked his tail and come running to me, shaking.

We were all off to the corn cribs. And I meant all of us: Noah, Jaxon, Liam, my parents, three siblings and their spouses, and thirteen nieces and nephews. I had to admit, not only was my inner child happy, but so was I. And it wasn't because I had downed three pumpkin-spice doughnuts already. Though they definitely helped my mood. It was this place, and my people. I realized this was my family's place long before I'd ever brought Ben here. He'd only haunted it because I had let him. Noah was right, it was time to make new memories here. Except not with him. He'd been hanging out with my brothers most of the time we'd been here. I don't think he liked the advice I'd given him on the drive over. I highly recommended he stop with the photo shoots already.

He'd mumbled something about it being a romantic gesture and to let it alone.

I had no idea how any woman was going to find that romantic. But what did I know?

What I did know was that I was smitten with Liam, who hadn't left my side the entire time and held my hand as we walked to our next destination. I also knew how to get to my nephews Corey and Ryland. "Hey guys, who's your BAE?" I teased them.

They were walking in front of me and turned around with scowling red faces.

"You know you love me," I sang.

"I love you." My niece Melody came and hugged my side.

"Now you're my favorite and I'm buying you anything you want today."

"What!" Corey and Ryland both roared.

I shrugged. "I guess you should have said I was your BAE."

Chandler, Corey and Ryland's dad, paused his conversation with Noah and turned around. "Torturing my children again?"

"She specializes in torture," Noah said jokingly, but I sensed a hint of truth.

What was his problem? Regardless, I owned it. "It's what I live to do."

My sister-in-law and Chandler's wife, Katie, jumped in on my behalf. "Torture the boys as much as you want. Feel free to spread the love to your brother." She playfully smacked Chandler's butt.

"Ew, Mom," Anna, their ten-year-old daughter squealed. "You guys are disgusting."

Our large group laughed.

After that, the older children ran ahead, probably afraid their parents would embarrass them more. It was a good assumption. That left me with little Liam, who held up his arms to me. It was his usual naptime. I didn't miss a beat and picked him up, although he was quite heavy. He was all muscle like his dad. I didn't mind. I'd been carrying kids around since I was sixteen, when Ryland was born. I swore I was part pack mule.

My dad sidled up to me. "Hey, kiddo." He wore a look of

contentment. These kinds of days were what he and Mom lived for. Family time was sacred time, they would always say. I'd missed out on a lot of it the last few years.

"Having fun?" I asked, even though I knew the answer judging by the smile on his face.

"Yes. Looks like you are, too." He rubbed Liam's head. "I would say you even have some of your sparkle back."

He had no idea. I partially blamed him for my dual personality. It wasn't until he'd talked to me, that Miss Sparkly had appeared.

Uh, I was totally here first, thank you very much. You are the interloper, she was happy to remind me again.

"I feel a little sparkly." I gave Sparkles a shout-out, hoping to keep her quiet for the rest of the day. And I felt bad for her. She was having a hard time. On one hand she was depressed about Noah, but on the other hand, she was overjoyed to be back at Peterson's. Meanwhile, I was excellent at repressing my emotions—and there were doughnuts, bunnies, and most of my minions, so I was doing just fine.

"It shows, kiddo. I hope it lasts."

I did too.

I was glad we made it to the corn bins. Liam was killing my back. I set him down in the bin Jaxon and a few of my minions were already in. I jumped in too. That gave them the go-ahead to tackle me, while trying to bury me in dried corn kernels. Oh, I dished it out too. I wasn't sure who laughed harder, me or them? It wasn't all fun and games—my bra was getting inundated with kernels. I probably should have worn a turtleneck. I'd forgotten how sneaky corn could be and how ruthless my nieces and nephews were. I was totally proud of them. I had taught them well.

After I had enough kernels down my sweater and bra to plant an acre of land, I called a truce, meaning I started picking up children and setting them outside of the bin. My parents took mercy on me and grabbed the minions. Not sure where their parents had wandered off to. That left me with Jaxon, Liam, and Noah, who decided to show up out of nowhere. He had promised to jump in the bins with us, but I wasn't holding him to it, as I obviously wasn't his favorite person today.

I wasn't sure why, but I felt a little nervous around him, almost as if he knew my alter ego had a crush on him.

How many times do I have to tell you that I'm not the alter ego? You are! Miss Sparkly made her point.

Or so she thought. I was still in control.

"Oh. There you are," I said, as if I were out of breath. "Can you take the boys? I think I've gone from a size C cup to a D. Who needs tissues when you have corn kernels?"

Noah's eyes zoomed in on my chest.

"Are you staring at my bre—" I went to tease him, but remembered there were little ears around.

Noah's cheeks reddened; he obviously knew what I was going to say. "Uh, no," he spluttered.

"If you say so." I messed with him. He deserved it for going back on his promise.

He hastily helped his nephews out of the bin and took their hands. "I was just wondering if you wanted to do the corn maze next."

"I want to do the hayride," Jaxon voiced his opinion on the matter.

"That's fine with me." I had mixed feelings about the corn maze. I used to love it. As a teenager, I would come here at night and play hide-and-go-seek in the maze. I'd kissed my fair share of boys during those nights too. But there was one boy, man—I guess you could call Ben that—who had set my world on fire in that maze.

Half of me (the sparkly side) wanted to face my demons in there and vanquish them, but the other half feared what she would find in that maze. What if I wasn't strong enough to defeat Ben?

Don't think like that. Please. We can do it. Or at least I can. Just set me free, woman.

If I set her free, there would be trouble afoot. She'd want to date, and heaven forbid visit the holly jolly aisles at Hobby Lobby and probably hit every craft fair she could in November. She'd for sure OD on candy canes. She'd probably want a tree. My throat closed up thinking about it.

"Oh, okay." Noah seemed disappointed. "I thought we could walk and talk."

"Are you feeling guilty for ignoring me most of the day?" I evilly grinned.

He scrubbed a hand over his chiseled, stubbled face.

Those were Miss Sparkly's observations of him. She forced me to stare. Not sure why. We both knew it was a lost cause. Whoever this woman was, he'd told her he loved her.

I'm really surprised Annika hadn't mentioned it in our meeting this past week. She normally loves to tell us of the men who fall at her feet before she stomps all over them. Maybe Noah was different. Perhaps she loved him, too, but was having a hard time coming to terms with it because of her ex-husband. I totally got that.

If someone told me they loved me right now, even if I had feelings for them, it would be a shock to the system. How do you trust anyone after the kinds of betrayal Annika and I had endured?

"I haven't ignored you. I've been catching up with your brothers."

"You're such a liar." I carefully exited the corn crib. My breasts were starting to itch from all the kernels. "Anyway, I need to de-kernel myself. I'll be right back."

Noah chuckled. "We'll be by the apple cider stand."

I waved at the three of them and hustled over to the restrooms, corn kernels falling out of my sweater as I went. That had to be attractive. Thankfully, I found an empty stall where I could privately scoop kernels out of my bra. I had no idea what to do with them, so I started shoving them in my pockets. I supposed I could deposit them in the trash near the sinks.

As I picked the corn out, I thought about Noah and his offish behavior. Normally he was a happy, fun-loving guy. I realized the way he was acting did kind of hurt my feelings. It made me feel even worse for treating him so horribly the last few years. I had probably hurt his feelings too. I guess the thing that bothered me most was that, typically, Noah was a constant. I'd always known what to expect from him. Except after Ben and I had gotten engaged. He was offish then too. His reasoning was that there wasn't room for three people in a marriage. Amen to that. Although I never looked at Noah as an intruder. Some of the best times Ben and I'd had together, Noah had been right there with us.

What depressing thoughts. I tried to shake myself out of them. I was there to have fun with Liam and Jaxon and my family. Noah, I wasn't so sure about.

I walked out of the stall looking like a fool with hands and pockets full of corn kernels. A few women chuckled, and some nodded appreciatively like they'd been in my position before. Anything for the kids.

De-kernelled, I walked out into the crisp autumn day with plenty of sunshine. Laughter and squeals of delight filled the air, as children ran from place to place to enjoy each activity the pumpkin patch had to offer. Behind the children lagged parents holding pumpkins and juice boxes, tired, but with smiles on their faces. Sure, there were some tears and even tantrums, but for the most part it was a happy scene.

I meandered down the dirt path to the apple cider stand, where they sold a variety of flavors, both warm and cold. I was a sucker for warm cinnamon apple cider and planned to get some before we headed over to the hayride.

It didn't take me long to spot Noah, as he towered over most people. He stood near the stacked shelves where they offered gallons of their cider for sale.

Noah held up two lidded cups as I got closer.

Meanwhile, I frantically looked around for Jaxon and Liam. "Where are the boys?" I asked, my heart racing.

"Relax." Noah handed me a cup of steaming apple cider. The cinnamon and apple scents tickled my nose. I loved that smell, but how could I relax when the boys were missing? Better question was, how come Noah wasn't panicking? Shanna was going to kill him, and possibly me.

"The boys are safe," he put me at ease. "Your parents offered to take them on the hayride."

I tilted my head. "I wanted to go with them."

Noah gave me a pressed-lip smile. "I hoped we could talk."

"Listen, let's just forget about earlier. I have no business giving anyone relationship advice. And you're allowed to get grumpy and act like a jerk sometimes." I smirked.

He grimaced. "I don't ever want you to think I'm a jerk."

I shrugged. "It happens to the best of us." I held up the apple cider. "Thank you for this."

"It's the least I can do." He kicked at a rock near his feet. "You've been great with my nephews today. Watching you in that corn crib with all the kids was a beautiful sight."

"Because they were trying to take me down with brute force?"

His eyes met mine. "No, because you let your guard down around them."

I took a sip of my drink, not sure what to make of that observation, although I knew it to be true.

"Let's walk," Noah suggested.

I silently followed him away from the crowd. He headed toward the back of the property, the same direction as the corn maze. I still wasn't sure it was the best idea for me to revisit that part of my past today, yet I kept putting one foot in front of the other.

When Noah didn't say anything, I responded to his observation. "It's easy to be myself around children because I know that it doesn't matter what I do or say, they will still love me. And even if I mess up, they easily forgive my mistakes."

"Kids are great that way."

"Agreed."

"You know, there are plenty of adults in your life that feel the same way about you as those kids do. I think they miss you."

"Is this part of my parents' intervention?" I cringed, thinking about them recruiting Noah to their cause. Worse, my mother trying to throw us together. I'd told her he was in love with another woman.

"No, no," he stammered. "This is me telling you how much I loved seeing the old Cami today."

See, I told you, you should just give me control, Miss Sparkly bragged.

"Then why didn't you join in on the fun like you promised?" I threw back at him.

"I was having too much fun watching the kids obliterate you." He nudged me.

I rolled my eyes. "Gee, thanks."

"Honestly," his tone softened. "I was admiring you. There is something special about you, Cams. I hope you know that."

"Thanks," I whispered, not sure if I believed him. "So, should we see if we can catch the hayride?" We were getting closer and closer to the corn maze, and I was getting itchy. And not from the residue of corn kernels.

He stopped and looked between me and the sign directing people toward the maze. "I was hoping we could talk. I know you say you're the last person who should be giving relationship advice, but honestly, I think in this situation your advice and insight would be valuable to me."

I drank and drank my apple cider until my insides burned, trying to stall. When every taste bud I had was burned, I cleared my throat. "I really don't think I could offer anything of value to you. You know my history, and how I feel about relationships now."

"That's what makes you perfect. This woman and you have eerily similar pasts." He wasn't giving up.

This was my opportunity to see if it really was Annika. "Did her husband cheat on her too?" I grabbed my stomach.

Noah nodded gravely.

"With someone she knew?"

He nodded again.

Yep, it was Annika.

"I'm sorry to hear that." Truly I was, even if half of me was jealous.

Let's be honest, lady, three-fourths of us.

Please keep your opinions to yourself. Thank you and goodbye. I tried to dismiss my nemesis.

"What more do you want to know about my situation?" I asked. "I mean, you kind of had a front-row seat for it all."

"It's a ticket I never wanted," he said with an air of protectiveness. "That said, if you would be willing to open up and give me some deeper insight, I'd really appreciate it." He was practically begging me. He must really have it bad for this woman.

I wanted to be a good friend, but did he know what he was asking of me?

"Please, Cams?"

I hemmed and hawed some more. This was serious business. It might actually make me confront my past head-on. Who wanted that?

He sighed before giving me a wicked grin. "You never did send a condolence card."

See! I told you so, Miss Sparkly gleefully derided me. *But really, you should talk to him. Be honest with him, and yourself. Please.*

"Okay. Fine."

Twenty-One

UH . . . EX-FILERS, I'M about to enter a corn maze with this sign at the entrance: Do what scares you until it doesn't. *Not sure this bodes well for me. Wish me luck.*

Lots of love,

Cami

Honestly, how apropos was that sign? Not sure who thought it was a good idea to place a sign like that in front of a maze you could get lost in for hours. It gave me second and third thoughts about entering, and not because I was worried about getting lost—at least not physically. Emotionally drowning was definitely a possibility.

Noah said his goodbyes to Shanna, who had called to check on the boys. I felt guilty for shirking my duty with them. Not to say I didn't trust my parents with them. They were certified pros. I just wished the boys were with us so I could be fun Cami and give them silly answers to the hundreds of questions they asked—instead of having to face the hard questions I knew their uncle was going to throw at me.

"Sorry about that." Noah shoved his phone in his pocket.

"No worries. Feel free to take or make as many calls as you need to." I was totally serious.

Noah chuckled. "You'll be fine."

Easy for him to say.

He waved his arm toward the entrance. "Ready?"

"Nope." Inside that maze lived part of my past. Beautiful parts and ugly parts that both scared me.

Noah studied me for a moment, as if I perplexed him. His eyes searched my own, looking for the map to the maze that was my life. I supposed he thought if he could figure me out, he could better understand the woman he loved.

Noah pointed at the maze. "Ben's not in there." Then he gently rested his finger on my forehead. "Ben's in there. Don't you think it's time to let him go?"

"I've tried," I whispered. If you count running away from everything connected to him, even myself.

"Let's try harder, together."

Please. I have this feeling he could help us, Miss Sparkly implored.

You just like him, I argued.

I do like him. Very much. And so do you. Can't you feel his goodness?

He's in love with someone else.

This has nothing to do with that. Think about every time he's been there for us.

That's a lot of times, but how do we trust our feelings? That was the million-dollar question.

Do what the sign says. Do what scares us until it doesn't anymore.

Easy for you to say, you're on the inside.

Let me out.

Miss Sparkly didn't know how tempting that sounded. I let out a deep breath. "Lead the way."

"How about we do this side by side?" He offered a better alternative.

I liked that. A lot.

We fell in step, side by side, as we walked through the maze's wide entrance, which significantly narrowed the farther we got in. That didn't stop teenagers from whizzing past us. It meant a lot of bumping into Noah. Which wasn't bad. He smelled delicious and was a steadying force. Which was good as I grappled with my thoughts, trying not to let Ben overcome them. But then I wondered if I should just let my mind live out his memories. Maybe it just needed to work him out of our system, but I was always stopping it because it was painful and it scared me.

We came to our first crossroads where we had to choose whether we went left or right. Once we decided to go left, that's when the questions came.

Noah shoved his hands in his pockets. "So, I don't want to be a jerk like you accused me of earlier, but—"

"You were totally being a jerk but proceed." I smirked.

"All right," he conceded. "I apologize. Anyway, I know these questions won't be easy for you, but I really need the answers." He sounded like this was life or death.

"Okay." I cringed, knowing what was coming.

"First question." He swallowed hard. "Why don't you trust yourself?"

I came to a halt and grabbed my heart. "How do you know I don't?"

He dipped his chin to his chest and gave me a meaningful look.

"Okay, but you could have gone with a softball question first."

"I'm way past that stage," he said, frustrated.

My eyes widened. "Wow. This woman has really gotten under your skin. I take it she doesn't trust herself either."

"You guessed right. It's ridiculous, she's so capable and incredible."

Okay, okay, we don't need to know all the gory details about her. Answer his question already, Miss Sparkly demanded.

I started down the trail again, thinking it would be easier to answer if I wasn't looking directly at him. It was a complicated and layered answer. While I thought of how to put it into words, I focused on the crunch of cornstalks beneath my boots and the earthy smell of Peterson's. "Noah," I began, "most of my life, I intuitively knew the right things to do. What classes I should take, which friends to pick, the school I should go to, who I should marry," I whispered. "With every fiber of my being, I knew Ben was the one for me, and I for him. I trusted myself, and him, implicitly. And then," my voice hitched, "he violated that trust. At first it was little by little, a criticism here and there. Things I could brush off. But as the months wore on, the slights cut deeper, and I started to believe they were true." My eyes welled up with tears thinking about that woman.

Noah took my hand. "Cams," his voice ached, "I didn't know."

"How could you have? I was so ashamed and felt so lost. Worse, I allowed it to continue. I did everything I could to try and be worthy of him. I lost weight and did my hair just the way he wanted it. I even spoke softer around people because he said I was too loud and obnoxious." I cringed saying those words. Words I had never spoken out loud, not even to Mara. "I was so pathetic."

"Don't say that. He was the pathetic one."

"I was pathetic," I disagreed. "I was going to stay with him, because how could I be so wrong?" I pleaded, knowing full well Noah didn't have the answer. "It took me walking in on him with another woman before I could leave him." I had even gotten pregnant with his baby. I couldn't say that out loud. That I couldn't own, yet. Maybe someday. I squeezed Noah's hand, trying to absorb all the comfort I could before letting go. "So, you see, I have a good reason not to trust myself. This woman of yours probably does too."

Noah stopped and ran a hand through his hair, shaking his head as if I'd just shocked him. Perhaps I had. Without warning, he drew me to him and embraced me like that would somehow magically put all my broken pieces back together again. If only that would do the trick. Not to say it wasn't helpful. I found myself wrapping my arms around him, my head landing on his chest. Unsurprisingly, it was rock solid, yet somehow it was a soft landing place. Or was that safe?

Yes. I felt safe in Noah's arms. I always had. Because no matter what, he liked me for me, even when I was awful to him. And there had never been any expectations with Noah. We were friends, nothing more, nothing less.

He rested his chin on my head. "I knew something was wrong. I didn't know how wrong. I'm sorry, Cami."

"It's not your fault. I'm to blame."

"Don't you dare say that," he roared.

By now several onlookers had passed by. Some immature teen boys even called out, "Move out of the way and get a room."

After that, Noah and I broke apart faster than the speed of light, both blushing.

I bit my lip. "So, there you have it." Well, most of it. "I hope that helps."

Do I really? Miss Sparkly asked.

We do. You more than anyone know why we can't open ourselves up to possibilities like Noah or other men. We really messed up. Remember when we even agreed not to gain a bunch of weight if we got pregnant and we promised to be back to pre-pregnancy weight by six weeks postpartum? How could we do that?

I know. I know, Miss Sparkly cried. *I screwed up, but please don't keep punishing me.*

I'm not, I want to protect you. You created me to do that.

And there it was. I'd just admitted to being the interloper.

It's not that I don't want you. Maybe I still need you. I don't know. Sparkles was as confused as me. Or her. Who were we?

I held my stomach while it churned with so much uncertainty. I wasn't sure if purging my secrets was the best thing. I started briskly walking, looking for a way out of the maze, both in real life and in my head.

"Cams, I know that must have been difficult. Thank you. It was more helpful than you'll ever know. I know exactly how to proceed now."

Great. I was glad someone knew what to do. Meanwhile, I didn't even know who I was.

You do know. You just have to be willing to let go.

Oh. Is that all?

Twenty-Two

Dear Ex-Filers, Happy Halloween! Are you ready to party? The ballroom looks amazing. A huge thank-you to Bloom Events! And our very own planning committee. I can't wait to see so many of you tonight.

Lots of love,

Cami

"So, you are finally going to renovate?" Mara was flipping through one of the many designers' books Noah had given me to peruse. This particular one was all about cupboards. Who knew how many different types there were? And the colors, so many colors. White, sage, cream, gray, blue, black. Plus, you could mix and match, which was popular. I had no idea what to choose.

I set my phone on the still-mauve countertop. Speaking of countertops, there were so many varieties of those too. I was dreaming about granite, quartz, and woodblock. They each had their pros and cons. What if I chose unwisely? It was enough to make me wake up in a cold sweat. Don't even get me going on the cupboard dreams. Those had to be picked out first so that I could match the countertops to them. Let's just say I'd had a nightmare about furry cupboards and leave it at that. At least I had decided on the flooring—distressed white wood plank. It was going to be stunning. You know, as soon as I decided on everything else.

"Yeah." I picked up some of the wood samples. "I figured it was about time."

Mara set the book down. "I assume Noah helped you come to this conclusion," she said nonchalantly, being anything but subtle. I knew exactly what she was getting at. Yes, Noah and I had been spending a lot of time together lately. He'd needed a lot of help with his nephews over the last several days. Who else was going to make Rice Krispies treats that looked like candy corn, or spiderweb cupcakes? And not to brag, but I'd made some pretty snazzy LEGO costumes for the boys, using boxes and spray paint. I had officially become an honorary room mom for Jaxon. Yesterday at his class party, I think I'd spun what felt like a hundred kids for pin the nose on the pumpkin.

I inadvertently smiled over at the jack-o'-lantern sitting on my table that I'd carved with the boys a few days ago. It looked like it was high on weed with a goofy askew smile and cross-eyes. It was perfect, as the evening had been. We'd watched *Hocus Pocus* with the boys and their parents while stuffing our faces with caramel popcorn. "He's just returning the favor for me helping him with his nephews."

"Right," she said with an air of skepticism as she, too, looked at the carved pumpkin. "You are becoming awfully chummy for friends."

I rolled my eyes. I'd heard that from my mom and even Shanna. "Men and women can be friends. Believe me, that's all we are." He'd made sure to mention, every time we were together, how nice it was that we were friends. He'd even become less touchy-feely. I think he had taken what I'd said to heart, about making sure this woman of his knew he was completely available. His plan was to help her feel comfortable so she would come to him. Which reminded me to add, "Besides, he's in love with Annika."

"So you think. You don't have any actual proof."

"We will tonight. You saw how Annika was behaving this morning when we set up for the party. She was positively glowing with excitement."

"It could be because she stabbed someone and hid the body." Mara grabbed one of the leftover spiderweb cupcakes I had sitting on a platter and began peeling back the paper.

"This is true," I laughed. "But I'm telling you it's because of Noah. He wouldn't even tell me what he's coming as. He hopes the woman he loves will know it's for her."

"You know, that could be you," Mara said carefully.

Miss Sparkly perked up. She, like me, thought it was a lost cause, but I had a feeling she'd been holding out some hope.

"It's not me," I said uneasily. "He told this woman he loves her. Like you, he's just helping me figure myself out. That's all."

"Okay." Mara shoved half the cupcake in her mouth. "It's just, you sound disappointed by that," she said with her mouth full, which was super attractive.

I squirmed where I stood. "No, I don't."

You totally do, Miss Sparkly sang.

Hey you, I thought we were on the same side now. You've had one heck of an October, lady. And three trips to Hobby Lobby, so zip it.

You've had an amazing October too, she fired back. *Don't deny it. You are happier than you have been in a long time, so you zip it, lady.*

She had some points. She always had her points. And a lot of the time she was spot on. I was happier than I had been in a long time. There were even times I didn't feel like the interloper, that Sparkles and I could be one again. Or maybe it was that she was letting go of me. I wasn't sure. But she was for sure right about one thing, I should zip up some of my thoughts. Our thoughts. Thoughts like what a stable force Noah was. Or how adorable Noah was when he read stories to his nephews and acted out all the voices. Or how sweet he was to take his sister to her doctor's appointments when Adonis had to work. It's weird how I had never noticed what a good guy he is. I blamed it on my Ben vision. He'd consumed my every thought. I realized now how dangerous that kind of love was. I think it was one thing to be wrapped up in one another as new love tends to do, but I think real love, the truest kind of love, makes you want to be a better person and make the world a better place. To do that, you have to see outside of the two of you. Ben and I never got there.

Mara rubbed my arm. “Okay. If you say so.”

“I totally say so,” I said too quickly. Noah and I were friends, plain and simple. To think otherwise would complicate everything.

Mara gave me a placating smile.

“Enough talk about men; let’s do your eyes, Aries, and catch up on *Cosmetics and Crimes.* We have a party to attend.”

Mara smiled and grabbed my hand. “You are happier, just so you know.”

“I know.”

“You know that makes me happy, right?” she asked.

I wrapped my arms around her. “Of course I do. You’re my person. The big enchilada in my life.”

She giggled. “I do look good covered in cheese.”

I leaned back, eyes wide. “How do you know that?”

She gave me an impish grin. “It’s probably best not to talk about it.”

If Mara didn’t want to talk about it, it must be either really bad or too good, so I let it drop.

We ended up sitting on the floor in my living room with *Cosmetics and Crimes* playing in the background while I did Mara’s flame eyes. I’d practiced on myself, so I knew what I was doing. Hopefully. I’d even made a stencil using a label and X-ACTO knife because I was clever like that, or maybe because I’d seen someone on YouTube do it.

I readied my makeup palette with all sorts of fun liquid eye shadow colors. Everything from reds and oranges to hot pink. Mara was going to look truly like fire.

While I carefully applied the stencil to Mara’s left eye, she said, “Thanks for letting my mom come tonight.”

“I’m glad she asked. How is everything going with your parents?” I hesitated to ask, while I started to feather in the orange eye shadow.

“I think my dad is in denial. He’s trying to buy his way out of it, like he does everything in his life. But Mom isn’t having it this time. Though I think it killed her to refuse the anniversary band with three rows of diamonds that my father gifted her.”

"That had to hurt." Kellie had once quoted Zsa Zsa Gabor, *"I never hated a man enough to give him diamonds back."* At the time, she had been trying to convince me to keep the two-carat stunner Ben had given me. But I hated Ben so much that I didn't want the reminder. Not even the money I could have gotten had I sold it. To me that felt like blood money. Instead, I donated it to the women and children's shelter. Ben was livid about it, which made it even better.

"Don't worry, she went on a shopping spree. A little retail therapy. She and my dad need some real therapy."

"I think everyone does." I dabbed my brush into the yellow shadow.

"This is true. But at least Mom is sticking up for herself this time. Dad doesn't know how to deal with a backbone. We all usually end up bending to his will." She sounded ashamed to admit it.

"Family is complicated."

Mara's eyes popped open and hit mine full-force. "I'm just glad you left my brother. Idiot," she snarled.

"He is an idiot," I agreed.

She closed her eyes and let me continue my masterpiece. "Horrifyingly, his wife is worse. Sadly, the #CannClaudia campaign did not work. She ended up donating a bunch of money to charity and then posting a half-naked picture of herself, so all is forgiven." Mara stuck a finger in her mouth, pretending to gag. "That earned her a spot on PREPARATION H hemorrhoid treatment's mailing list. She should be getting a free sample any day now." Mara laughed like a mad scientist.

"My hero. I adore you."

"I just do what I can for society."

She had me giggling.

"But," she turned more serious, "I think there's trouble in paradise."

My ears perked up. "Really? Why?"

Mara's pretty hazel eyes fluttered open. "Well . . . because of you."

I dropped the brush on the palette. "Me?"

"This new, old you"—Mara waved her hand in front of me—"has my brother in a tailspin."

"I don't understand."

Mara tilted her head. "Don't you? The woman he fell in love with has reappeared."

"He didn't like that woman," I said, without my voice hitching. That was progress.

"No. He, like my dad, wanted to control that woman. But unlike my mother, until recently, you let him know he couldn't."

"It took me longer than it should have."

"The important thing is that you got there. Give yourself credit for that. Maybe even forgive yourself," she added.

Yes, please. Please forgive me, Miss Sparkly pleaded. Again.

"I'm working on it." This time I was telling the truth. That said, it was hard work. I'd even started putting little notes on my mirror to read every morning like self-affirmations. They said things like, *Believe in yourself, Let it go, You're in the driver's seat, Live life intentionally,* and my favorite, *You're such a weirdo for doing this.* That was my love note to Miss Sparkly.

"It's showing, and my brother notices. And Claudia notices that my brother notices. You probably inspired that half-naked picture."

"Ew." I wrinkled my nose. "Don't say that."

"You know what I mean. She was trying to show my brother what he had to lose. Little does she know what a winner he'd be if he lost those hundred and ten pounds."

"Do you think he would leave her?" I wasn't asking because I wanted him back. More like a little sweet revenge. Except I would love for him to find Claudia in his beloved Audi having sex with, like, her trainer, or better yet, his trainer. Just thinking of it made me giddy and pukey and perhaps guilty. Okay, so maybe I wouldn't. No matter how much I hated Ben, I didn't wish that for anyone.

Mara shrugged. "I think it's a possibility. He's been talking to my mom a lot. He feels like he's missing out on having a family of his own, and just so you know, he doesn't like your *friendship* with Noah."

"I told you, we are platonic with a capital *P*."

"So you keep saying." She smirked.

"It's true." I rolled my eyes. "You'll see tonight. It's Annika."

"You want to bet on that?" She wagged her brows.

I held out my hand and matched her toothy grin. "I bet my life on it."

Twenty-Three

DEAR EX-FILERS, SOME words of advice for tonight: Remember, men and women rarely do right by each other at parties. Don't drink and drive. Don't drunk date either. Alcohol is the leading cause of bad hookups and morning regrets. But if you fall prey to the charms of another on this All Hallows' Eve, just remember I'll be here when you've sobered up to crop that mistake right out. As for your hangover, that one is on you. Stay safe, sober, and single.

Lots of love,

Cami

Before I could click publish, the Miss popped up in my head. *Do you really have to add the single part? Don't you think that's a personal decision? You could be keeping people from a happiness like they've never known. Like yourself, cough, cough. Besides, if everyone stayed single, your little photoshopping business would be obliterated.*

Thank you for your little PSA. I clicked publish before I could think too much about Sparkles's lecture. I admit that was a dilemma for me. Not like I was thinking about getting into a relationship, but the Miss was all for entertaining the thought. But yes, that could put a serious damper on our brand. What would I say—all for me and none for thee? I would be a total hypocrite if I let Sparkles have her way.

Yes, but you would be so much happier. Come on, I need a good make out session and some slow hands. Remember how that feels?

A shiver went through me at the thought of how amazing a man's touch could be.

Stop it, I begged her. *I'm in the middle of hosting a party and fundraiser. See all the good that's come from our tragedy? Don't you want to keep helping these causes we believe in so much? We need the Ex-Filers to do that. We never had this reach before.*

You don't know that it would go away if you decided to date again. She refused to be quiet.

I had to settle for ignoring her as several people were walking in and I was currently greeting each guest, handing out drink tickets indicating a two-drink limit, with a list of gift baskets and packages they could bid on. All proceeds were going to the shelter. People in the community had been more than generous. They had donated season ski passes, spa packages, and even a trip to Disney. Sometimes I really loved humans.

Like the human coming my way, dressed as one sexy leopard—meow. Kellie was rocking the skintight, spotted bodysuit with a tail and ears to match, especially for someone close to sixty years old. She slinked my way with her head held high. She knew she was a babe. I wondered what Jay thought of her getup. It probably turned him on, but I bet he didn't want her to leave the house looking like the women he would hook up with on the side. The pig.

Kellie was to me in no time, wrapping me up in her arms. "Darling, how are you?" She squeezed me tight.

"I'm good. I'm so happy you could make it tonight. Look at you, hot mama."

She laughed like she was purring. She kissed my cheek. "You look absolutely stunning. You'll have all the schoolboys running your way tonight."

I looked down at my prep school getup, complete with a short plaid skirt and knee-high socks. My mom had even found a Gallagher patch for my tight pink sweater. I'm not sure anyone got who I was, except Mara. I had a feeling, like Kellie, people just thought I had come as a naughty schoolgirl.

"No boys tonight," I responded.

She patted my cheeks. "We shall see," she said in a sing-song voice.

"No couples allowed," I reiterated.

She laughed. "Good luck with that. I'm off to find my daughter."

Ugh. Why did everyone think we couldn't prevent hooking up? Not like I really needed an answer to that. But come on. It was one night. We were here for the women and children's shelter. I didn't sponsor this thing so I could drum up more business for myself later on. Did they not know that, statistically, Mondays were made for breaking up and we were only six weeks away from December eleventh, which is the biggest breakup day of the year? It's true. Look it up if you must.

Anyway, people had been warned. But just a glance at this soiree would tell you that no one was heeding my words. I thought this would be more of a single mingle thing, but people had already pushed tables out of the way and made a dance floor. Fabulously stunning decorated tables, I might add, with black roses and candelabras. Our committee had worked very hard on those. It didn't help matters that the DJ had gone from playing the Halloween-themed playlist I'd given him to some thumping booty-grinding music. And was there ever some grinding going on.

Mara warned me this was probably going to happen. But I didn't think so, as we had the two-drink limit in place and we were Ex-Filers. Not to mention, we were barely twenty minutes into this bash. I hadn't even been able to give my welcome speech yet.

Mara sauntered my way, looking sizzling hot in her white goddess dress and golden ram horns. I had to say, the flame eyes were killer. And people say YouTube isn't educational. She was also wearing an I-told-you-so smile. "You doing okay?"

I looked apprehensively at the makeshift dance floor; it was a four-alarm party. Someone had dimmed the lights and turned a strobe light on. I'd told the civic center it would be more of a sophisticated mixer. It was looking more like my college days. I bit my lip. "Well, at least no one's clothes have come off yet." I had to practically yell so she could hear me.

Mara laughed. "The night is young," she teased. At least I hoped she was teasing. She lasered in on her mom, who was already engaged in conversation with a couple of men who were half her age. "I just pray it's not my mom's. Can you believe what she's wearing?" Mara smacked her head.

Before I could answer her, a favorite voice crooned, "Am I at the right party?"

I turned to find my old teenage dream come to life. There stood Noah, unmistakably dressed as Damon Salvatore, the vampire my seventeen-year-old self would have been willing to let suck all the blood out of her. I had a major obsession with *The Vampire Diaries* books, TV show, you name it, during high school and college. I literally cried when it ended. Hallmark movies had nothing on my love for the angsty young adult show. I mean, who could compete with Ian Somerhalder? Well, Noah was certainly in the running, in his black leather jacket and tight black jeans with black boots. He even wore Damon's ring on his finger. Oh baby, I was speechless.

We definitely just popped another egg, Miss Sparkly sighed.

Oh, I felt it this time. Oy vey, I was in trouble.

"Hi," I said like a breathy teenager. I might as well have twirled my hair and licked my lips.

Mara looked between the two of us with a look that said, "You just lost the bet. You owe me your life." With his appearance, I had all but forgotten that Noah had said his costume was for the woman he loved, and I had bet Mara my entire life that I knew it wouldn't be for me. But . . . that couldn't be. Right? I mean sure, Noah knew I loved *The Vampire Diaries.* He and Ben even used to watch it with me sometimes. They made fun of it the entire time, but my love for the show had never waned.

Miss Sparkly didn't want to think about the past. She was thinking of all the possibilities this opened up for her; she was definitely going to off me. Probably in my sleep. Or perhaps she would make me embarrass myself so much, by doing all the things she was thinking of doing with Noah, that I would go crawl in a hole and die of my own accord. She was seconds away from grabbing that sexy jacket of his, pulling him to her, and seeing if Noah's breath was truly as good as it always smelled. I actually ended up licking my lips thinking about it. *Crap.*

Noah smiled, and I think he perused me with his eyes, before he returned my greeting. "Hi there. You look—"

"Oh. My. Gosh. Noah!" Annika squealed as she came running at him.

It was then I remembered who she had come as.

"Look at us all matching." She practically pushed me out of the way and threw her arms around Noah, looking like the love of Damon Salvatore's life, Elena Gilbert. Well, at least the TV show version of Elena. In the books she was blonde and a totally spoiled, stuck-up brat. I wanted to think that way of Annika now. Or at least Miss Sparkly did. Sparkles was checking to see how sharp our nails were. But Annika was lovely. Disgustingly so, with her shiny long cocoa-colored hair, olive skin, and eyes so brown they looked like pools of chocolate. And given the way Noah leaned back and stared at her in her own cropped tight leather jacket and plunging red V-neck shirt, it looked like he wanted to dive right into those chocolate pools.

"Remember how much I raved about those books in high school? I even teased you once and called you my Damon." Annika pulled Noah to her again and squeezed the life out of him.

There it was—the proof. Noah did, indeed, love Annika. His costume was a tribute to her.

I could hardly bring myself to glimpse at the pair, but all it took was seeing Noah reciprocate the hug. I glanced at Mara and her face said it all—she knew she'd lost the bet.

I gave her a faux smile. I should be happy I'd won. I mean, now the next month's Thai takeout was on Mara when we watched *Cosmetics and Crimes.* Yay.

So how come I felt as if I had just lost?

"I have to go welcome everyone," I said, all flustered.

"I'll come with you." Mara zipped my way, and we left the two lovebirds alone to fawn all over each other.

Once we were out of earshot, which was like two feet away thanks to the loud music, Mara looped her arm through mine and semi whispered in my ear, "I guess you were right."

"Yeah." I nodded.

"You're upset?" Mara guessed.

"No." I waved away her insinuations all while Miss Sparkly was near tears. A deep sadness emanated from her and began to seep into me. I tried to reassure her it was for the best, but it was a half-hearted plea. I knew things would change between Noah and me now. Judging by Annika's reaction, she was ready to take the next step. I was happy for Noah.

No, you're not, the nagging voice in my head cried. *Be honest with us and own this.*

I don't know if I can. I don't want us to hurt.

We are hurting. We've been hurting for years. We will keep hurting unless you go through the pain.

I have been working through it.

Not all of it.

I know, but I can't deal with the Noah thing now. I have a party to host.

Fine, but we will discuss this later.

"I'm happy for Noah," I added in. It was the truth. He'd been in love with Annika forever. To hold a flame like that and never let go, no matter how much it flickered, that deserved a happy ending—even if I didn't know if I believed in those anymore.

Mara pursed her lips together, Judgy McJudging the truthfulness of my words. "You could tell me the truth, you know? I wouldn't fault you."

"I know that. But there's nothing to tell. Noah and I are friends with a capital *F*."

"Just remember, we are best friends with a giant *B*."

"You don't know how grateful I am for that." I hugged her, needing someone to hold on to for a moment. It wasn't as comforting as I'd hoped, as my line of vision included Noah and Annika. They weren't touching now, but Annika was animatedly talking with her hands. Noah seemed to be keenly paying attention to her. While I clung to Mara and studied the pair, the tagline to *The Vampire Diaries* popped into my head—Love sucks. Yep, with a capital *S*. Not that I was in love with Noah, but it was a reminder of how, often, when love begins to bloom, in the wake of that budding relationship is someone who feels as if they are wilting.

Yes! Miss Sparkly shouted. *You are finally getting me.*

I didn't want to. I didn't like this withering feeling inside. It was so confusing. Noah had always been my friend. But more-than-friendly feelings stirred within me as I looked at Noah and was reminded of his goodness. I had begun to wonder if all along it had been Noah who made Ben shine so bright. So bright I was blinded to the source.

Unfortunately, I gazed too long. Noah's eyes zeroed in on me, as if he knew I had been shamelessly observing him. He flashed me his most charming smile and waved.

I was embarrassed he had caught me staring, so I let go of Mara and headed for the stage. I couldn't get up there fast enough. Mara trailed behind me.

My first stop was at DJ Smiley's booth. Smiley wore a sheepish smile. He'd totally gone off the rails. He was supposed to be playing Halloween classics like "Thriller"; instead, we were bumping to Bruno Mars's "That's What I Like." Admittedly, I felt like breaking out some Bruno moves, but I refrained. I had some serious business to take care of first.

"I need a minute," I shouted.

He gave me the thumbs-up before turning the music down, to the rowdy crowd's dismay. It was amazing how differently people behaved when in costume and with the lights lowered. That felt like a metaphor for life that I should probably pay attention to. In fact, it felt like my marriage. Sometimes I wondered if dating-Ben and engaged-Ben were all just an act. That he stripped off each persona like a costume after we were married, to reveal his true self. I had no time to ponder that. It was showtime for me.

"All right, all right, listen up, our beautiful hostess and spy girl would like to impart some wisdom to all of you."

I wasn't sure how wise my words would be, but I took the mic DJ Smiley handed me. "Hello, Ex-Filers," I shouted. Even though I knew they weren't all Ex-Filers. There were quite a few men in the crowd, and our local chapter was mostly women, as were most of my online followers.

A deafening roar of greeting came back my way, making me grin and, for a brief moment, forget the ache inside of me that I was desperately trying to ignore.

"First of all, I want to say thank you for coming. Because of you, and those who donated online, we have already exceeded our goal of raising fifty thousand dollars for the women and children's shelter. And the night is still young. Please be sure to check out the auction table to bid on the packages and gift baskets. All the money we raise tonight will not only help provide basic needs for these brave women and children, who find themselves in frightening and unknown circumstances, it will also provide crucial job training and childcare. Again, thank you. You are the most amazing group of people."

Cheers and applause ensued.

"With that said," I sang with an air of teasing, "I have a feeling I will be very busy in the near future cropping out some mistakes from tonight's shenanigans."

Everyone laughed.

"Anyway, I love you all. Please be careful and remember it's okay to be a party of—"

Do not say it! Miss Sparkly interrupted me.

I have to say it. It's my job. Whether you like it or not, it affords us our cozy condo on the slopes.

You could be doing lifestyle shoots. Remember how good we are at those?

I can't do this with you right now. "One," I squeaked out, since someone was strangling my vocal cords.

I received another round of applause before I handed the mic back to DJ Smiley. He wasted no time cranking the tunes back up. I felt the bass course through my bones.

Mara and I stood on the stage for a moment longer, looking over the crowd. Okay, mainly we stared at her mom, who knew how to bust a move. She was dancing with some man dressed like a surgeon. He looked like he wanted to play doctor with my ex-mother-in-law.

Mara closed her eyes and shook her head. "Please just tell me this is like a midlife crisis, or something that will pass."

I put my arm around her and gave her a squeeze. "The good news is that with the way she's moving at her age, she'll probably need a bottle of Advil tomorrow and to lie in bed all day. It will be a good reminder for her."

Mara groaned. "I just hope no one is recording this."

I hoped not either. "Come on, let's go show everyone how it's done."

Mara took another peek at her mom and cringed, but then some Justin Timberlake came on and Mara's face lit up. She could never resist a Justin song.

We found a spot on the dance floor toward the middle and got our figure-eight sways on like our hips were born for swinging. You know who else had some moves? Annika. Several feet away, I saw her up close against Noah like this was *Dirty Dancing* or something. I'm sorry, but she was no Baby. But Noah seemed to be enjoying himself, like Patrick Swayze, judging by the stupid grin on his face.

I had to turn around and avoid the scene. I was being ridiculous. Noah was my friend. I was happy for him. Annika was a good person, even if her shiny hair was extensions and her boobs were fake. She was always the first to volunteer, and she was a family lawyer; her life's mission was to help kids. She was perfect for Noah.

She also keeps a photo of her impaling her ex on her nightstand, Sparkles reminded me.

Well, we can't all be perfect.

You know who is good for Noah? Me.

I pushed away her thought, my thought. I didn't know whose thought that was, but it didn't belong in my head—or worse, my heart. My heart that was beating wildly out of control, and not because I was shaking my hips like a Shakira wannabe. I had made a vow to stay a born-again virgin. I screwed up so badly last time. And now here I was, having feelings for a man whose heart belonged to another. I had serious issues and obviously could not be trusted in matters of the heart.

When the song was over, I told Mara I needed some water. I

slipped away and found a quiet table in the back to be alone with my thoughts. More like I desperately tried to push them away, but the sparkly side wasn't backing down. She demanded to be heard, to be trusted. She wanted grace to learn from her mistake. Let's be honest—our mistake. Okay, my mistake. I had to stop feeling like two people. I knew I had to decide who I was.

While I contemplated this complex issue, Noah threw himself in the chair next to me. All smiles.

"I've been looking for you."

"You have?"

"Why do you sound so surprised? We've hardly been able to talk."

I scanned the room to find Annika at the auction table. "It looks like you were having fun with Annika, or should I say Elena?"

"What a weird coincidence, huh?"

"Totally weird," I lied.

Noah laughed. "She was an even bigger fan of those books than you were."

"How funny," I said, strained.

"Anyway." He leaned toward me. "You look great. I love the costume. It's you, Gallagher Girl."

My cheeks pinked. "I'm surprised you know what that is."

"Are you kidding me? Don't you remember when we . . ." He cleared his throat.

I knew who the *we* was.

". . . helped you move back home after you graduated? You made us take extra special care of those books. Then you proceeded to give us a play-by-play of the entire series on the drive back to Nevada. That was a long ten hours," he teased.

"Excuse me. You seemed to be awfully interested in chicks who went on kick-butt missions."

He tugged on a strand of my hair. "I was definitely interested." His voice turned low all of a sudden, which sent a streak of heat through me as if I'd been struck by lightning.

I gripped the table, feeling stupid and vulnerable. "Well, I appreciated you indulging me."

"Anytime." He grinned.

I inched away from him as far as I could on my seat without looking like an idiot. "So, did the boys have fun trick-or-treating?" Noah had taken them because Shanna wasn't feeling well and Adonis wanted to stay with her.

"We crushed it. Four big bags," he bragged.

"I'm sure Shanna loves that."

"Not so much." He laughed his infectious laugh.

"How is she feeling?"

"Better. Except she's blaming you for her addiction to pumpkin cupcakes."

I smiled, not only because Shanna liked the cupcakes I'd dropped off to her yesterday, but because I had remembered how much she'd liked them in the past and thought to make her some. It was very sparkly of me.

"I'm proud to be your friend," Noah added.

There was that word—friend.

"You've been amazing this month, helping my family and still pulling this off." He waved his hand over the large crowd. "You do so much good for others."

"I had a lot of help," I responded, uncomfortable with his compliment. I felt very unworthy of it. Especially in light of the last few years.

"Don't do that," he begged.

I tipped my head to the side. "Do what?"

"That thing you do where you refuse to see what a good person you are. I don't know where you got the impression you are anything but amazing."

"Ben," I said without thinking.

Noah clenched his fists, his gorgeous face turning fifty shades of angry. "He's a prick. You need to kick him out of your head."

"I'm trying."

"I'm here to help." He rested his warm hand on my knee. Ay, ay, ay, it felt good.

"Thank you," I stammered, so overcome by these feelings for him that I'd never had before. Feelings I hadn't had for anyone in a long time.

"Do you want to dan—"

"There you are," Annika interrupted.

Noah's hand popped right off my knee.

Annika stood by Noah and placed her well-manicured hand on his shoulder. "Can you believe we came as the best couple of all time?" she asked me, all aglow.

I stood. "It's fabulous. You make a stunning couple." Unfortunately, that was true.

Annika giggled, while Noah shifted in his seat.

"It's like high school all over again," Annika gushed.

"So fun," I tried to keep the bitterness out of my voice. "Anyway, I better go uh, you know, check on Kellie. I'm worried about her hips."

Understandably, they both gave me strange looks.

"You know, because she's old, I mean older." Seriously, I was a dunce. I just wanted to be anywhere but with the two of them. "I just don't want her to have any regrets in the morning." Like the ones I would be having.

"Bye." I waved.

Noah caught my arm as I tried to escape. "Save me a dance."

I blinked a few times, not sure that was the best idea, but Noah's eyes got to me—maybe he was part vampire. "Okay." I felt as if the sun landed on my face. Really my entire body. Something burned within me. Was that desire?

Yes! Yes! Yes! Miss Sparkly was obviously thrilled about it. *Let it burn, baby.*

I was thinking more like stop, drop, and roll.

Twenty-Four

Dear Ex-Filers, if you're looking for someone who will be semi obsessed with you and might even pee a little when you walk in the door, get a dog. No man or friend has ever peed because they were so happy to see me. I'm telling you, it's the mark of true love.

Lots of love,

Cami

P.S. Thanks for making the Halloween Bash such a success. We raised over $70K. You're amazing. Well, everyone but the guy who thought he was at a Magic Mike audition last night.

I added a picture of me cuddled up with Neville on my bed before I clicked publish. I still couldn't believe some guy jumped on the stage and started doing a striptease. Noah and a couple other men had to tackle the jerk and get him off the stage before the police had to get involved. Of course, someone recorded the entire thing, and it was making the rounds today on social media. But it wasn't the semi-nude man who garnered the most comments—it was the hot guy dressed like Damon Salvatore.

While Noah was getting his fifteen minutes of fame, I finally uploaded his latest pictures to my laptop. I hadn't had the heart to do it until today. But after seeing him with Annika last night, I knew I had to. It looked like his I'm going to let her come to me approach had worked. She'd stuck to him like gum on the bottom of a shoe. Well, except the one dance Noah and I had shared. "I Put a Spell on You" by Annie Lennox.

I certainly felt as if Noah had put a spell on me. The way he'd held me close, his hands resting on the small of my back, as we'd swayed to the sensual beat of the music. The way he'd whispered, "Trick or treat," in my ear—and I'd found myself burning with desire, pulling his body closer to mine—and before I could stop myself, I was replying, "Treat." In the moment it felt right, especially when he'd given me a seductive grin, but as soon as the song was over, the spell was broken. Annika appeared, out of what must have been thin air, because I didn't remember anyone else around Noah and me as we danced.

I felt like such an idiot as I watched Annika lead him away to do whatever lovers do. He had glanced back at me, wearing a look of confusion. He was probably wondering why I had behaved so flirty when he was just trying to be friendly and fun. I surely had mistaken his grin for seductiveness when it was only Noah being Noah. So now I was curled up in my bed feeling hot shame for coming on to my friend, worse for going against my principles. Which Sparkles had reminded me wasn't true. In our heart we believed in love and the power of a good Hallmark movie. It was the perfect time to edit Noah's photos with what I was sure would be yet another beautiful woman. I had a feeling after last night, this would be the last photo shoot I would be cropping for him.

Unless Annika really is a psycho. I have my suspicions. The sparkly side of me was clinging on to some hope. She interpreted our dance with Noah very much like I had at first.

All I knew was my head hurt and I had zero clue who I was supposed to be. Sparkly or snarky? On the love train or the plane to virgin paradise? The beaches were quite lovely there, albeit lonely. But lonely was safe. There were no STDs or cheaters on that beach.

But I knew what Sparkles would say: there were no hands to hold or feverish kisses in the night. No chance of babies. She was sure one day we would walk that virgin beach and regret we never lived the life we'd dreamed of—a beautiful life of working through all the hard things with your second self.

Ugh. Regardless, I knew one thing, if I ever hopped from the plane to the train, Noah wouldn't be a fellow passenger. He was taken and that was that. Friends forever.

I settled Neville next to me and opened Noah's file. I wasn't prepared for what appeared on my screen. Holy amazingness. There Noah stood, in his swim trunks, showing off why many women thought he was a gift straight from God. Each muscle he owned was on display. Most notable were his chest and rock-hard abs. I think I drooled and probably popped another egg. I barely even noticed the bikini babe standing next to him, who resembled a sexy pixie. Not to say it didn't sting. It didn't help that they were in one of my most favorite spots—Soldier Meadows Hot Springs. The amber waves of grass, with the hills playing in the distance at sunset, made it a gorgeous spot. I could feel the warm water and see the millions of stars that shone there at night.

I had to give it to Noah—he had good taste in where to take his dates or girlfriends. Who knew? I think every photo shoot of his I'd ever edited had been at a prized spot for me. Whether it was the hot springs or the slopes.

I stared a bit longer at the couple, mostly Noah. He'd done his body good. I noticed, though, how he didn't touch his date even though she had a rockin' bod. Not even Claudia looked as good as this woman.

"Sorry, honey," I said to the screen. "You never had a chance. But don't worry, Annika is just as beautiful as you."

Bad thoughts of covering this bikini-clad woman in boils filled my mind. But mainly, I was annoyed with Noah for leading these poor women on. Even if she did look bored, which said there was something innately wrong with her. If Noah were standing next to me with hardly a stitch of clothing on, I would be pretty dang excited. Yet, I had to remind myself, I had been around Noah plenty like that. How had I been so blind? Sure, I was in a relationship, so it would have been bad form to ogle Noah. But seriously, how had I never noticed him?

While I painstakingly began to crop the woman out of the picture, my phone buzzed. I looked over to find it was Noah calling. I debated on whether or not to answer. I was kind of thinking of ignoring him from here on out. Last night was awkward to say the least. Besides, he would surely be busy with Annika now. She had totally put her number in his phone last night. I debated too long, and he hung up.

Not to be deterred, he called again and again. I finally answered.

"Did you know I'm editing your latest photo shoot and annoyed with you?" were the first words out of my mouth.

"You know, I was getting that vibe." He laughed.

"What do you want?" I said, half-annoyed. His laugh was pretty charming.

"Since you asked so nicely," he oozed sarcasm. "I was calling to tell you that I'm bringing you dinner tonight."

Uh. I wasn't expecting that. "You don't need to do that. I have a lot of work to catch up on." And I need to avoid you.

"It's perfect, then. You don't have to worry about dinner now."

"I was just going to eat cereal or something."

"That's a crime against humanity. Especially when you hear that I've ordered dinner from Nico's."

Ooh, I loved Nico's. "Did you order shrimp carbonara and their homemade breadsticks?"

"Uh-huh. With a side of chocolate and pistachio biscotti. I thought it would go perfect with your hot chocolate. We're supposed to get our first snow tonight."

It was an old family tradition that when the first snow of the season fell, we would make hot chocolate and turn on the fireplace. I was surprised Noah remembered I used to do that.

That all sounded lovely. Too lovely for friends. "You probably don't want to drive up here, then, if it's going to snow."

He chuckled. "Good thing I have four-wheel drive and have been driving in the snow since I was fifteen. Besides, I'll already be up there. I'm switching out some of Annika's light fixtures for her."

Sure, he was "switching out light fixtures."

"Is that what people are calling it these days?"

"What?"

"Never mind. I don't want to put you out."

"Are you kidding me? You've done so much for me and my family. I'll see you at six. Oh, and I'm bringing Luna. She can't wait to meet Neville." He hung up before I could object.

Great. Now I had hours to overthink this and argue with Sparkles about what this all meant. All while thinking about what he was doing at Annika's. Which was none of my business. I guarantee, though, some of those light fixtures were in her bedroom. And not to be catty, but it's not that hard to switch them out on your own. She was capable. I shouldn't be like that. Annika was a wonderful person.

I set my laptop to the side and picked up Neville. "Hey, buddy, if you could do me a favor tonight and run and hide from Luna, I would really appreciate it. You don't need to show off in front of your pal Noah. I don't need to be proved wrong about anything else. You got it?"

He gave me a look that said he might pee a little when Noah got here.

Traitor.

I found myself getting ready like this was a date, which I knew it wasn't. For crying out loud, he was coming straight from Annika's. I truly did wonder if she was okay with us being friends. Did she really think I made Noah a better person? He was pretty great all by himself. You know, except for his weird obsession with dating women and doing photo shoots with them. I had to believe, though, that Annika would not appreciate some of the thoughts I'd had about him. Or the way I had ogled that picture of him in his swim trunks, especially after I cropped out his latest goddess divine. I'd even had the thought of adding myself to that photo, right up next to him with my hand on his perfectly hairy chest.

I had to stop this.

Yet, I still put on an off-the-shoulder black tunic and jeans that hugged me in all the right places. I wasn't proud of it. I just couldn't get over the way I'd felt in his arms while we'd danced. Almost like I had come home. But I knew that was wrong. He wanted to make a life and home with Annika. And who I was, I didn't know. And if I didn't know who I was, how could I even contemplate being with someone? I knew the sparkly part of me would say that the real me was just trapped inside, but the fact was, we both existed, for better or for worse.

Worse, she gave her two cents.

Maybe she was right.

Or maybe I was cuckoo for Cocoa Puffs. It was a toss-up.

Either way, I didn't look half-bad. My hair had the perfect amount of bounce, and I had that natural makeup glow going for me. And it was starting to snow. There was something magical about the first snow of the season. I opened the curtains in my living room and admired the bits of heavenly-shaped ice softly landing on my balcony. I should have been working, but I was mesmerized by how quickly and beautifully the landscape could change. There was something hopeful about it. It felt like the holidays. I swallowed the lump in my throat.

Do you remember when the first of November meant it was fair game for all things holly and jolly? How everyone made fun of me for listening to Chris—

Not even Miss Sparkly could say the word. It wasn't surprising. It was she who had taken the blow.

I want to. I miss me. Will I ever come back?

That was a good question. I was obviously still hanging on for a reason. Sparkles would have offed me by now if she didn't need me.

You're right. She sounded so ashamed.

I was ashamed. I used to be so strong. I felt so weak for not even being able to face the most wonderful time of the year.

My phone buzzed, bringing me out of my head. Something I was grateful for.

Mara: *SOS. My mom has been reliving her glory days and making me watch old eighties music videos, the most disturbing of which is Olivia Newton-John's "Let's Get Physical." Watch at your own risk. I've never seen so many gyrating Speedos in one room. But now we're online, shopping for the workout outfits Olivia wore because everyone used to tell my mom she looked like her. What do I do? Help.*

Of course I had to google the video first. Oh my. I'm pretty sure Olivia Newton John wasn't talking about exercise when she sang "Let's get physical." The video was half-fascinating, half-disturbing, and probably the most eighties thing I had ever seen. However, I could see the resemblance between the singer and Kellie. Not sure, though, that she needed to revisit the white leotard and purple leggings. I mean, the white tennis outfit was cute.

Me: *Just watched the video. I need to go disinfect my eyes now. Steer her toward the tennis outfit. I'm praying for you.*

Mara: *Pray harder, she just struck eighties gold. The purple leggings exist. I can't live through another parent's midlife crisis. Especially since my dad is still going through his.*

Me: *I'm sorry, girl, do you want me to come over?*

I was praying she said yes—it would get me out of seeing Noah. He would understand if Mara needed me. The only good excuse I had now was that I couldn't trust my feelings around him. He would never, ever know that.

Mara: *You're the best, but the village idiot, a.k.a. my brother, is on his way over. My dad called him in like some hostage negotiator since my mom took over the west wing of the house, including his beloved theater room. Apparently, he can't watch sports on only a ninety-inch screen.*

Jay did love that theater room. And according to Mara, Kellie had literally put a strip of tape down the middle of the house that Jay wasn't allowed to cross. When my parents were mad at each other, my dad just slept on the couch. We never had wings in our house. And, thankfully, I also had a dad who worshipped the ground my mother walked on.

Me: *Just keep thinking, in fifty-three days we will be in virgin heaven.*

Mara: *It can't get here soon enough!*

Me: *Amen.*

I sighed and turned my gaze back to the falling snow, wishing life were as gentle as the tiny flakes multiplying on the exposed surfaces. But life was more like a blizzard that at times left you unable to see what was in front of you, and in its wake, you were left with a whole lot of shoveling and even some meltdowns. I wondered how the Scott family would see their way out of their situation. And when the storm inside me would end.

Twenty-Five

Dear Ex-Filers, it's snowing here, and I couldn't be happier. Snow means ski season is just around the corner. However, I realize for some of you, the first snow brings on an innate desire to enter the world of coupledom. It's actually a scientific fact. But remember, you are stronger than your bodily urges. In fact, it's great to be alone on snow days. You don't have to share the remote or your food. Besides, solitude sparks creativity and even improves your mental health. So get in some sweats, pull up your favorite show to binge, and feel the creativity and healing power of being alone.

Lots of love,

Cami

I clicked publish before Miss Sparkly berated me. Oh, I knew it was coming. She was furious with this post.

You totally read my mind, she mocked. *By the way, you're a hypocrite. You have the most gorgeous man you know coming over here, all while you're telling people to go it alone. And being alone isn't good for everyone's mental health. And let's not forget that being in love with someone can actually make you more creative. You know that more than anyone. You did your best work when you first started dating Ben.*

Don't say that to me, I begged.

You think I like to admit there were good times with Ben? I don't, but it's the truth. You're good in love, Cami. Award-winning good.

I know. I wanted to cry, but I couldn't. Noah was knocking on the door.

I composed myself as best I could, trying to take comfort in convincing myself I wasn't a hypocrite. Noah was my friend and there would be no coupling or cuddling. I stood tall and took in several deep breaths, which did zero to help me. I still felt guilty for the post. And for some other thoughts, like how nice it would be to cuddle with Noah. All while my dog was running for the door. Seriously, how did he know it was Noah? But then I remembered Noah was bringing his pooch and that I better grab my little guy before I opened the door. I didn't see Neville reacting well to Luna. In fact, I was hoping for it.

With Neville securely in my arms, I opened the door with a fake, albeit friendly, smile.

There Noah stood, with his dazzling smile, holding a large bag of food in one hand and his dog's leash in the other. Oh, and he was wearing a tight blue sweater that said he had definitely just been on a date with Annika. Flecks of snow danced in his gorgeous hair. Holy schnikeys was his body a wonderland. I was sure Annika had enjoyed the trip there today.

I averted my eyes and instead focused on his beautiful dog. She lived up to her breed's reputation, golden retriever. Her coat looked as if it had been spun from gold. Her big, gentle brown eyes immediately won me over.

"Can we come in?" Noah asked, when I stayed as silent as a mute.

"Of course." I waved them in, flustered.

Noah stepped in, and instantly my place smelled like a mix of snickerdoodles and homemade bread. There was no doubt that's what heaven must smell like.

Thankfully, my pooch was freaking out enough that I couldn't get lost in that scent or the person who accompanied it.

I held Neville to me, trying to calm him. He couldn't bury his head far enough into my chest.

Noah hurried to set the food down on the kitchen counter before approaching us with Luna, who was up on her hind legs trying to check out my baby.

"Luna, sit," Noah gently commanded, and she obeyed. "Hey, buddy." He scratched Neville's head, trying to soothe him. "Let me have him."

"Uh. I don't think so." My poor baby was shaking so badly. "I just betrayed him by letting another dog in the house. Though she is lovely." I smiled.

"You look lovely too." He playfully wagged his brows.

I knew I should have worn the sweats. Now he knew I was trying too hard. Crap. He was probably thinking about how flirty I had been while we danced last night. That left me no choice but to ask, "Did you have fun with Annika?"

"Yeah," he responded without fanfare. "It was great to catch up. Did you know she keeps a picture of herself stabbing her ex-husband on her nightstand?" He shuddered. Probably thinking about where she was stabbing her ex.

I shuddered, too, but for other reasons. "You were in her room?" I blurted without thinking. What was wrong with me? Of course he would go in her room. They probably spent the entire time in her room "switching out light fixtures."

He gave me an impish grin. "I had to switch out the light in there."

Right. "That's great. So great." I had to keep myself from having visions of clawing Annika's eyes out for touching Noah in such a way. I mean Miss Sparkly did. Noah and I were friends. Just friends.

Noah's left brow arched. "It wasn't a big deal."

Is that how he felt about sex? That was disappointing. Sex was like a monumentally huge deal. It involved intimacy, trust, vulnerability, and let's not forget oxytocin. That bonding hormone didn't mess around, which was why I cautioned people not to mess around. Bonding, unfortunately, was too easy—true intimacy is much more valuable and rare, which is why it's so beautiful. But also, so devastating when it's violated and severed.

I held Neville closer to me, feeling the sharp pain of that violation. And because I had thought Noah would be someone who valued intimacy. Maybe he did. Or perhaps he and Annika had already been doing the horizontal mambo and so it wasn't a big deal for him. Still, that was disappointing. Each time Ben and I had sex, even though we were married, it was a big deal for me. To give yourself to someone like that required it to be of significance.

"Are you hungry?" It was all I could think to say.

The corners of Noah's eyes crinkled. "Starving, but let's make Neville comfortable first."

Neither Neville nor I were going to be comfortable tonight. Of that, I was sure. Or at least pretty sure.

Noah snatched my dog from out of my arms. "Come here, buddy."

The traitor nearly leaped into his arms, to Noah's delight.

Noah smirked at me.

I gave him the evil eye and he laughed. I stood pensively and watched while Noah loved on Neville, whispering things in his ear, like, "Let's show your mommy how wrong she is."

"Excuse me, I can hear you."

"I know." Noah chuckled.

"Fine. Prove me wrong." I folded my arms. I wasn't being snotty; I was praying that Neville wouldn't prove Noah right.

Noah knelt with Neville, who shook a little less in Noah's arms. That didn't bode well for me. Luna seemed to know not to lunge at my pooch, but she did take a few sniffs. I swore the beautiful dog smiled like she enjoyed what she got a whiff of. For a dog, Neville did smell pleasant. It was the lavender-scented fabric softener I used. Neville loved to snuggle into the blankets.

Noah held Neville out to Luna, while still keeping a firm hold on him. What happened next, I couldn't have ever imagined. Luna gave Neville a big old sloppy lick and that was it, Neville was hooked. We are talking he licked her right back. And kept on licking her, like he was trying to get to the center of a Tootsie Pop. I was almost embarrassed for him. Meanwhile, Noah was laughing and giving me the gloatiest of grins.

"I knew it," Noah bragged, "they were meant to be."

I threw my hands up in the air and headed for the carbs. I seriously couldn't believe my dog was a lover. He was supposed to stay single like his owner. I was never living this down with Noah. Thankfully, breadsticks and carbonara were in my immediate future to help ease my pain. I didn't even bother with plates. I grabbed a fork, removed the lid from the aluminum serving container, and dived right into the carbonara—while I watched my dog run around Luna like a lovesick puppy, playfully nipping at her, as she returned the gesture. I was disgusted.

Noah stood with wide eyes and watched me shove a large bite of twisted-up noodles into my mouth. He made his way to me, shaking his head. "Come on, Cams, this is a happy occasion. It should give you hope."

"Hope for what?" I chewed while my hand dove into the takeout bag for the breadsticks.

"The future." He took the breadstick bag from me and opened it, giving me easier access. He truly was a good friend.

I grabbed a breadstick and ripped it in half. "The future?"

Noah leaned across the counter, coming within inches of my face. "Yes. If your dog is brave enough to fall in love, maybe you will be too."

I started choking on the carbonara.

Noah rushed around and patted my back. "You okay there?"

I nodded, so not okay, while I got my food down. "Neville isn't in love," I managed to get out. "They barely know each other."

"Look at them." Noah pointed to the living room.

My jaw dropped. Neville had already taken her to his bed, like it was his love shack. My dog was a freaking gigolo. I was going to have to get him a gold chain to replace his collar. Good thing he was neutered, or we would probably have puppies on the way before the night was over. You know, if Neville could figure that out—he was quite small compared to Luna. Regardless, there he was sharing his toys and letting Luna cuddle up on his bed. I was appalled. I shoved a breadstick in my mouth. Neville was supposed to be as neurotic as I was. What was next? No anxiety meds? Was he going to want to watch Animal Planet now, to search for girlfriends?

"I can see you need a moment. I'll grab the food and some drinks," Noah offered.

I did need a moment, or like several. I walked like a zombie to the couch, holding my breadstick like it was the only comfort I had left in the world. How could I be so wrong about my dog? What else was I wrong about?

A lot, girlfriend. My alter ego was happy to answer and rub it in.

I sat numbly on the couch, nibbling on my breadstick, hoping the carbs would breathe life back into my soul.

Noah soon joined me. He set two bottles of water and the breadsticks on the coffee table, before sitting next to me. Like a good friend, he held up the container of carbonara, two forks sticking out of it. "Help yourself."

Oh, I did. I grabbed my fork and twirled that baby until it would twirl no more, then shoved it in my mouth. That had to be so attractive.

Noah watched, most likely in horror, wondering how I could fit so much food in my mouth. But he never judged me. He just kept holding the container up, only taking a few small bites himself, as I shoveled food in while contemplating my life. And staring at Noah. He was so handsome and good. Not even Mara had served as a human food tray for me. In his eyes I could see he thought I was crazy. He wasn't wrong.

"Thanks," I said, after I swallowed down another huge bite.

"I'm sorry I was right." He didn't sound sorry at all.

I looked at my traitorous pooch, curled up next to Luna on his bed. It was an adorable sight. "It's fine. I mean, she is a beautiful dog."

Noah set the food on the table. That was a good thing—my stomach was starting to hurt from being overstuffed.

"Yes, she is. Don't worry, she doesn't sleep around."

I giggled and stuck my fork in the food. "I'm sure Luna and I will be good friends." But no sleepovers.

"I'm glad to hear that. Annika didn't appreciate me taking Luna over there with me today."

I perked up. "She doesn't like dogs?"

This is good news for us, Cami, don't screw it up. Miss Sparkly was scheming. There was a statistic out there that said most dog owners were willing to end a relationship if their significant other didn't like their beloved pet.

"She's not a big fan of them. And Luna had jumped on her dark comforter and left hair all over it."

Oh my gosh. Noah was totally on her bed. Why else would Luna jump up on it?

"It's nothing a good lint roller can't fix." I was getting irritated on behalf of Luna. Poor thing was probably subjected to some explicit images today. Images I didn't want to think about.

"Exactly!" Noah exclaimed. "See, you get it."

Unfortunately, I totally got it. "Well, maybe she'll warm up to Luna."

Noah shrugged. "I don't know if I'll take her with me when I go back to caulk her tub and shower next week."

Caulking. Sure. That's an even better term for sex than light fixtures.

"That's probably a good idea." I grabbed another breadstick from off the coffee table. "Does she have a lot of work for you to do?" Not like I didn't know the answer. She probably wanted him to work all night long.

"A long list, but don't worry, I'll still make time to do your renovations—if you ever decide on anything." He nudged me.

I didn't want to be his side project. How could I stand in the way of true love?

Oh please, you do it all the freaking time. Why don't you start spouting your single crap that you push on your followers like a sad drug dealer?

He is a follower, I reminded her. *He's obviously not listening. He loves Annika. We have to deal with it.*

Ugh.

"That's okay. Maybe it would be best if I just held off until the beginning of the year. I mean, you're so busy, and it's great that you're *helping* Annika. That's got to make you happy."

His face pinched. "It's always good to make money . . ."

She was paying him? That's kinky.

". . . but, Cams, I said I have the time to help you, and I meant it. Are you trying to cheat on me with another contractor?"

"No." I smiled.

"Okay then. Now pick out some cabinets, woman."

"I'm working on it." I bit my lip. "Speaking of work, I have your latest photo shoot cropped and edited. I'll go grab the flash drive for you." I went to stand up, but Noah placed his hand on my knee. A little thrill went through me. That was so wrong.

"You can get it later. We have serious business to take care of first."

I tipped my head. "What's that?"

He looked out the window, the darkness was accentuated with spectacular white flecks. "It's the first snow. Traditions must be kept. I'll start the fire and find a cozy movie while you make hot chocolate."

"Bossy much?" I teased.

He caressed my knee, or maybe he was trying to wipe butter off his hand or something. Whatever it was, it was nice. "Please," he crooned.

"Since you asked so nicely," I stuttered, and popped off the couch before I did something both Annika and I would regret. "I'll be right back."

"I'll be here." He grabbed the remote. "Are you still boycotting Christmas movies?"

I stopped in my tracks and cringed. "You know how I feel about that word." I scratched my neck.

"I do, and I think you need some exposure therapy. It will be good for you."

"I've been exposed plenty today." I rushed to the kitchen.

Noah jumped up. "Exposed how?"

I tilted my head. "How do you think?"

His ears pinked. "I don't know. Like a guy looked down your shirt or something."

I grabbed my middle and laughed. "Definitely not that. I was home all day, if that makes you feel better. You're acting like one of my brothers."

"I'm not one of your brothers, Cams," he growled.

"No, you're not," I whispered. "I appreciate it all the same, though, that you were worried I had been compromised in some way. But no need to worry, no one is looking at me."

"That's not true," he grumbled, before turning on my TV.

"Well, certainly not like how women are looking at you. Did you see you've gone viral? You could have your own harem."

He ran a hand through his hair. "Annika mentioned something about a video from last night. I don't care what people say about me online. Besides, I'm already taken." He gave me a furtive smile.

I felt as if I'd been sucker punched. I gripped my counter. "Do you want whipped cream in your hot chocolate?" I asked, five octaves too high. It was either that or, "Are you sure Annika's the one? She doesn't even like Luna."

"I love whipped cream." He smiled.

I took my time making the hot chocolate. I used real dark chocolate and milk. It was a process, but well worth it. It also gave me a moment to breathe. To think about how important it was for me to act normal. If not, I risked losing Noah's friendship, and that was the last thing I wanted to do. Men and women could be friends. I believed that with all my heart. Noah had been my friend for many years. With that said, I had no right to interfere with his relationship with Annika. I worried that I was being skanky by even hanging out with him, especially when more than friendly feelings kept popping up like a game of whack-a-mole.

By the time I was done with the hot chocolate, Noah had turned off the lights in the living room. The glow of the fire and the TV made for an intimate setting. Too intimate. But I didn't ask him to turn the lights back on. With the lights off, it was much easier to see the snow that was steadily coming down. It felt so, well, so C-wordish. So much so, I had to stop and catch my breath.

Noah glanced my way, and a soft expression washed over his face as if he knew how hard this was for me. He patted the seat next to him. "You got this, Cams."

"You just want the hot chocolate." I used humor to deflect how crazy I felt inside.

"You got me, now get over here."

I found myself zipping his way as if he were a tractor beam. I handed him a big, steaming mug of hot chocolate bursting with whipped cream and curls of chocolate on top.

"You are an angel." He carefully took his mug.

If only he meant that for real and not just because I handed him a thousand calories of delight.

I sat a properly friendly distance away from him. "I don't know, I'm feeling kind of devilish."

"Devilish can be good." He wagged his brows.

"Not that kind. Like the truly evil kind," I admitted.

Noah's eyes narrowed. "Cams, you're not evil. What has you feeling exposed today?" He swiped some whipped cream off my cocoa and dabbed it on my nose.

"Hey, don't waste my whipped cream." I took a swipe of his and licked it off my finger.

Noah seemed mesmerized by my lips, and I think he might have stopped breathing.

"You okay?"

"Damn," he whispered and swallowed hard before letting out a heavy breath. "I'm fine. Answer my question." He put more space between us.

I was totally being skanky. I knew I'd sat too close. And the whipped cream thing was kind of flirty. I sipped on my hot chocolate, trying to ease my soul. It wasn't helping.

"Cams." Noah reached over and tugged on my hair. "You can open up to me."

Be open. Like wide open. Don't let me down this time. Miss Sparkly was demanding.

I did need to talk to someone, but I wasn't sure Noah was the right person. After all, I was having a lot of conflicting feelings for him.

He's the perfect person. Spill your guts, woman!

Before I could stop myself, I found this flying out of my mouth: "Do you like the old me or the new me better?"

If you're trying to get rid of me, it won't work. Noah totally likes me better, babe.

Don't get your panties in a wad, I'm just taking a poll here. You know, maybe I should do a big survey and whoever wins stays.

Get ready to pack your bags, sweetheart.

She was probably right, but I needed to do more research. I could put up a fight too.

Noah set his hot chocolate down and inched a tad closer. "Cams, there is no old you and new you; there's just you, and I like you."

That was a little heart-melting. But he didn't know the ugly truth yet.

"Noah, that's sweet, but I feel like there is a before-Ben and an after-Ben version of me. And I don't know who to be. Honestly, I feel crazy."

"You are a little crazy." He smirked. "But it's part of your charm."

"Thanks," I said, chagrined.

"I'm being sincere. You've always had this crazy, wild side to you. That's who you are. And as far as you before and after Ben," he hissed his name, "the only difference is you seem to be afraid of who you are."

"I am afraid." I sounded so pathetic. If he only knew about Miss Sparkly and how rude she was.

Hey, I'm not rude. I'm giving you tough love.

Noah took my cocoa and set it next to his before wrapping me up in his arms. Like the skank I was, I burrowed right into him. Oy vey, was it nice. Much less scary in his arms. Well, until I thought about it. It was scary how good it felt. Even how right it felt.

Noah ran his hand down my hair. "Cami, just hold on. You're going to figure it out. I promise."

"How do you know?" I sounded like a damsel in distress, which I hated, but it was kind of working for me, so I went with it and snuggled in a little more.

Noah obliged and tightened his grip on me. Oh baby, I was feeling all those muscles he had shown off in his latest photo shoot. Which reminded me, he was in love with Annika. Reluctantly, I wiggled out of his arms. His eyes, though, didn't let me get far. Those babies grabbed ahold of me like the jaws of life holding me hostage right next to him, where I could breathe the same breaths as him.

"Cams, I know you'll get through this because deep inside,"—he pointed to my heart, really my boob, but I got the sentiment—"no one loves life like you do. That fierce love is just waiting to be unleashed. I can feel it."

"Can you really?" I whispered.

He nodded. "You just have to keep following my plan."

I laughed softly. "You mean there's more?"

"Oh yeah. Get ready for the most Thanksgiving month you have ever had."

"The holidays," I groaned.

"Come on, Cams, you love the holidays." He held up a pumpkin pillow to prove his point. "Not only love them, but need them. We're going to start tonight with watching *A Charlie Brown Thanksgiving.* Then we're going to move on to signing up for the 5K Turkey Trot, and we'll see where life takes us. I'm thinking snow angels."

I hemmed and hawed a bit. "I do love a good snow angel. And it is a first snow tradition."

That's my girl, Miss Sparkly sang.

You win this time, but don't get any ideas about the C-word. Also, do you think I'm a skank?

No, no. Not at all. She didn't sound very convincing. *And Annika did say you were good for Noah.*

That's true. And Noah and I can stay friends, right?

Of course, honey. You have nothing to worry about.

Did that sound like she was leading me to my death, or was that just me?

Twenty-Six

Dear Ex-Filers, I heard that remodeling is like pulling a loose thread on a cheap sweater. I should have listened. I'm accepting prayers, thoughts, and/or burnt offerings on my behalf, whatever you got.

Lots of love,

Cami

In the last few weeks following my cabinet choice it seemed like it was one thing after another. I went with a muted shade of gray, by the way. Well, that's what I thought. Noah had placed the order two weeks ago, but we found out yesterday they are no longer making that style. This is after I was told all the pipes need to be replaced in my kitchen and I have mold. Not the bad kind that will kill you, which I guess is good, but all the drywall in my kitchen had to go. If that wasn't bad enough, one of the subcontractors Noah had hired helped himself to all my wine. Needless to say, he got fired.

I now lived in a demolition zone. I blame Noah. He promised this would be fun. He lied. Well, not exactly. It has been fun hanging out with him most nights. I never knew you could get so much pleasure using a sledgehammer to take out drywall. I would have bought a sledgehammer a long time ago, had I known. Or invited Noah over to use one in front of me. Oy vey, was he attractive.

Of course, this was creating a huge internal conflict. I was becoming more and more of a skank. Noah had also been spending a lot of time with Annika doing "home improvement" projects. They had now moved on to polishing her wood floors and building shelves. He could have just said they were having sex. I knew what that was, and I was a big girl. I could handle the truth. Well, sort of. I felt as if I were desperately clinging to my friendship with Noah, knowing all this time together would eventually come to an end. The writing was on the wall. Noah had even quit doing photo shoots. That meant he had quit dating other women. He'd said it was time. He'd been awfully hopeful since Halloween night.

Yet there I was, feeling things for Noah that I shouldn't. Things that scared me. I was blaming the snow and hanging out with Jaxon and Liam, making toilet paper roll turkeys and candy cornucopias. Add in some pumpkin and apple pies for their mommy, who was still dutifully and restlessly on bed rest. All this cozy cheeriness made me want to snuggle. And not just anyone—Noah. I started to wonder if this was how it all began with Claudia and Ben. Claudia had become his client, his very needy client, wanting his opinion on everything from how she should rearrange her furniture before I took the freaking pictures for her listing, to analyzing every last number to come up with the asking price. Did I question all the phone calls and Ben's attentiveness? No, because I blindly trusted him. It didn't matter that he had made me question who I was—I knew he would never betray me like that.

Now here I was having cuddling thoughts about a friend's lover. I assuaged my guilt by telling myself that Noah wasn't married, he hadn't even made his relationship with Annika Facebook official—or official in any sense of the word. And we had done nothing inappropriate. Nor would we ever. I was the single guru, after all. And for Noah's part, I was sure hanging out with me was like hanging out with his guy friends, minus the beer and incessant sports. I mean, I could out-burp any man.

"What did you tell your ever-loyal followers?" Noah shook me out of my thoughts.

I turned and smiled at him, well really Luna, who had her head between us in Noah's truck. She went with us a lot now on our hardware store runs. I'd never been to the hardware store more in my life than I had the last few weeks.

I rubbed Luna's head; we had become besties, even though she was trying to steal my baby. My baby who still refused car rides unless he was sedated. We had tried, but it wasn't pretty. I was happy Neville was still somewhat psychotic. That was normal. However, as soon as we got back with Luna, he would be acting like Barry White showing his lady to his pad. I'd gotten him a bigger bed so they had more room to cuddle.

"I'm just lamenting about this renovation. Thanks again for talking me into it." I laced my words with so much sarcasm, they were dripping in it.

Without missing a beat, Noah replied, "You're welcome. You're lucky we caught the mold when we did. Besides, you need a good shake-up in your life."

"Says the person who isn't washing his dishes in his bathtub." I had no sink or running water at the moment in my kitchen.

Noah chuckled. "You're welcome to wash your dishes at my house anytime."

Huh. Noah had never invited me to his house before. I knew he'd bought a place a couple of years ago. But he never said much about it.

"Do you like your new place?" He used to live in a dive. His excuse for living there was that as long as he had space for a big TV and bed, what more did he need.

"Yeah, it's great. Four bedrooms, three baths, big backyard with a pool."

My eyes widened. "Wow. Why so much space?"

"Just thinking about the future."

He meant Annika and all the beautiful babies they would have together.

I kissed Luna's head, trying not to be bummed out.

"You should come over sometime," he added, nonchalantly.

I wasn't sure I could do that. I wasn't sure why. It's not like I couldn't keep my hands off him if I went to his place. I hadn't accosted him yet at my own. But my tiny condo screamed that I was living the single life for eternity. If that didn't do it, my pink couch cemented my intentions.

We could buy a new couch, someone reminded me.

Noah would still be in love with Annika, so the couch was staying.

"I don't know, do you still use beer crates for furniture?"

His laughter filled the cab of his truck. "I've matured now. I only use them for my nightstands."

I rolled my eyes.

"I'm kidding. I think you might be surprised by my bedroom furniture," he said with an air of allurement.

I gripped my seat, doing my best not to think about going into his bedroom. "If you say so." I cleared my throat.

"I do." He left it at that.

I was grateful for the reprieve, except now I was curious about his bedroom, how soft his bed was. Bad, bad thoughts. So bad, I jumped out of the cab of his truck as soon as he pulled into a spot at his favorite hardware store in Carson City. He was like a VIP there. He even had special contractor privileges and could use the exclusive checkout lines, where every woman cashier would check him out. I could hardly blame them. He looked like a freaking rock star.

Luna followed me out. I had become her favorite. I was pretty smitten with her too. I held on to her leash and waited for Noah to join us. He was in his signature "Look at my tatted arms" shirt and hug-me-right jeans. Meanwhile, I was already layering with a long-sleeved shirt and a hoodie and was still cold.

Today we were picking out paint. I think Noah thought I needed a renovation pick-me-up even though we were nowhere near being ready to paint. But paint offered me some hope this renovation might end on a good note.

The three of us walked in together like Noah owned the place. Everyone waved at him, a few women swooned. Noah took it all in stride like he was used to the attention. It was one of Noah's many finer points: he was beautiful, and he totally knew it, but he didn't care if other people knew it. He treated everyone as if they were his best friend. Even me.

As we walked toward the center of the store where the paint was, I had this odd feeling someone was following us. But every time I turned around, there was no one obvious. Why would anyone follow us anyway? I was sure I was just being paranoid. I was a little twitchy from the holly jolly decorations they were selling and the music being played over the PA system. Why did a hardware store need to jump on that bandwagon? Even when I was crazy for the C-word, I never once thought, "Let's hit up the hardware store for all my holiday needs."

I refrained from scratching my neck. It was the time of year; I would be itching all over anytime I went anywhere. Which was why I had mostly hibernated the last few years. Noah was changing all the rules for me though. He wouldn't allow me to wallow at home. My mother was using this to her advantage too. I had been roped into the Jenkins Thanksgiving feast next week. She'd put me in charge of the green bean casserole knowing I would have to come through or else my brothers would storm my condo. It was weird, but my family had a long-standing obsession with green beans, cream of mushroom soup, and fried onions. Every family had their quirk, and this was ours.

By the time we made it to the paint samples, I felt as if I had been on my morning run, training for the 5K Noah and I were doing on Thanksgiving with his nephews. Thanksgiving was going to be busy for me.

I took some deep breaths and reminded myself that holly and jolly didn't own me. The problem was, part of me wanted to deck the halls and falalalala. I rubbed my flat abdomen, the invisible scar I was trying to keep from ripping open. I knew it meant in some small way that Ben still owned me. The past several weeks I had taken back what I could. Even enjoyed myself. More like rediscovered my sparkly side who was all for doing away with me. I had to admit, I did like her.

Why thank you. By the way, did you notice they decorated the tree all wrong on aisle 10? Hello, did you see all those gaps? Maybe you should go fix it.

Miss Sparkly was looking for a hit of pine. I would not be her dealer.

Instead, I settled Luna next to me and grabbed some greige paint samples. Sparkles could get high off paint fumes later.

Noah sidled up to me. "You doing okay? You looked like you might hyperventilate there with all the—"

I placed my finger on his lips. I was good at catching him now before he used the C-word. Unfortunately, his supple lips felt way too good. Don't even get me going on his stubble. Forget the pine, we were going to get high off Noah's charm.

Noah grinned, and I dropped my finger before I did something skanky like run my hand across his chiseled jawline.

Just do it.

We are not a Nike commercial, Sparkles.

"I'm fine. Thank you for asking," I answered, before holding up some paint tiles. "What do you think? Ginger Sugar or Cotton Gray? I'm thinking Ginger Sugar."

"Sounds like a good stripper name," Noah teased.

I snort laughed. I laughed a lot around Noah. I always had. "So, no Ginger Sugar." I placed the tile back and picked up a few more samples. While I was comparing the five shades of white, my phone exploded with noises and notifications. I handed Luna's leash over to Noah and reached in my bag for my phone. My social media pages were going wild with comments. I had no idea why. My daily posts did well, but not like this. Before I could log in to my accounts, I got a message from Mara.

Mara: *Don't panic, but someone just posted a picture of you and Noah on your pages. Also, is there something you want to tell me?*

Her words had my stomach dropping to the floor. So much so, I couldn't respond to her. I had to see what I was dealing with. From the sounds of it, I wasn't going to like it. With shaking fingers, I got on my Facebook page—that's where most of the notifications were coming from. Sure enough, someone had posted a picture of Noah and me in the hardware store. We looked, in a word, coupled. His hand was on the small of my back, and we were both smiling. Luna only added to it. We looked like a danged Hallmark Channel movie poster. Title: *Hardware Magic.* Wait, that sounded more X-rated. Regardless, it was getting two thumbs-down.

My breaths became shallow as I read the comments the photo was garnering.

I have to say, I'm kind of disappointed.

Was it all just a lie, Cami?

I thought she really understood what it meant to be single. I'll miss her posts.

I grabbed my chest, tears filling my eyes.

"Cams, what's wrong?" Noah was obviously concerned.

I looked up into the warm, inviting eyes of the man who had gotten me into a huge mess. "Noah," I squeaked. "People think we're dating. Someone just posted this picture of us." I held up my phone and looked around for the creepy culprit. I knew someone was watching us.

Noah grabbed my phone and grinned. "We look good."

I swiped it back from him. "This isn't good, Noah. This is bad for both of us." Annika was probably going to flip her lid. And we know she likes to stab things.

Noah's brow crinkled. "Bad how? Like I said, I don't give a damn what people say about me, in person or online."

"You're lucky that way. This could be the end of my business," my voice hitched.

Noah pulled me and Luna to a more out-of-the-way place near some large buckets of paint. He placed his hands firmly on my shoulders, searching my eyes like he was looking for the right words to say. His face went from pinched to pursed to tight, finally landing on a soft smile. "Cami, I get why you do what you do, but someday you are going to have to quit letting other people rule your life, whether it's Ben or your followers. I know you're trying to figure out your life right now, so go tell the world whatever you need to, to make yourself feel better. But just remember, until you own your life, you're never going to get better." He kissed my head and walked back toward the paint samples, leaving me without any air to breathe.

Dang, girl, he just told it like it is. Now what are you going to do?

That was a good question.

While I was trying to think of the right thing to do, my phone buzzed again. I looked down to see a text from Annika. My heart stopped. I hesitated to open it, but I knew if I didn't, I might go into cardiac arrest.

Annika: *I know this might be awkward, but I need to know if you and Noah are more than friends. I thought maybe he and I were going to rekindle. Again, awkward.*

I knew then what the right thing to do was.

Twenty-Seven

Hey, Ex-Filers, I know many of you have seen the picture of me with my FRIEND and CONTRACTOR, Noah. That's right, we're friends with a capital F. *Add a* P *for platonic. I've known him for years. In fact, he is my ex-husband's best friend and was the best man at my wedding. Awkward. And look at the man. Do you think I would leave the single life for someone like him? I know some might find him attractive—okay, a lot of you based on your salacious comments—but pictures can be deceiving. The bottom line is, we aren't a couple. I'm more single than the number one.*

Lots of love,

Cami

I stared at the message, there in the middle of gallons and gallons of paint. I knew I wasn't telling the full truth, so help me God. But it was the right thing to do. Noah needed me to do this for him and Annika. I was probably just having feelings for Noah because he was safe, and I knew it would never go anywhere.

Seriously, stop lying to yourself. You know that's not true. Own your life and your feelings, Miss Sparkly begged.

Fine. I care about Noah, but he's in love with Annika. We will not be the other woman, ever.

Sparkles went silent. She knew better than anyone, the damage the other woman could do. Once I silenced myself, I clicked publish before I thought about it too much.

My head popped up to see Noah reading his phone. Maybe I should have thought about it more, judging by how he shook his head, his face getting redder by the second. But then he took a deep breath and let it out, his shoulders rising and falling. He shoved his phone in his pocket and made his way to me with Luna.

I braced myself for what he was going to say. He really should be saying thank you, but judging by the perplexed look on his face, I knew that wasn't happening. Instead he sighed, then smirked. "The lady doth protest too much, methinks."

My mouth dropped and I spluttered. He was so, so right, but I couldn't admit to that. I threw my hood on my head and cinched it up tight. "I probably shouldn't be seen with you."

Noah crinkled his brow. "You're not that famous, Cams."

"Yeah, well, famous enough."

"More like infamous," he growled.

"I didn't do anything wrong," I pleaded with him to understand. "I just did us both a favor, so you're welcome. Can we go now?"

"Fine, Cams." He was clearly unhappy with me, judging by the way he marched toward the entrance, leaving me in the dust.

I trailed behind him and Luna, feeling like there was a tail between my legs. What was I supposed to do? I'll tell you what I didn't want to do, and that was get in his truck. He didn't open my door like he normally did. That was good. But watching him, sitting behind the wheel stewing, didn't give me any warm fuzzy feelings. I didn't understand why he was so upset. He had to know that picture of us hurt Annika. Maybe I should show him the message she sent me, even though it was totally embarrassing. And if he didn't care what people online thought about him, he shouldn't take issue with the fact that I basically indicated I didn't think he was godlike. Maybe I would tell him he was pretty to try and smooth it over. Because the one thing I knew was that I couldn't lose Noah as a friend. It pierced my heart even thinking about it.

As I approached the vehicle, I saw that he was taking a call. I stood by and watched as the blood drained from his face. Oh no. Annika was breaking up with him, and it was all my skanky fault. I wanted to rush to him to tell him I would make it all better and talk to Annika, but I felt as if my shoes were plastered to the asphalt. Maybe I was better off in hiding. Look how much I screwed everything up.

It didn't take Noah long to get off the phone. As soon as he did, he started his truck and rolled down his window. He lasered in on me with his steely gaze. "I need to go. They think my sister's in labor and they don't know if they can stop it this time."

My hands flew to my mouth. She still had five weeks until her due date. "I can take Luna for you and watch the boys, whatever you need me to do."

He let out a heavy breath, wisps of vapor playing in the cold air. "I have it covered. I just need you to get in the truck so I can take you home," he snapped.

That was it, the piercing blow. He was done with me. I could hardly blame him. Yet, I was stunned by the sting of it all. I stepped back, hoping he wouldn't see the misty sheen in my eyes. "You should go. I'll call Mara for a ride."

For a split second, regret lined his features, but exasperation took over. "If that's what you want," he sighed.

"I think it's for the best. Please tell Shanna and Adonis they are in my prayers. And if it's not too much trouble, please keep me posted about the babies." My voice hitched unnaturally. There was a lump in my throat the size of Mars.

Noah only nodded and rolled up his window. With that he took off, leaving me standing there feeling more alone than I had ever felt, and that was saying something. The tears I had been holding back softly trickled down my face. I pathetically stood in the parking lot for several minutes, crying, not having a clue what to do. All I kept asking myself was, how did I just let one of the best people I know walk out of my life? The answer didn't come right away, even as the snow began to land on my cold, red cheeks. Though I was freezing, I couldn't move. I had to know. Then the cold hard truth hit me.

Because you don't own your life. Miss Sparkly haunted me with Noah's words.

I felt as if I had been trying. But obviously not hard enough.

That was going to change.

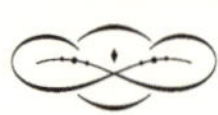

I shoved a huge spoonful of peppermint ice cream in my mouth while I blubbered, "He just left me there. I mean, I told him to, but he didn't even hesitate."

Mara made circular motions on my back with her hand, while I hovered over the large bowl of ice cream like I was hoarding it. Which I was. Mara was a saint and had picked me up from the hardware store and brought me back to her place. I cried the entire way there, preventing me from telling her my sad, sad tale.

"I'm sure he's worried about his sister, and your post about him wasn't all that flattering."

Ugh. The stupid post. I dropped my spoon in the bowl, sat back on her comfy couch, and curled into myself. "I had to write that post because I'm a sneaky skank."

Mara pressed her lips together, trying not to smile. "How are you a sneaky skank?" Her lips twitched up. "Try to say that ten times fast."

If only I could laugh over this, but there was nothing funny about it. "Mara," my voice cracked. "I . . . well . . . the truth is . . ." I knew I had to own it. "The truth is that I like Noah."

Mara stilled, but her eyes were riddled with questions. "When you say *like*, do you mean like or like like?"

"Like like," I said dramatically.

"Holy hella."

"I know." I cringed. "What's wrong with me? He loves Annika, and she's hoping they'll rekindle their romance."

Mara scrunched her nose. "Their high school romance?"

"I guess so. Noah is caulking her and polishing her floors."

"Caulking her?" Mara giggled.

"You know what I mean. I shouldn't have been spending so much time with him and harboring these feelings."

"Did you act on those feelings?"

"No," I whined.

"Then you did nothing wrong. But let's go back to the fact that you have feelings for a man." Mara sat up straight, eager for the 411.

I curled more into myself. “I didn’t mean to. What’s wrong with me?”

Mara laughed and rubbed my arm. “There’s nothing wrong with you. Noah is admittedly freakishly hot, and honestly, I’ve been wondering lately if he has feelings for you.”

I grabbed one of the afghans she’d crocheted and squeezed the life out of it. “He doesn’t. You saw him and Annika at the Halloween Bash. His costume was obviously for her.”

“Yeah, I also saw the way you looked when you danced together. I’m surprised someone didn’t post a picture of the two of you that night.”

I sat up a bit, feeling extra squirmy. “That night I was ridiculous and flirty.”

“Cams, you’re not ridiculous. I’m actually shocked it’s taken you this long to jump back on the man train.”

“I’m not jumping on any train.”

Mara scooted closer and took a dramatic breath in and out. “I know better than anyone what you lost and what my brother did to you, and as hilarious as you’ve been doing the single thing, I wonder . . .” She paused.

“You wonder what?”

“Well, I wonder if it’s really you.”

I sat up and fell against her.

She wrapped an arm around me.

“Mara,” I whispered. “I miss me.”

“Where do you want to look for her?”

I thought about that for a second. And what my mom said about the song in my heart. It wasn’t going to be pretty, but I knew what I had to do. “Will you watch a Chris . . .”

Say it. You can do it! Own it.

“. . . Christmas movie with me?”

“Does it have to be Hallmark?” she groaned.

“No,” I laughed. “How about *Die Hard*?” That was a good one to ease into it.

“Now we’re talking. Nothing says merry Christmas like a good old-fashioned hostile terrorist takeover.”

"I kind of feel like that's my life right now."

Hey, I heard that. I'm not a terrorist. I'd like to think of myself as more of a motivational speaker.

I smiled to myself.

Mara squeezed me tight as if trying to protect me. Man, I loved her.

"So," she hesitated, "what are you going to do about Noah?"

I rubbed my heart; there was this ache and emptiness there. "There's nothing I can do. He loves Annika."

"Are you sure?"

"Yes," I whispered.

"Well, men suck."

"Not Noah," I defended him, even though I was pretty sure he hated me. "Regardless, I think I'm going to date myself first."

Mara laughed. "I'm dating myself too—we should totally go on a double date, like to the spa."

"Now you're talking."

"I love you, Cams."

"I love you, and I think I'm going to love myself too."

Twenty-Eight

Dear Ex-Filers, I know for many of us these big holidays can be hard. It's so easy to focus on what's missing. My dad says that gratitude is like medicine: sometimes it's hard to swallow, but once you take it, it cures almost any ill. So today I want to say how grateful I am for all of you. You have helped me through some of my deepest, darkest moments. If you are alone this day, I hope it's by choice and you enjoy every SINGLE second of it. You see what I did there? Anyway, see my pinned post and highlight reels about ten things to do if you're alone on Thanksgiving. As for the rest of you, sweats are always an option, and don't forget people placement in pictures should be intentional—you know, just in case you need some cropping done. Wink, wink. Because you know I'll be here winter, spring, summer, and fall to remove them all.

Happy Thanksgiving!

Lots of love,

Cami

I read over my post to make sure it reflected me. The me I was trying to become. I was still trying to find the balance between sparkly and snarky. I still wasn't sure my brand would survive the change, especially if I ever decided to jump on the man train, as Mara called it. Not like anyone was handing me a ticket to board. Especially not Noah. Our only communication was a few texts updating me on Shanna, who after being in the hospital for several days, did have the babies very late last night. The girls were tiny at only four pounds each, but they were breathing on their own, which was a huge blessing. Shanna texted me pictures of her tiny angels, Amayah and Camila. They were gorgeous and oh so squishy.

Shanna was doing well and overjoyed that her daughters had made it to the party.

I assumed Noah was happy. I wanted so badly to see him today. We were supposed to run the Turkey Trot with Jaxon and Liam this morning, but Noah had canceled via text. His excuse was the babies being born, but I knew it was more than that. I'd exhausted him with my craziness, and he had Annika. She canceled helping at the homeless shelter because she was making Thanksgiving dinner for Noah. As happy as I was for Noah, the thought of them together hurt in ways I didn't know I could still hurt. My mom said that was a good sign. I wasn't so sure, but it was where I was at.

I finished getting ready at the ungodly time of 5:00 a.m. I never understood why races needed to be so early. Especially when it was so freaking cold out. The air was for sure going to burn my lungs. The good news was all the calories I would be burning would mean I could eat more pie. My mom and I had made seven yesterday. Everything from pecan to pumpkin. I licked a lot of beaters. Mom was so ecstatic to have my help. She'd blasted Christmas music all day. I had even found myself humming to a few songs while we'd worked. She was still trying to talk me into getting a tree, but I wasn't there yet. I still had visions of Ben and Claudia under the boughs of pine I had lovingly and carefully decorated. Besides, I wouldn't be here for Christmas. Mom wasn't thrilled with that. But I think she understood at least some of it. She had no idea the loss I had sustained on Christmas. I couldn't burden her with that knowledge.

I looked in the mirror one last time. I looked ridiculous in my bright turkey-feather tutu and my *Run Now and Gobble Later* shirt. I even had the matching gloves and hat. While I looked like a nutjob, and probably was, I felt more like me. It was why I was still going to run, despite Noah canceling on me. I wanted to face my demons, even if it was alone. The last time I'd run the Turkey Trot was with Ben. He'd asked me not to dress "weirdly" that year. He was already sleeping with Claudia, Miss Perfection. Yet he'd still made love to me that night. The thought made me want to vomit.

But today was going to be a new day where I embraced my "weird" side and let go of another piece of my past.

I looked down at my feet to find Neville holding Luna's favorite toy, a squeaky hot dog, in his mouth. He was about as forlorn as I was. I knelt down and scratched his head, "I know you're missing her, buddy. I miss Noah too. He would love my outfit. Maybe he'll let us have Luna over for a playdate. If he ever forgives me. Sorry, I screwed this one up. If you want, I found a YouTube channel about big beautiful dogs that you can watch."

Neville curled his lip. I would take that as a no.

I stood and headed for my kitchen, which was a disaster area, to grab a protein bar. At least Noah had sent someone over this week to work on the countertops. I had a feeling he wouldn't be doing any more of the work himself. So much for him trying to be a safe landing place and helping me to figure it out. I didn't blame him; he had tried. It was for the best. I realized it was something I needed to figure out on my own. I was the only person who could give myself permission to love me. To even love the holidays again.

So, I was off to make a fool of myself. That's how I rolled.

There was nothing that made my own worries seem so small like serving at the homeless shelter. As I looked into some of the vacant yet grateful eyes of those so in need, I appreciated my life more than I could express. Especially as I sat there with Hector after taking him a tray of food. His frail, scarred hand held my own as if he never wanted to let go. He said he hadn't held anyone's hand in at least twenty years. My eyes filled with tears thinking that even in my darkest hours, I always had a hand to hold.

The only thing I could do was sit there and listen to him tell me his story, one of many triumphs but too many bone-crushing tragedies. He was born to wealthy parents and had every advantage given to him, but he got lost in the world of drugs. Drugs led to prison, and prison led to more crimes and more incarcerations. Any family he had all but disowned him, even his children. He'd been living on the streets for years.

"You know my biggest regret in life?" his shaky, gruff voice asked.

"What's that?"

"That I was too stubborn to ask for help. Don't ever be afraid to ask for help." Then he winked. "And I wish I would have kissed more pretty girls like you."

I smiled and kissed his cheek. "I think you are a flirt."

His free hand rose and touched his rough, worn cheek where I had just kissed it. Tears filled his eyes. "Young lady, that right there was the best gift I've been given in a long time."

He had no idea that he was the best gift I'd been given in a long time. Perspective was such a beautiful thing. In that moment I realized how lucky I was. I didn't want to blow that by letting Ben rule my life. No, I hadn't taken drugs, but I had given control over to a powerful substance—fear. Fear of who I am.

I walked out of the homeless shelter with even more determination to not let fear rule me. And to be so thankful. So very thankful.

One of the people I was most thankful for, Mara, texted me as I got into my 4Runner.

Mara: *Please send wine, it's a crap show over here. Here's the highlight reel for you. Claudia is livestreaming my spread and complaining how there is nothing worse on Thanksgiving than not being able to eat anything, all while giving tips about what to do about that. She can shove a piece of celery up her tight butt.*

I giggled because I wouldn't mind seeing that.

The text continued: *My dad is being judgmental per his usual, now my mom is eating her weight in mashed potatoes. Ben has zoned out, looking like he's questioning all his life choices, which he should be. Ugh. Anyway, happy Thanksgiving from the Scotts. If you see me on the nightly news, don't worry about bailing me out, prison has to be better than this.*

I felt awful for her. She was really hoping she could plan the perfect Thanksgiving to make her dad see how wonderful her mom is and I think to show him how capable and impressive Mara could be. As always, Jay was a blind jerk.

Me: *I'm so sorry. You are still more than welcome to come to my parents'. I'm heading over there now. It will be a zoo, but I can guarantee good pie and I know where my mom hides the liquor. Love you.*

Mara: *Thanks for the invite, but I just found some celery and I know exactly where it should go. She can livestream that. Love you more.*

I would head over to her place and bring her some pie after my family's festivities were over. It was weird how much I was looking forward to it this year. Maybe it was the turkey headbands I had bought for all my minions. Or perhaps it was me. The real me.

No matter the reason, I made my way back to Aspen Lake. I had to make a quick stop at my place to check on Neville, who was back to bingeing *Beverly Hills, 90210.* I think he was depressed, and Dylan and Kelly brought him comfort. I'm pretty sure he was ecstatic to find out that Dylan really was the father of Kelly's son. Believe me, we were all happy for that piece of news. I also had to grab the two pans of green bean casserole I had assembled in between running the 5K and helping at the homeless shelter—they just needed to be baked. By the way, I had rocked my run. A seven-minute-mile pace, baby, and no tears. Not to say Ben didn't haunt that trail, but there was something about facing him that helped give me the courage to push through.

I wished I could take Neville with me, but he would go into cardiac arrest with so many people. Besides, he was mourning Luna. I, on the other hand, was trying not to think of Noah and Annika. It wasn't going so well. I kept thinking they had probably skipped dinner and gone straight to caulking. Ugh.

With Neville taken care of, I headed to my parents' place; I even put some Christmas music on the radio. I wasn't doing the hard stuff yet, like Bing Crosby and Andy Williams. I started out slow with some Trans-Siberian Orchestra. No words, just some head-banging-worthy Christmas jams.

I dispensed with the pep talk I had needed to face my family on the holidays the last few years and just went for it. Me, the headbands, and the coveted casseroles. Corey and Ryland were going to kill me. I couldn't wait to see them with felt turkeys on their heads.

When I walked in with my hands full, still wearing my turkey feather tutu, though I had upgraded to a black sweater, it was as if time stopped. I swore my entire family was there waiting for me to arrive, like they were throwing me a surprise birthday party. Everyone rushed me, and Dad grabbed the green bean casseroles to keep them from harm, before everyone else began hugging and kissing me, so happy I had come. It's not like I hadn't been to Thanksgiving in the last few years, but it was the first time since my divorce I hadn't snuck in wearing sweats and a scowl that could melt butter. All I knew was I felt loved and hungry. Sage, thyme, and homemade rolls wafted through the house.

With sheeny eyes, I hugged and kissed everyone back, from my big dopey brothers to the cutest tot and, of course, the best parents a girl could ask for. Daniel and Ilene Jenkins—the world didn't make them any better than those two. And someday I might forgive them for inviting the unexpected guest who walked in the door looking way too good, and oddly shell shocked, in his photo shoot outfit. I guess that meant he and Annika had taken the next step. Good for them. I'll tell you this, I didn't care if they did break up, I was never cropping another photo shoot for him.

My family peeled away from me like a blooming onion, leaving me exposed to the gaze of Noah. I swore every head, even my little minions', ping-ponged between us. All Noah did was peruse my ridiculous getup, his lips twitching, until he turned his focus to my mom—the main instigator, I was sure. She'd pestered me with questions about him yesterday and was disappointed to hear that we weren't really speaking and he was spending Thanksgiving with Annika. Or at least he was supposed to have been. Why was he here?

"Sorry I'm early for pie, Mrs. J. My dinner plans were cut short," he sounded relieved.

That cleared up why he was here, sort of.

Did Annika have a headache? Not in the mood for caulking? Maybe she tripped and fell while taking pictures. Okay, that was petty on my part. Annika was a good person.

Mom pranced her way toward him. "We're so glad you're here. I'm sure you have more room for turkey."

Noah rubbed his washboard abs. "*Your* turkey sounds great."

What? Had Annika's not been good?

"Perfect. You can sit next to Cami." My mother's eyes gleamed with deviousness.

Oh no, no, no. I would not be the ho. Not ever. No matter how much I liked Noah or wanted to catch up with him, tell him how sorry I was. "Uh, I'm sitting at the kids table." A.k.a. the island.

My mother wasn't to be deterred. "You like kids, don't you, Noah?"

All the adults chuckled. This was getting ridiculous.

Noah returned my mother's conspiratorial grin with one of his own. "Love them, Mrs. J."

Mom clapped her hands together. "That's settled, then. Let Thanksgiving begin."

I think she meant, "Let the games begin."

Twenty-Nine

Dear Ex-Filers, if anyone wants to know what holiday dinners are like with my family, it's a beautiful time where we all gather and talk over each other at the tops of our lungs. It really brings a tear to the eye. Also, if it makes you feel any better, just remember most pies count as a serving of fruit, so don't be shy, eat that pie. And if you need to escape any setup attempts from your mother, remember that talking and plotting to yourself is always a fan favorite. Good luck.

Lots of love,

Cami

I had escaped to the bathroom for a few minutes. Dinner had been awkward so far, to say the least. Like hella awkward, as Mara would say. Noah still hadn't talked to me. Sure, he had looked my way, smirked, observed, even laughed when I forced turkey headbands on Corey and Ryland, but he'd said not a word to me as he'd sat across the island from me, chowing down like he hadn't eaten in weeks while wearing an extra turkey headband. It was adorable, but I hadn't mentioned it. Mom had definitely outdone herself this year. The turkey was melt-in-your-mouth amazing, and the green bean casserole was yummy. But hadn't he just come from dinner with his girlfriend? I wasn't going to ask him.

I slipped back onto my stool between my nieces Michaela and Toby. They were Ashton's kiddos. Thankfully they were cuter and more well behaved than my brute of a brother, who was already talking smack and wanting to get out on the court for a game of three-on-three.

Saylor, my youngest niece, toddled my way and put her arms out, wanting me to hold her. I felt Noah's eyes on me as I picked her up and cuddled her.

Say something to him, please. Miss Sparkly begged. She'd been quiet as of late—I mean, why would she need to talk when I was doing most everything her way?

Not quite everything, dear. But we're getting there, she threw in for good measure.

Don't expect everything to go back to the way it used to be. I don't even know if that's possible. Also, I don't know what to say to Noah. I already texted him congratulations about his nieces, and all I got was a simple "Thank you" back, I defended myself.

That didn't stop my head from turning to meet his gaze. When we locked eyes, a rush of heat trailed down my entire body. His lips parted like he might say something, but my dad stood and cleared his throat loudly.

"I have an announcement to make."

My head whipped in my dad's direction. My mom was now standing next to him. Dad smiled at the love of his life and wrapped an arm around her. How could they be so cute and still so in love? I knew it should give me hope but considering my track record and the fact that the man I liked was already taken, I wasn't feeling all that hopeful about love. Yet, my parents made me smile even if they had made my holiday hella awkward.

It took my family a hot minute to quiet down. By that I mean my siblings and their spouses yelling at their children to hush for a good three minutes, then some crying ensued, followed by bribery. Good times.

I held on to sweet Saylor, wondering what kind of announcement my dad had to make. Last time he'd done this, he'd announced he was taking us all on a Disney cruise. I could live with that. But from the way my mom was beaming up at him with her hand resting on his chest, I had a feeling I wouldn't be packing my bags anytime soon. At least not for a family vacay. I was still hitting the Virgin Islands with Mara in twenty-six days. Not like I was counting.

When the noise level was down to a quiet roar, Dad peered into Mom's watery eyes and said, "We've come to a decision."

I braced myself.

"I'm retiring. Jay," he groaned, "wants to take the firm in a different direction, so he's buying me out. It's almost a done deal."

The noise level erupted to breaking-the-sound-barrier-level.

I had no idea Dad was even thinking about retiring. It made me wonder if Jay wanted to do something shady and Dad was having no part of it. Regardless, we were all in shock. Then Dad caught my eye, and between his smile and nod, I knew what he was telling me. He was moving on from Jenkins & Scott, so I had permission to as well. In part, his retirement was a gift to me. I popped off my seat with Saylor still in my arms and headed straight for my dad, passing off Saylor to her mom as I went.

Dad opened his arms wide, and I fell right into them. "Thank you, Daddy," I cried into his chest. I hadn't called him Daddy in a long time, but this was a total daddy moment.

He kissed my head. "I figured it was time for both of us to move on."

"I'm officially turning in my resignation." I laughed.

Dad chuckled. "I figured that would probably be the case."

I felt such a weight lift off my shoulders. I mean, I would have to figure out health insurance and ways to replace that income. My heart stilled. It knew exactly how I could easily replace that income. Oh. It was definitely something to think about—doing lifestyle shoots again.

But I didn't have time to think about it, as Kellan stood and yelled over the crowd. "We have an announcement too. We've got a little Elvis cooking! We're due in March."

Wow. Tonya didn't look pregnant at all. They'd done a good job of keeping that under wraps.

Everyone diverted their attention and rushed Kellan and Tonya, well mostly Tonya. Mom was to her first. She was already bawling like she always did when someone announced a new grandchild. Next, she would bring out her *Blessed Grandma* shirt and wear it for days on end. I so badly wanted her to wear that shirt for me. I'd had visions of telling her I was pregnant and the shopping spree that would have ensued, along with decorating the nursery.

For now, I stood back and watched the joyous scene and wondered if I would have one to match. Don't get me wrong, I was so happy for new life, but as always, it made me think of the life I never got to bring into the world. That didn't stop me from hugging my brother and congratulating him, but after that, I slipped downstairs, grabbed one of Mom's long coats, and headed outside to catch my breath. I headed for my favorite spot by the lake. With the crunch of snow beneath my feet, I breathed in the cold air that smelled of pine and for some reason apple pie. Maybe a neighbor had gotten adventurous and made pie on the grill.

I carefully made my descent to the firepit Dad had built near the lake, with large boulders and tree stumps for seating. The lake was still, and reflected the half moon. With the snowy trees surrounding it, the water looked like a pool of silver. The clear night showcased the array of stars. It was quite perfect. I swiped the snow off a stump and sat down to absorb the peace of the night while watching my breath play in the cold air. So many beautiful memories lived in this place. Memories like sleeping out under the stars with my dad while he made up stories about the different constellations. Until I was nine, I believed with all my heart that the Little Dipper and the Big Dipper were married and their babies were the stars surrounding them. Dad and I had even named them: Dot, Jasper, Dippity-do, etc. To be so innocent again.

I closed my eyes and let the cold sting my cheeks. It was refreshing and made me feel alive. I'd felt more alive the last few days than I had in a long time. Now I had new possibilities in front of me. More chances to be myself, if I was brave enough. Today my dad had helped me crop out another piece of my life with Ben. I wondered if Jay had made the same announcement at their Thanksgiving meal. I was anxious to get Mara's take. See what her dad was up to.

For now, though, I continued to soak in the magic of this place. The place where I'd believed that dreams could come true, and I could do and become anything I wanted to be. I longed for that girl. She was making an appearance more and more, but life had made her more cautious.

Amid the calm, I heard the crunch of snow. I opened my eyes to find Noah walking down the trail. His hands were shoved in his pockets, and his turkey headband was gone; instead, he wore a pensive expression. I seemed to bring that out in him. Regardless, my heart pitter-pattered while I begged it not to. Noah wasn't meant to be mine.

I rubbed my cold hands together. "Hey," I whispered.

"Hi," Noah's deep voice rumbled in the dark. "Happy Thanksgiving, Cams."

"You're talking to me now?" I didn't mean to be snarky. I knew I had screwed up last Saturday, but the feelings I had for him made his silence hurt.

He ran a hand through his hair and closed his eyes. "Cams, you frustrate the hell out of me."

"I know. And I'm sorry." I stood and trudged through the snow to the water's edge. A memory so sweet hit me. It was the magic of this place. Or maybe it was Noah. He lived in so many of my memories. I thought back to a night long ago when Noah, Ben, Mara and I, along with a few other friends, had all decided to camp out down there. Everyone else had fallen asleep but Noah and me. We lay in our sleeping bags, heads propped up on our arms, and talked for hours and hours, until the sun began to rise. We talked about everything from if we believed in God to if we thought the Dodgers would make it to the World Series that year. I wanted us to be able to be friends like that again. I would forget that I had any romantic feelings for him, if only we could go back to how things were. I realized how much I wanted him to be a part of my life.

"Cams." He came up behind me and wrapped his arms around me.

I turned around and naturally snuggled into him and held on like he was a lifeline. I didn't say anything. I just soaked him and his goodness and friendship in. I did my best not to wish we could be more or to revel in how intoxicating his warm breath felt across my skin.

Noah broke the silence. "What's troubling you? Why did you come out here alone?"

I leaned away and was caught by his intense blue eyes boring into my own, begging to understand me. The consternation I caused him was apparent in the lines on his face. He needed to know the truth about why I was so neurotic. And I knew I needed to be the one to tell him.

"Noah, I know I've screwed up and frustrated you and been a terrible friend, but I have my reasons. Reasons so painful, I couldn't tell you."

He rested his forehead against mine. "Cams, you can tell me anything."

I tried my best not to think about how close our lips were or how inviting his breath was. "How's Annika?" I asked out of the blue. I needed a link to reality something fierce.

"I don't want to talk about her right now," he snarled.

Was there trouble in paradise? I tried not to be too giddy about that.

"Just tell me what you need to. Please," he begged like his life depended on it.

Do it, please. Let the poison out. It's been festering for so long.

Sparkles was right. I had let it build up over the years until it poisoned me against myself. "Noah." My lips quivered, and not from the cold. "I was pregnant." I hadn't said those words in so long. Tears streamed down my face, letting the poison out a drop at a time.

Noah leaned away, and his strong hands worked their way up and cradled my face. "When?"

"The night I came home early to surprise Ben," my voice trembled. "That was the surprise."

"Cams." Noah's thumbs gently wiped away as many tears as they could.

"It made his betrayal a thousand times worse," I stammered.

"That bastard," Noah raged, but only for a moment. He kissed my forehead. His warm lips were like a balm to my soul. "What happened to the baby, Cams?" he hesitated to ask.

"I lost it," I blubbered. "I woke up early on Christmas morning in so much pain. And then the bleeding started. And it kept going and going and going. Mara took me to the emergency room, but there was nothing they could do—other than tell me my hormone levels indicated I had been pregnant but I was miscarrying. They sent me home and I felt as if I'd lost everything. I never wanted another Christmas. I didn't even want to be myself anymore. Something inside of me broke."

"Cams." He held me tight.

My head fell on his chest, and I soaked it with my tears. "No matter what Ben had done to me, I thought it would have been worth it just to have my baby. That baby offered me light in a darkness so black, I thought I wouldn't see my way out of it. And then my baby was gone too. The light turned off and it wasn't until recently that I wanted to turn it back on." I burrowed my head into his chest as deep as I could. "Noah, I'm so sorry I've ignored you and frustrated you. You've been a wonderful friend, and I know I'm kind of screwed up, but I want you to know how much your friendship means to me. Please be patient. I swear I'll get it all figured out."

Noah stilled, but his heart pounded so heavily, I could feel it. It made me nervous.

"We can be friends, right?" I pleaded.

"Cams," he whispered and kissed the top of my head, and then he leaned away and kissed my forehead, then my nose, next each cheek.

All while I held my breath. This was all very friendly of him.

His eyes captured my own, willing me to pay attention. "I don't want to be your friend." He articulated it so clearly, it pierced my heart.

"But—" I began to beg him to reconsider.

He silenced me with his lips as they brushed my own.

The world and my heart stopped. Noah kissed me. I didn't have time to think about what that meant because he kissed me again and the pleasure center in my brain exploded, making all reason go out the window. This time when his warm lips pressed against mine, he drew me against him. He groaned as his lips glided and teased. His kiss was intimate and sweet before it became deep and incredible. Like the most amazing kiss I had ever experienced. His tongue danced magically in my mouth, making me feel all the things from dizzyingly warm to hungry. So hungry. I wanted more and more. I gripped his jacket and wound my fists in it, begging him silently not to stop. I wanted to endlessly drown in the cinnamon on his breath.

But then I remembered what I should have remembered all along. I pushed away from him. "I'm a shameless skank and you're . . . you're a man whore."

He blinked and caught his breath. "What?"

I pointed and spluttered. "You . . . you . . . you're dating Annika. You love her. How can you kiss me like that?"

He gave me a devilish grin. "You did kiss me back."

"Ugh. I know! What's wrong with me. I'm the other woman now." I backed away from him.

He grabbed my hand and pulled me right back to him.

I half-heartedly struggled to release myself from his grip.

"Cams, will you calm down? You're not the other woman. You *are* the woman."

"What?" Was he high?

He drew me closer and rested his cool hand on my cheek. "Cami, I don't love Annika. I love you." He let out a long breath like he had been holding it for years. "Damn that felt good to say."

Either the air suddenly vanished or it was so cold my lungs froze. All I could do was stare blankly at him. This couldn't be real. When I forced some air into my lungs and could finally form words, I responded, "No. No." I shook my head. "We're friends. You've never said anything."

He dropped his hand and sighed. "When would have been a good time for me to tell you I was in love with you, Cami? When you started dating my best friend? When you got engaged to him? Maybe before you walked down the aisle?"

"Well, I can see how that could put a damper on it. Wait. How long have you been in love with me?" I could hardly believe I was asking that.

He gathered me in his arms and chastely kissed me once. "Since the moment you said, 'Hi, I'm Cami.'"

"Oh," I squeaked. "That's a long time." I still couldn't believe this. "But you've been doing photo shoots with other women, and you and

Annika came as a couple to the Halloween Bash, and she told me you were going to rekindle, annnddd . . . you've been caulking her and polishing her floors."

Noah spat out a laugh. "Caulking her?"

"Yes, caulking her tub. I know what that means."

"Cams, I don't think you do." He grinned before letting out a heavy breath. "I don't know where to begin, but I only did those photo shoots because I couldn't think of any other way to see you. After your divorce, I felt like you divorced me too, and I was desperate to change that."

Oh man, he was right. I would think those photo shoots were romantic.

"So, you weren't dating any of those women?"

"Not one. They were just acquaintances, willing to help a guy get his girl."

"But what about you and Annika? You were the Damon to her Elena."

"Ugh," he groaned. "That was a terrible coincidence. I came as Damon because of you."

"So, you aren't caulking her?"

"No." He snorted. "That said, I feel guilty. She told me today she wanted more, and I had to tell her I didn't feel that way about her."

"How did she take it?"

"Not well; but Cams, I'm more concerned about how you're taking this." He pointed between us.

"That's a good question. The kiss, definitely an A-plus. I don't know if you practiced licking the beaters when you were a child, but it paid off."

His hands slid down my back, inching me closer to him. "You want to go for round two?"

Did I ever. "Yes. But . . ." I placed a finger on his inviting lips. "Love, Noah. That's huge. You're in love with me." I could barely say it.

He kissed my finger before he removed it from his lips. "Yeah, Cams, I love you. I've tried not to, but there's been no getting over you, even when I knew it was Ben you would choose."

That was obviously a grave mistake on my part, but I didn't even know I had the choice. Except, at the time, I know I wouldn't have chosen differently. Ben called to my soul. I hated to admit that, but it was true. But how was I so blind to the man in front of me?

"Does Ben know about the baby?" Noah whispered.

I shook my head. "For days I tried to tell him, but how could I when he threw me away so easily? And I hated myself for believing a baby would solve our problems. I was so stupid," I choked out.

Noah stroked my hair. "He was the idiot, not you."

"But I was. I let him own me and destroy me with hardly a fight. That scares me, Noah." What if I allowed that to happen again?

"I know," he sounded resigned. "Which is why I walked away on Saturday. I realized it wasn't me who could heal your heart, as much as I've wanted to. That's so damn frustrating."

I rested my hands on his chest. "Your frustration makes a lot more sense to me now."

"Yes, you're maddening, but I wouldn't change you for anything."

My eyes stung with happy tears. "You don't know how much that means to me. How much you have meant to me, but . . ." I paused. "This is a big deal. I feel like I'm trying to get to know who I am right now. I don't want to frustrate you in the process."

His lips pressed against mine. My tears landed on our melded lips, making the kiss salty and sweet.

"Find your Christmas, Cami. Find you. Whoever she is, I'll love her," he spoke gently against my lips.

A swell of emotion filled every fiber of my being. He had no idea what that meant to me. "I know this isn't fair of me to ask, but do you promise?" I didn't want to lose him, not when I had just found out he was an option.

"I'm not going anywhere. As long as there is breath in me, I will have hope that we'll be together."

My hands wandered up his chest, wound around his neck and ran through that gorgeous hair of his. This time *I* kissed *him*. I was anxious and greedy and begged him with my tongue to devour me. He did a thorough job while his hands owned all my curves, pressing ever deeper, as if he couldn't believe he could touch me. Yet, he was quick to pull away.

He swallowed hard and inhaled deeply. "We need to stop before I think about caulking with you." He winked.

I giggled.

"Cams." He tenderly ran a finger down my cheek. "I think you need to tell Ben about the baby."

He caught me off guard. "Why? He won't care."

"I don't think that's true," he whispered. "Regardless, do it for you. You deserve to be free of him, and he needs to be accountable. Don't let him own any part of you for another day."

I knew he was right. As weird as it sounded, for so long it seemed easier to hold on to it. The pain gave me a cover to hide behind. But as I looked in front of me at Noah, I didn't want to hide anymore.

Psst. Psst, Cami, Miss Sparkly interrupted my moment. I'm actually surprised she hadn't popped up earlier. *You better hurry up and find your Christmas. I need some more of Noah.*

You and me both.

Thirty

Dear Ex-Filers, "Who in the world am I? Ah, that's the great puzzle." —*Lewis Carroll,* Alice's Adventures in Wonderland. *Do you ever feel like a puzzle with missing pieces? Or that you have all the pieces but you don't know how they all fit together? Or maybe you've been trying to force the wrong pieces into the empty spaces. Sorry to wax poetic so early in the morning. I'm just over here trying to figure out who I am, while I watch a group of women in a parking lot at 2:00 a.m. diagramming their store route for when the doors open at 4:00. Now they just swiped black makeup under their eyes. It's straight out of a locker room scene in a football movie. I'm not sure if I'm impressed or disturbed.*

For anyone Black Friday shopping, please remember, don't wear red if you're going to Target. You're welcome for the reminder. Stay safe out there, friends. By the look of these ladies in the parking lot, people mean business.

Lots of love,

Cami

I clicked publish and looked up to find Mara walking back to my car with two gigantic cups of steaming hot chocolate, hopefully with a bunch of whipped cream, from the nearby coffeehouse. She'd taken one for the team and blazed her way into the only open store in the vicinity. They were taking advantage of all of us crazies. I hadn't done the craziness in a few years, but Mara begged me to come with her and be the voice of reason. She was addicted to coats and yarn, and I was the gatekeeper to her credit card. Besides, how could I sleep knowing Noah was in love with me and he had kissed me. And kissed me. And kissed me. And kissed me some more. Kissed me until he'd stolen my breath and I lost all feeling in my toes. That was probably because it was cold, and we were standing in the snow. But I'm open to testing that theory.

This was a life-changing event. And not just because I had never been kissed so thoroughly or wonderfully. Seriously, the man should make a YouTube tutorial on how to kiss. He would be a millionaire with all the views. However, it wasn't just his technique. There was something in his kiss that spoke to my broken soul. That said, "I don't need to fix you; I'll take you as you are for now and who you decide to be forever."

It was the forever part that scared the living daylights out of me. Noah wasn't just looking for a hookup or a girlfriend—he wanted me for every trip he would take around the sun until the end of his days, and knowing him, all the days after that too. He didn't say that last night, but I couldn't help but play over and over again the time he'd said he already knew who Mrs. Cullen would be. He was talking about me. That meant I had to know if a relationship was a part of my puzzle. When I'd married six years ago, I thought I knew everything I needed to know about life. Oh, how wrong I was. I knew absolutely nothing. Even now I knew very little. But what I did know made me skittish.

Mara jumped in the car, looking as if she'd just survived the Hunger Games. "Here." She handed me a cup so large I needed two hands. With it also came the smirkiest smirk. She'd been giving those to me ever since I picked her up an hour ago.

"What?"

"I'm still thinking about the fact that after he kissed you, you called yourself a skank and him a man whore. If you end up together, that will be a great story to tell your kids." She laughed hysterically.

I rested my head on my steering wheel and groaned. "I know. It's so embarrassing. But how was I to know he wasn't in love with Annika?"

"That's another thing—caulking?" She giggled. "From now on that's what we're calling sex."

I lifted my head and smiled over at her.

"Which reminds me, you didn't get to the part about how Annika took it."

"Not good." I cringed. "Apparently she shoved a large knife in the turkey while laughing maniacally."

Mara shuddered. "Did he tell her he was in love with you?"

"No. Not only did he fear for my safety, but he knows how much I'm struggling with who I am and what that means for the Ex-Filers. You saw all those comments when they thought I was dating Noah. Some of them were vicious and questioned if I was deceiving people and just an opportunist." I let out a heavy sigh and took a sip of my hot chocolate. Yep, the whipped cream was there. "It's all so confusing. Then there's the question of how I support myself if it all goes away. But I don't want it to go away. I feel like what I do helps people. I get messages all the time of how healing it was for me to remove an ex from what they considered a living reminder they didn't want anymore." I took several more sips and let the chocolate soothe my soul.

"So, you've already decided on Noah?" she hesitated to ask.

I bit my lip. "I mean, I could kiss him all day and be a happy woman," I teased. "Honestly, though, I don't know. I'm scared. What if he changes like Ben? And what if I don't stick up for myself? And I am worried about losing my business, and for some reason Noah isn't into sneaking around. But doesn't that sound like fun?" I half-heartedly laughed.

"Secret liaisons do sound sexy," Mara agreed. "But as much as I hate to agree with Noah, a person who keeps you a secret usually has other things to hide. And if you can't be open in the light, there is no hope for you as a couple when things get dark."

"Wow. That's really deep." I giggled though I meant every word. She was right. Love flourished in the light.

She held up her cup to me. "You know my family, we're all about secret relationships," she snarled.

I rubbed her leg. "I'm sorry. Listen to me rambling. Tell me about your Thanksgiving."

"I'd much rather talk about yours. At least yours was happy," she sighed. "I'm so over my family and the holidays. You're lucky, Cams," some emotion laced her words. "At the end of the day, you have an entire army that would hunt down and maim anyone who hurt you. I'm not even sure anyone in my dysfunctional family would know if I disappeared."

I set my drink in the console's cup holder and took her hand, my heart breaking for her. "Mara, your family loves you. I love you. I would notice the second you were gone and search for you until my dying day if I had to."

"This is why I love you and will never sign you up for any spammy email lists."

"I do appreciate that." I grinned.

Mara pulled out her phone. "Which reminds me, Claudia is getting added to a few more after she livestreamed herself from my living room and made fun of my basket full of yarn."

"What a witch."

"She's going to pay. I happened to learn of a device that people put on their tongues so they can lick their cats."

My face scrunched. "Ew."

"It's called a Lick Me-ow. She's so going on that list of weirdos, and I've been saving the herpes control for a special occasion. Today is that day." She cracked her knuckles, ready to get to business.

"What about Ben?" I was eagerly anticipating what lists he would go on.

"Honestly, I'm going to give him a break. He was pretty depressed yesterday. He watched his wife with this vacant stare that said, 'What have I done with my life?' He also asked about you and Noah. He saw that picture of you together at the hardware store."

My brows raised. "Does he follow me?"

Mara shrugged. "That I don't know, but I get the feeling he checks in on you from time to time online. Selfishly, I want you to date Noah just to vex my brother."

I ran my fingers through my hair. "Noah thinks I should tell Ben about the baby."

Mara's brow quirked. "Really? What do you think about that?"

"I'm not sure, but I know before I even think about starting a relationship with Noah, I can't let Ben haunt me anymore."

"So, what you're saying is that you have to vanquish my brother. I like it." She laughed evilly. "How fast can you do that? And how can I help you?"

I threw my arms around her. "I'll let you know. Now let's go get in line. Those crazy ladies out there have friends and they've brought their own bags."

Mara clung to me. "Cams, don't be afraid to forge your own path, even if that means Noah is a part of it. Those who are meant to follow you will always follow you. Why worry about anyone else?"

That right there gave me all the feels. Like, I felt those words in my soul. "Wow. You're like my own personal spiritual guru."

"Nah, it's all the private crocheting groups I'm in. Mark my words, crocheters are going to save the world."

Knowing Mara was part of them, I had no doubt.

When I said those ladies meant business, I wasn't kidding. They were running some crazy formations, snagging all the good deals the department store had to offer. They were even throwing things to each other. One had just made a pretty spiral pass with a bottle of perfume, only to have it intercepted by an opponent. Now there were some personal fouls being called, along with security. All I could do was watch in utter fascination as these women fought over Gucci Guilty Black, which did smell divine, while Mara was trying on all the coats.

While I observed, it got me to thinking that instead of the impersonal across-the-board Visa gift cards I had gotten everyone the last few years for Christmas, I could actually make a list and check it twice, make sure everyone got something super special and personal like I always used to do.

Yesssss, Miss Sparkly purred. *Now we're talking. Also, Mara is about ready to sneak her extra credit card and buy that gaudy puffy jacket. Stop her.*

I hopped to my duty and practically vaulted over a clothes rack. "Step away from the coat," I called to Mara.

She clutched it like a child. "But I don't have a lime-green puffy coat."

I pressed my lips together. "Say that sentence again and think about why you don't own one."

She thought for a moment. "Fine. I don't even like lime green." She hesitantly put the coat back on the rack.

I laughed while she hunted down another coat. Meanwhile, my phone buzzed. I looked to see that Rachelle had messaged me. I hadn't heard from her since her breakup with Dave.

Rachelle: *Hey, I just read your puzzle post. Dave and I are headed to the airport for an early flight. He's taking me to meet his parents. I know you probably think I'm crazy for getting back together with him, but some things are worth fighting for, even men. Anyway, I got the vibe that you have some difficult choices to make. I just wanted you to know that for me, the most beautiful puzzles are always the most complicated ones, and just because it's hard it doesn't mean it's not right. I don't know why, I just thought I should tell you that. Take care, Cami. Thanks for being a piece in my complicated puzzle.*

I sniffled a bit. I apparently had the wisest friends of all.

I knew then what I had to do to complete my puzzle. Well, right after I stopped Mara from buying a tacky leopard-print coat.

Thirty-One

Dear Ex-Filers, I have made a grave, grave mistake. I thought it would be smart to use an at-home Brazilian wax kit. Let me repeat, this was a mistake of epic proportions. Please pray and send ice. And I beg you to never, ever do this to yourself.

Lots of love,

Cami

I clicked publish and lowered an ice bag onto my lady parts. This was not how I'd envisioned my night going. Not like I had huge plans, other than editing some photos I took. Yes, I had taken photos, and no, they were not of houses. That part of my life was done, seeing as Jay was already moving on with the firm. Apparently, he wanted to expand his horizons in the real estate game. Whatever that meant. I'm sure Mara would tell me more about it when she came over later to probably laugh at my predicament. She had tried to talk me off the crazy ledge of doing my own Brazilian wax. I should have listened to her.

Thankfully, while I was writhing in pain, I had the cutest children imaginable to look at. Those being my minions and then Jaxon and Liam. I hadn't gotten to see Amayah and Camila yet, as they were still in the hospital until they learned how to eat, but Shanna, who was spending her time between home and the hospital, had shown me pictures. All I could say was they were the sweetest and made my ovaries scream that they wanted to make one. Funny, Shanna screamed that I should make one with her brother.

Noah. I swore I thought of him all the time, even though I hadn't seen him since last week on Thanksgiving. I was still reliving every kiss and his words of love and acceptance. Sure, we'd talked, but he was trying to give me my space. I appreciated it more than he would know, even though I missed him. But I knew that I had to know who I was before I jumped into a relationship. Of course, Miss Sparkly was pretty adamant that we were her and I should get with the program already, but as much as I did love her, this other part of me lived, and there was a reason she kept sticking around.

With that said, I decided to start conquering some of the things I had been avoiding the last few years. To find my Christmas, as Noah called it. I started with doing some lifestyle shoots for the minions and the boys. My plan was to have some canvas prints made of my siblings' kiddos as my Christmas gifts to them and my parents. Yep, I was doing Christmas gifts this year. Still no tree. They were still making me a bit rashy, though I had forced myself to go down the tree aisles at Hobby Lobby. It was only slightly painful, as I remembered how carefully I had chosen the last Christmas decorations I had ever purchased, in a muted green-and-red palette, for that fateful tree that Ben and Claudia had desecrated.

It was weird, but the thought of Noah eased a lot of the uncomfortableness as I strolled the aisles, trying to refrain from rearranging some of the ornaments. My mind had often drifted to him taking me to the Christmas tree farm and helping me pick out the perfect tree. He'd also helped me decorate it as we'd sung all the Christmas songs out loud. Who knew all that time he'd been torturing himself because he loved me, knowing he could never have me? Yet he'd done his best to make me smile, knowing how sad I was that Ben had neglected me and my annual traditions and chosen work, well really Claudia, instead. That was a special kind of love, more like the essence of love. For love is never supposed to be selfish.

I wondered if I could love like that again. Or allow myself to be loved again without feeling insecure. Sure, I loved Noah, but it was like how I loved Mara. Not to say I didn't have romantic feelings for Noah.

Believe me, I did. But I still hadn't given myself permission to fall in love with him. I knew it wouldn't take much, and that scared me.

I carefully shifted to reach my laptop, sitting next to me on my bed. Poor Neville was hiding from me. I had let out such a deafening scream when I'd ripped the wax off that he'd run for cover under my bed, where he was probably still sitting and shaking. I couldn't blame him; I didn't even know I could scream in such a guttural way. The directions recommended not drinking before you tortured yourself in such a manner, but I'm going to say, it might not be bad to have a glass or two of wine before giving it a try.

While I pulled up my editing software, Noah called. My heart did a few flips just seeing his name on the screen. I put him on speaker so I could continually shift the ice bag. I'm not lying when I said I felt as if I were on fire.

"Hello."

"Hey, Cams, I just called to check on you. Sounds like you're having some issues." He cleared his throat.

"You could say that." I laughed. He must have read my post.

"I'm assuming there's nothing I can do for you."

I could hear in his voice that he was begging me to say no on this one. "I'm good, but thank you for checking in on me. How was your day?"

"Busy between work and the boys. I miss you." The longing in his voice was apparent.

"You know, I was just thinking that I miss you too."

"This is good. Progress."

"Yeah. I'm making some progress. It felt really good to get behind the camera this week and not have my subject be a gourmet kitchen. Speaking of kitchens, when will I get a working sink again?"

"My guys are on it, I promise."

"Uh-huh. You know, you could do the work."

He paused. "Cams, you don't know how much I want to, but I can't promise that I'll keep my hands off you, and I don't want us to start out that way. I want you to want me for all the right reasons, and I want you to know that I want you for all the right reasons."

"Are you saying I can't keep my hands to myself?" I was faux offended.

I told you, you were handsy.

Oh please, you were begging me to be.

Miss Sparkly sighed long and hard thinking about the wonders of Noah.

"Judging by Thanksgiving, I'm going to say yes." He playfully laughed.

He was probably right. And sweet. I loved that he was wonderful and wise enough to know how easily a physical relationship could, at the very least, complicate it all.

"Okay, fine," I pouted.

"Well . . . if you can control yourself, I was thinking that since tomorrow night is Aspen Lake's annual Christmas tree lighting and Christmas parade, you might want to run into me and the boys there. I promise not to get you in trouble with your fans."

"Oh." That came out high-pitched. "My parents and siblings asked me to go with them, but I'm still thinking about it. I don't want to go totally Christmas crazy."

"What frightens you there?" He could read me so well it was scary.

I swallowed hard before whispering, "Ben told me he loved me for the first time there." I remembered like it was yesterday. As soon as the lights had come to life on the fifty-foot tree, Ben had wrapped his arms around me from behind and whispered in my ear, *"You are magical like this tree. I love you."*

"I could see where that would be hard. But . . . if it makes you feel better, I loved you on that night and I still do."

Tears pooled in my eyes. A rush of warmth encompassed me and not because my lady parts were on fire. "Noah, you may not think you can heal me, but you are part of the healing process. Thank you." Those were the only words I could think of to convey my gratitude to him, though they were wholly inadequate.

"So does that mean I will see you tomorrow night?"

"Yes," I found myself saying, without a second thought.

"I won't be offended if you pretend like you don't know me," he teased.

"Noah, I wouldn't do that to you. I'm sorry I ever did."

"You give me hope, Cams," his voice was full of emotion, "that my Christmas wish will come true."

"What do you wish for?"

"The same thing I've been wishing for ten years—you. Good night."

"Good night," I whispered, not wanting to say goodbye, but knowing it was probably for the best. Besides, he'd ended it on a beautiful note, one I would keep singing into my dreams that night.

Please let us make it a merry Christmas for him and, you know, us, Miss Sparkly begged.

I'm working on it.

You are and I'm proud of you.

Wow, Sparkles, a compliment?

You have to love yourself first, right?

Yes. And I promise, I'm getting there.

Then promise me we will never, ever do the Brazilian wax thing again.

Oh, I promise. Now excuse me while I go get some more ice.

Thirty-Two

DEAR EX-FILERS, I never thought I would say this, but here is a poignant thought from Mike Ditka: "If you're not in the parade, you watch the parade. That's life." I'm not saying it's bad to be a spectator. There would be no need for the parade if there was no one to watch it and cheer and catch the candy. Cheerleaders play a huge role in life, but if you want to be in the parade, so to speak, don't let anyone keep you from jumping in. Grab a trombone and get down with your bad self. Or whatever instrument floats your boat.

By the way, thank you for all your messages of concern. I have to wear loose clothing, but I think I will survive. Stay safe and don't do wax.

Lots of love,

Cami

I clicked publish as I wended my way through the large crowd, mostly made up of my family, to get a good spot on the main parade thoroughfare. It was a cheery scene with everyone bundled up; the streets boasted twinkle lights and wreaths on every lamppost. Everyone seemed to be smiling, and anxious children wiggled in their parents' arms, longing to see the wonders of the parade floats, especially the one that carried Santa. Our town had the best Santa too. His beard was his own and his suit was hand sewn. My minions who were still believers were convinced he was the real Santa.

My main purpose in getting a good view of the route was to find Noah. He'd said he would try and be near Thompson's Barbershop. I looked across the street at the barbershop and didn't see him or Jaxon and Liam.

Mom wrapped an arm around me. "Looking for someone, dear?" she sang.

I adjusted my beanie to cover my cold ears. "Maybe." I smirked.

"Maybe, she says." Dad laughed on the other side of Mom. "Look how she sparkles." Dad winked at me with a knowing twinkle in his eye.

"Do we need to tell Noah the rules for dating our sister?" Derek boomed too loudly into the crowd.

I whipped around and glared at him. "Shhh. And no. I'm a grown woman; I make my own rules, thank you very much."

"No one is saying you can't have your rules." Seth fist-bumped Derek. "But as your brothers, we are sworn to not only protect you but humiliate you."

All five of my brothers guffawed while their wives told them to behave and leave me alone.

At this rate, everyone would know there was a little something, something going on between me and Noah. While I wouldn't deny it, it would be a lie to say I wasn't worried about what it meant for my future. Would my business disappear? Would that part of me disappear? Was I supposed to let that part go? I knew I should be brave and blaze my own path and trust that those meant to follow me would. It's not like I didn't have a bunch of built-in groupies with my family. But they didn't pay the bills. And honestly, I loved my job, as weird as it was. Just yesterday I got a request from a man to crop out his ex-fiancée, who turned out to be a convicted felon who had escaped from prison and had been on the run for five years. I couldn't make this stuff up.

I also couldn't deny the inexplicable happiness and comfort I felt when Noah came into view. He was adorable with Liam on his shoulders and holding Jaxon's hand. It didn't hurt that he looked like a sexy lumberjack in his plaid flannel shirt, jeans, and his beanie that showcased the curls above his ears. How he wasn't freezing, I didn't know, but I enjoyed the view all the same.

As I stared at him, it hit me. More than the holiday scene around me, Noah felt like Christmas to me.

I waved at him and the boys, longing to keep that feeling of Christmas he invoked.

The boys enthusiastically waved back.

Noah flashed his charming smile at me.

"Come over here," Mom yelled, as she waved them over.

Noah glanced at me, his eyes asking if that was okay.

I nodded and smiled. I would never again make Noah feel as if I were ashamed to be seen with him. He deserved at least that from me.

He and the boys pushed their way out of the crowd on that side and crossed the street, and just in time too. One of the local high school marching bands started to play, "We Need a Little Christmas." How fitting for me. I felt that need so acutely as Noah neared.

The excitement level of the crowd went up with the lively tune.

My excitement increased when Noah came to stand by me and Jaxon took my hand. It felt like the Christmas mornings of my childhood.

"Hi," I shouted so they could all hear.

"I'm going to catch some candy!" Liam squealed.

My younger minions were excited about that, too, and were eagerly waiting near the roadside, with their parents trying to hold them back before they got maimed by a tuba player.

A palpable tension hung between Noah and me. It was the delicious kind, filled with longing. Like a child waiting for Santa, knowing he knew exactly the gift to bring you. With every glance and gaze, my desire to draw near him grew, even though we were in public. I found myself not caring. That spoke volumes to me. But sweet Jaxon snuggled deeper into my side, placing a cute barrier between me and his uncle.

My parents and siblings shamelessly gawked at us. Noah took it all in stride, smiling and gazing frequently at me. He never physically touched me, but he didn't have to. With each one of his glances, I knew how he felt about me. I realized he'd been looking at me like that for the last ten years. Yet he'd loved me enough to let me go, not once but twice. He was letting me choose him. What a beautiful gift.

As we watched the parade's procession of floats, bands, and convertibles—filled with celebrities who lived among us, waving like they were the Queen of England—it was hard not to absorb the magic of the Christmas season. It was as if hope lived and breathed. If that wasn't enchanting enough, when a local jazz band began to play "White Christmas," snowflakes drifted down. It was stunningly perfect.

I looked up to the sky and let the snowflakes catch on my eyelashes and melt on my cheeks. The boys stuck out their tongues to catch a few. Some of my minions danced in circles, enjoying the snowfall.

Noah watched me with that look that said I was the coolest girl he knew. Yet he patiently waited.

When Santa arrived, everyone cheered. Santa's elves threw candy out into the crowd, and as was the town's tradition, a chorus of "Santa Claus Is Comin' to Town" broke out.

I had missed this so much. So much that I was too choked up to sing. But I remembered many times with Ben and Noah at this very parade. Noah would sing as loud as me, just like he was doing now. Unfortunately, he wasn't the only person I could hear. Above the swell of music, the most grating voice on the planet pierced through my holly and jolly.

Noah and I must have heard it at the same time, as our heads jerked to the left. There she was near the street sign they changed to Santa Claus Lane each year especially for the parade, in her snug white jumpsuit with a white fur muffler. And she couldn't forget her brimmed hat to match. She pouted her lips like she was a long-lost Kardashian sister as she rambled on about the charm of Aspen Lake. She was so fake. I thought Claudia Cann can't do this side of the lake.

It didn't help when Ben came into view. He stood watching his wife, who constantly had a phone in front of her face. What a life.

I had to ask myself, what were they doing here? I looked up at

Noah, who must have been thinking the same thing. "Are you okay?" he mouthed.

I nodded, feeling like I might puke. I hated that they still made me feel off-center and like I wanted to scurry away. Yet, I made myself stay in place. The fact that he would bring her to a place that meant so much to me said it all. He had cared nothing for our relationship, for me. They were here for the photo op and that was all that mattered. He was a self-centered jerk.

I couldn't help but think, though, that I too often lived, not necessarily for the photo op, but for the laugh or validation. That I let virtual friends and strangers have a huge say in my life. Many who didn't care for me beyond my snarky and snappy posts.

Then there was Noah, who maneuvered himself to block my view of the pair. He was anything but selfish. He took care of everyone around him, never expecting anything in return. He was a living, breathing person in my world. A constant, no matter what I had done or would do.

I found myself switching Jaxon to my other side and reaching for Noah's hand. Not because I needed him, but because I wanted him and all his goodness. He was real, and when it was all said and done, he would follow me on any path I chose.

Noah's fingers entangled with mine. He pulled me to him. "Are you sure about this?"

"Yes." I realized if I was looking for Christmas, Noah was the very essence of the season. He was *my* Christmas.

Each one of my family members zeroed in on Noah and me. Many sly grins were passed between all of us, until they noticed my ex nearby. It was a good thing it was time to follow Santa to the town square, where he would light the Christmas tree—if not, there might have been bloodshed.

Ben and Claudia were so absorbed in themselves, they didn't even notice us. Fine by me. I decided to ignore them as well.

My parents took Jaxon and Liam, allowing Noah and me to walk hand and hand together in the falling snow. Noah stopped several times to kiss me, very innocently, given the public eye. His sweet kisses set my world on fire. More than the wax, even.

Town square was as beautiful as always, with the large gazebo aglow with twinkle lights. Every tree was covered in them as well. The shops and cafés that outlined the square were draped in boughs of pine and red ribbons. Kids skated on the nearby outdoor skating rink. It was quite Hallmark-ish. And I loved it.

The large crowd gathered round the fifty-foot real tree adorned in unlit lights and massive green and red ball ornaments. Noah wrapped his arms around me from behind, just like Ben had once upon a time. For a moment I stilled.

He's no Ben, Miss Sparkly reminded me.

She was right. I relaxed against Noah and reveled in his comfort and that snickerdoodle scent of his. Even as I watched Claudia get into the thick of it all, getting as close to Santa as she could. Kris Kringle flashed her an annoyed look before he got right back into character as his jolly self. Ben had to intervene and pull his wife out of the way.

Noah whispered in my ear, "Don't you ever compare yourself to her."

"I won't," I promised him. Not an ounce of jealously ran through me. Claudia was rude and only thought of herself. She and Ben were perfect for each other.

It was almost as if Ben knew his grip on me was evaporating. As he was pulling his wife to the side, his gaze happened to catch us. He let go of Claudia's arm and stared at us dumbfoundedly. Even from the distance, I could see his face explode in red.

I tilted my head to look up at Noah. "Does he know about us?"

"He does now." Noah sounded awfully satisfied. He kissed my cheek.

Ben still glared, behaving as if he were frozen in place.

The best thing I could think to do was ignore him. Instead, I focused on those around me who meant the world to me. And of course, Santa, who was now leading the countdown to flipping the switch. The crowd was counting down from ten to one. When we all shouted, "one!" the gorgeous tree lit up the square while Noah lit up my world.

"I love you, Cami," he whispered in my ear, before turning me toward him. He ran his cold hand down my cheek, wet from the snow and tears. His incredible blue eyes peered into my soul, making me believe in Christmas once again.

I stood on my tiptoes and brushed his lips with my own. I wasn't quite ready to say "I love you," but I wanted to give him hope. He must have gotten a shot of it, since his lips pressed against mine as he dramatically dipped me, making my family ooh and ahh . . . Okay, some said, "Ew."

Mom clapped her hands, before trying to wrap her arms around us both when Noah pulled me back up. "I knew it. This calls for a celebration. Moon Café for hot chocolate and pastries."

All the minions went nuts cheering for sweets, though many already had candy canes sticking out of their mouths. Poor Moon Café had no idea what shenanigans were in store for their employees. Thankfully my parents were generous tippers.

"Sounds good, Mom." I could see her eyes were already swirling with the possibilities Noah presented. I was beginning to see them too. Too bad I had to face my past first. Ben and Claudia appeared out of thin air. Ben, looking like a clone of his dad, with not a single hair out of place and dressed in a fine long, dark wool coat, even though it was snowing, got right in Noah's face.

My brothers all banded together like they were Noah's guard.

"Are you dating my wife?" Ben poked Noah in the chest.

Noah's face scrunched with revulsion when he glanced at Claudia, who stood there looking bored with a hand on her hip, tapping her foot. I'm sure this was impeding her Insta stories or something.

"Claudia?" Noah shuddered. "Hell no."

Claudia clucked her tongue, offended.

"Not Claudia," Ben raged. "Cami."

That did it. Not only did that set Claudia off, who began swearing, using all the four-letter words in what sounded like several languages—but Noah didn't take it too kindly that Ben was referring to me as his wife and touching him.

Noah gripped Ben's coat with two hands and got right in his face.

"Don't you ever refer to Cami as your wife again. After what you did to her, you have no business even saying her name. Are we clear?"

By now we had onlookers with camera phones, snapping pictures and recording. If Ben and Claudia were anything, they were ever aware of how the public perceived them. Ben pulled away from Noah, brushed off his coat, and cleared his throat. Under his breath he said, "We're done."

Noah's face was crestfallen, but he quickly recovered when he took my hand.

Ben shook his head in disgust before walking off in Claudia's direction. She already had her phone out, making her excuses for what had just occurred. The crowd around us dispersed, seemingly disappointed there wasn't a fistfight.

Noah directed his attention to me. "Are you okay?"

"Almost. I'll be right back." I had to do something. Something I should have done a long time ago. After this night, Ben would no longer haunt me. I was cropping him out of my life, once and for all.

Noah gave me a knowing smile.

My brothers, on the other hand, stood in my way. "You aren't going after Ben, are you?" Chandler was the voice for the brute squad.

"Only to put him in his place."

My brothers nodded. "You may proceed." They parted. They were ridiculous, but I loved them.

Ben was marching toward the gazebo when I caught up to him. "Ben," I called his name for what I hoped was the last time.

He turned around, stunned to see me, yet he wore his usual look of condescension. "What do you want?"

"I want to tell you the truth."

He folded his arms as if to say, "Thrill me."

I stepped closer, but not too close, disgusted with his arrogance.

"If you've come to tell me you're sleeping with my best friend, I figured that one out on my own. If you're trying to seek your revenge, I don't care," he obviously lied.

Normally that would have felt like a slap in the face, but his power over me was waning. And even though I wasn't sleeping with Noah, I didn't address that slight. It was none of his business. I glanced to the side at Claudia putting on some fake tears now for her fans. "If I were seeking revenge, I would say you did the job for me, but that's not why I'm here."

Ben was speechless, for once. It was apparent he didn't love Claudia. I questioned if he'd ever loved me.

"I need you to know something, and then you will never hear from me again."

He dropped his defenses and unfolded his arms.

"The night I came home early to surprise you," my voice shook while I pushed away the images that had held me hostage for far too long. "I came home to tell you I was pregnant."

He blinked a hundred times, as if he were trying to comprehend what I had said. His gaze drifted toward my abdomen.

"I miscarried on Christmas Day." I guessed that's what he wanted to know.

His fists clenched. "Why are you telling me this now?" his voice trembled. I noted the misty sheen in his eyes.

"Because I've carried your betrayal with me for so long. And now it's yours to own." I physically felt the release. This huge weight lifted off my chest. I took a deep breath in, like it was the first breath I had taken in three years. "Wow. Merry Christmas, Ben."

His jaw dropped but no words came out.

I turned to walk away.

Of course Noah was standing nearby, watching over me. Always watching over me.

"Cami." Ben's voice pleaded for me to turn around.

I gave him a half turn. "What?"

He swallowed hard and rubbed the back of his neck. "I am sorry," he stuttered.

I'm not sure how sorry he really was, but I found I didn't need his apology as much as I needed to let go. And let's be honest, I was getting the better end of the deal.

I rushed into Noah's waiting arms and didn't look back. While I snuggled into his chest I heard Miss Sparkly exclaim, as she drove out of sight, *Merry Christmas to all, and to all a good night. That was me trying to be humorous. But it's time for you to let go of me too.*

Wait. I thought you wanted to be the victor.

Oh darling, I am.

Thirty-Three

DEAR EX-FILERS, "KNOWING yourself is the beginning of all wisdom." —Aristotle

I'm sorry I've been missing in action the last couple of weeks. I thought it best to let the dust settle. By now I know many of you have seen the videos and pictures of what went down at the Christmas tree lighting ceremony in my hometown. I want to thank so many of you for your private messages of support. Even those who have stopped me in the store or on the street. It means the world to me and, yes, Noah. While many of you have been supportive, I know there are many who feel as if I have betrayed you or been an opportunist, claiming to espouse and promote the single life just so I can earn people's business; when in reality, I didn't mean any of it.

Here's the truth: Three years ago, when I caught my husband under the Christmas tree with another woman, I felt as if my life had been stolen from me. I lost my sparkle. The pain was so unbearable, all I wanted to do was hide from all the things that once made me happy, including men and the holidays. For a while that worked. The Holiday Ex-Files was born, and you will never know how much of a lifesaver that was. With every photo I cropped and every story shared, I felt less lonely and knew I would survive the inexplicable pain I was in. The thing is, though, I wasn't happy. I wasn't unhappy, but as someone I care about very much reminded me, it's not the same.

So, I went in search of my happiness, and guess what? I found me again. The me who loves cheesy Hallmark movies and pumpkin spice everything. I found the girl who dances in front of a roomful of strangers for no reason. I even found the woman who is willing to be vulnerable. Who wants to take a chance on love.

I know some of you might be saying it's a trap and how do you know this guy Noah will work out. The thing is, I don't know for sure. But this I know: Noah is like Christmas. Christmas is cozy and warm; it's about selfless giving and thinking about others; it makes you a better person and brings out the wonders of childlike faith. Christmas never thinks of itself—it only exists to make the world happy and a better place. Cheesy, I know, but it's true.

So, if you're still reading this and you can forgive me for knowing myself, I'll still be here winter, spring, summer, and fall to help you remove them all. I may be more sparkly now, but don't worry, there will still be plenty of snarky.

Lots of love,

Cami

I held up my phone to Neville. He was busy watching Animal Planet next to me on the couch and checking out a beautiful chocolate Lab. "Hey, look at this. What do you think? By the way, your lady love will be here soon, so put your tongue back in your mouth."

Neville paid me no attention, so I clicked publish. Maybe Neville didn't care that Luna was coming over, but I couldn't wait to see Noah. I had a surprise for him. Mara had called from Christmas Hell, as she had referred to it. A place called Carole Cove, Montana. Jay had sent her there on a business trip, and unfortunately things weren't exactly going as planned and she would probably be there through the holiday. But I had a feeling there was more to the story than just business. She wasn't being all that forthcoming, so I couldn't wait to get the full scoop when she returned after Christmas. But that meant no more Virgin Islands vacay. Noah was going to be ecstatic; he'd been begging me to stay. I'd almost given in but didn't want to disappoint Mara. Now it was the best of both worlds: sexy boyfriend for Christmas with no guilt.

I set my phone down and breathed in the pine scent that filled my condo as I stared at the bare balsam fir in front of my window. I'd had it delivered this morning. It was ironic to think that the beautiful seven-foot tree represented new life and a new beginning, especially when I'd had it chopped down and it was sure to die. But I never thought I would see another Christmas tree in my place. I wasn't even itchy at all. And it had nothing to do with the rumor that Ben and Claudia had separated.

Who cared about them when Noah was rushing over because he thought I was having a plumbing emergency? The truth is, I only wanted him here to help me decorate my tree and to tell him I was all his for Christmas. And . . . to give him his Christmas present early. I'd been working on it for days and was anxious for him to see it. I thought it was a fitting first gift of Christmas.

I jumped up when I heard a key being inserted into my door. Yes, he had a key to my place already—I mean, he was my contractor. That was my story, and I was sticking to it.

I hustled to the door, skirting around all the Hobby Lobby bags full of Christmas decorations. We are talking a maze of bags. I'd gone Christmas crazy there with Mom. It was the best present I could have given her.

When Noah opened the door, I full-on attacked him, throwing my arms around his neck and wrapping my legs around him. I pressed my lips against his before he could even say a word. I thought my way was the best way to say hello.

Noah must have agreed, since he let go of Luna and tangled his fingers in my hair while his tongue danced right into my mouth, making my holidays merry and bright. Oh, merry Christmas, could the man kiss. He walked us over to the kitchen and set me on my new butcher block counters while he decimated my hair and did magical things inside my mouth. I think I was going to start calling him Lucky Charms because he was magically delicious.

When he'd done a thorough job of taking my breath away, he groaned against my lips. "You are so handsy."

"I thought you liked that about me." I smiled.

"It's one of your finer qualities." He kissed my nose. "Did you get the water turned off like I told you to?"

"Wow. That's so sexy. If you're trying to woo me, considered me wooed," I teased.

He nuzzled my neck, his stubble giving me all the feels. "Water damage is no joke."

"Would you think it was funny if I told you I'm not having any plumbing issues?" I stuttered out. Kisses on the neck were my weakness.

His head popped up. "You lied?"

"*Lie* is such an ugly word. I just wanted you to hurry over here. I have a surprise for you." I pointed to the tree behind me.

Noah's eyes widened. "I thought you decided against a tree since you're leaving in a few days."

"Well . . . ," I purred. "What if I decided to stay?"

His eyes lit up like I'd hoped my Christmas tree soon would. "Merry Christmas to me." His lips crashed into mine and we started the entire dance over again, breathing the same breaths and tasting each other, like a fine meal you never wanted to end but that wasn't able to quite completely satisfy the hunger. It was a beautiful thing—Noah always left me wanting more, but in the best way.

My fingers danced in his curls while his slow hands took a trip down my curves. I wasn't the only handsy person in this relationship. All while every inch of my body tingled.

When the kisses eventually slowed to a heated simmer, he ran a finger down my cheek. "You know, you didn't have to make up an emergency for me to come rushing over here. I'll come anytime you call."

I peered into his eyes. He was so, so good. "Thank you, Noah."

He grinned his charming grin. "Should we decorate your tree?"

"Let's call it *our* tree."

He sighed a happy sigh. "Cami Jenkins, I love you."

"I know." I jumped off the counter, took his hand, and led him to the living room.

Our dogs were already cuddled up on Neville's bed. I really needed to have a talk with Neville again. I thought I had explained to him that it wasn't right for him to ogle other dogs and then take Luna to his bed. Totally bad form.

Noah eyed my tree. "She's a beauty."

"Yeah."

"This is kind of a big deal for you." Noah held up my hand and kissed it. "Speaking of big deals, I read your post before I walked up here." He choked up. "It was perfect, except you honored me more than I deserve."

He knew, more than anyone, how I had stressed about how to address my fans the last couple of weeks. "I don't think I'll ever be able to honor you enough. You gave me back my Christmas." I stood on my tiptoes and kissed his cheek. "Now let's get tangled up in some tinsel."

His eyes popped.

"Not that kind. The real kind." I winked.

"Okay, fine. Where do we begin?"

"With the lights. It needs its sparkle," I said with meaning.

We went to work and wound the white twinkle lights from top to bottom, intertwining them on top of and underneath each branch. Next came the glittery burlap, which made us literally sparkle. After that, we carefully placed each dusted pinecone, bright-white ornament, snowflake, and bauble with care, until the tree was a work of art.

Noah did the honors and put the white glittered star on top.

We stood back and admired our handiwork. Neither of us spoke of the last time we had decorated a tree together. The Ghost of Christmas Past no longer haunted my memories. I wanted to live in the present and look forward to the future. A future with Noah. Which reminded me.

"I want to give you your present."

He wrapped his arms around me. "Mmm. Now we're talking."

"Not that present." I giggled.

"Fine," he dramatically sighed.

"Don't be disappointed," I whispered in his ear. "You never know what will come later." I used all the seducing tones. I pranced away while he stood there with his tongue wagging like Neville. Men.

Noah's gift, beautifully wrapped in stark-white paper with a gold bow and ribbon, sat squarely in the middle of my snowflake comforter, waiting to be given. I snatched the gift off my bed and hurried back to Noah.

I found him sitting next to the tree, all sexy-like in his tight tee and his yummy jeans. Seriously, I could trace the barbed wire tats around his muscular biceps all day long. He was the best gift under the tree I could have ever asked for. I hoped he liked my gift as much as I enjoyed mine.

I cozied up next to him and leaned my head on his shoulder before placing the wrapped box in his hands. "Merry Christmas."

He stared at the box. "I feel bad. I didn't know we were exchanging gifts tonight or I would have brought yours."

"That's okay, you can just tell me what it is," I teased.

"That's not how it works." He kissed my head.

"Fine, be all by the rules. But hurry and open your gift."

"Anxious, are we?" He chuckled before popping off the bow and undoing the ribbon. Then, like a child, he ripped off the paper in two seconds flat. He tipped the lid open and pulled out the book. His fingers grazed the white cover and gold scripted letters. "Cami and Noah," he whispered. "I already love it."

"Look inside."

He reverently opened the book. The first page was a picture of us kissing while we skated on the outdoor ice-skating rink. We were the ultimate cute couple with our hand-crocheted scarves from Mara. The next pages documented our lives over the last two weeks. Us on the holiday Ferris wheel here in Aspen Lake, a few of us while we strolled the ice sculpture display, walks down Santa Claus Lane as we shopped. My favorites, though, were us holding Amayah and Camila, who had been able to come home a few days ago. Yes, I had popped some more eggs as I'd snuggled those little angels.

Noah looked longingly at us, each with a baby in our arms, smiling at each other. "This is what I want for us someday."

"I know." But I also knew I needed to take it a day at a time for now. Marriage and babies were definitely a possibility for us, but under the circumstances, I felt it was best to take it slow. "You can be patient awhile longer, right?"

"Cams." He caressed my thigh. "You're worth any wait."

I was seriously going to fall in love with this man any second now. But first I needed him to see the rest of the book. "Turn the page."

He flipped the page and kept flipping, his smile growing wider and wider with each picture. "I can't believe you did this."

"Well, you said every photo shoot you did was in a place you knew I loved; I thought it was only fair that I should be in the pictures."

"Look at you, using your Photoshop skills for good, not evil." He laughed.

"Hey, I can crop myself out."

"Don't you dare." He pulled me onto his lap.

I snuggled against his chest; his heart pounded clear and steady.

He pulled up the book and pointed to the last picture of the hot springs. I had photoshopped myself in a red bikini next to his beautiful abs and chest. "This one is my favorite," he crooned.

"Of course it is."

"Isn't that the bikini you bought for the Virgin Islands?"

"Yes."

"You know, we could go together for Christmas."

I sat up and met his sexy gaze, visions of Noah and me on the beach dancing in my head. "That is an idea." I bit my lip.

"What do you say?"

"I say, Christmas is wherever you are."

Christmas Day

DEAR EX-FILERS, FOR those of you feeling sparkly today, I say I hope you have a very merry Christmas. For those of you feeling snarky, maybe even a tad bitter or alone, I say think of all the money you're saving. If that doesn't make you feel better, for fun, watch all your married friends and family fight. It's bound to happen. Kids up too early plus alcohol always sparks a few good arguments. So, pop some popcorn and enjoy.

And please don't forget: placement, people. If you even think you'll need a picture cropped, for all the love, please don't let that person be in the middle of any photo. I will charge extra.

Lots of love,

Cami

I clicked publish and threw my phone into my beach bag while Noah slathered my back in suntan oil as we soaked in the sun and waves crashing against the shoreline. Merry Christmas to me. His plan was genius. A tropical vacation for two and Noah in his swim trunks.

"Baby, I think you missed a spot."

Noah gently rubbed my back. "Where?"

I turned around and pointed at my lips.

He gave me an impish grin. "I better take care of that."

"Like immediately."

He dropped the lotion and took me into his arms. He brushed my hair back before whispering, “I love you, Cams.”

“I love you too.”

New Year's Eve

DEAR EX-FILERS, FIRST of all, cheers to those of you walking into the New Year single. There is no shame in that. Remember, kissing frogs when the ball drops at midnight doesn't turn them into princes. But I mostly want to wish you each the happiest of New Year's! Words can't express my gratitude for those of you still sticking it out with me. Please don't drink and drive or drink and date. These are words to live by people.

Lots of love,

Cami

"Aunt Cami, hurry, we're going to start the movie," Aubrey called from the stairs.

I clicked publish, grabbed the humongous bowl of caramel popcorn, and headed down to the Babe Cave in my parents' basement. Noah and I had agreed to help my parents watch all the minions so their parents could do adult things tonight. My siblings figured I did enough adulting in the Virgin Islands.

It was fine. We were actually having a great time with the kiddos. Noah was never more attractive than when he had five kids hanging off him like a jungle gym.

I walked into the expansive room that held every toy imaginable. Dad had installed an even bigger screen along the back wall as a

Christmas present for the grandkiddos. Everyone was on beanbags or climbing all over my tanned man. The sun loved Noah like we all did.

The minions attacked me and stole the bowl of popcorn.

Noah motioned with his finger for me to join him on his beanbag.

"No hanky-panky in front of the kids," Mom warned.

"What's hanky and panky?" Toby asked.

I smiled evilly at my mom. She brought that one on herself.

Mom blushed.

Dad cleared his throat and said, "Ask your mom and dad."

I joined Noah and snuggled into him.

"When the clock strikes midnight," Noah whispered in my ear, "hanky and panky are coming out. I want you to be my first and last kiss of the year."

I drew circles on his chest with my finger. I couldn't wait to start the New Year with him. I had a feeling it was going to be a good one. "You have a deal."

Valentine's Day

DEAR EX-FILERS, I know for many of you this day is the hardest one of the year. Just remember it's a totally made-up holiday. A ploy by the florists and greeting card and chocolate companies. Maybe ploy *is too strong of language, but you get my drift. The point is, don't let a manufactured holiday make you feel any less about yourself. Take a romantic trip to the refrigerator or to the couch. Just don't Netflix and chill with somebody undeserving because the calendar says February fourteenth. You are worth more than that. Now for those of you happily with someone who is deserving of you, Netflix and chill is a great alternative to overcrowded restaurants.*

Lots of love,

Cami

P.S. Don't forget, all the chocolate goes on sale tomorrow!

Noah walked in from his gourmet kitchen that I had a secret love affair with. It was so much bigger than my kitchen, and he had a refrigerator that made pebble ice. Noah could have hands down won me over with that appliance. Right now, I loved him because he was bringing Chinese takeout and a bottle of wine with him.

"Are you sure you're okay not going out on our first Valentine's Day together? Or should I be offended that you see me as your Netflix and chill guy?" He set the bag of food and the wine down on the coffee table before he plopped down next to me.

"I would think that would be an honor for you." I kissed his beautiful face.

"I am honored to be with you." He got all sappy. I loved him for it.

"Aww. Now feed me, I'm hungry."

"Yes, ma'am." He reached for the bag and pulled out a fortune cookie first.

"I'm hungrier than that."

He leaned back and eyed the wrapped cookie carefully. "I just thought it would be fun to open your fortune first."

"I already know I'm the most fortunate girl around." I could be sappy too.

Noah leaned into me, our foreheads meeting. "I love you, Cams."

"I love you too."

"Good. Now open your cookie."

"So bossy." I plucked the cookie out of his hand. I leaned away and took off the wrapper before cracking the cookie open. With a dramatic flair, I cleared my throat before reading my fortune out loud. "Will you marry me?"

Noah slapped a hand against his chest. "I thought you would never ask. Yes. Yes. I will marry you." He pressed his lips against mine before I could say anything or comprehend that I was pretty sure I'd just gotten engaged. I mean, it wasn't a bad thought. But was this some Valentine's Day prank? Like, you know, do this and then film your girlfriend's reaction and post it?

I pulled away from him. "Uh . . . what just happened, and am I on camera?"

"Damn. I should have filmed that." His eyes danced with amusement. "Let's do that again. But this time, I want to try it a different way." He reached into the bag and this time he pulled out a Tiffany blue box. Like the Tiffany blue that means something. He opened the box to reveal the prettiest round diamond in a bead setting.

I nibbled on my lip and my breath became shallow. This was happening. Whoa.

"Cami Jenkins, I know this might be a little fast for you, but I've loved you for so long, I figured we could skip ahead a bit. I want to have and hold you for the rest of my life and Netflix and chill and whatever else you want to do. Because you are the coolest girl I know."

I smiled as tears filled my eyes.

"Will you be my wife?"

My heart raced like we were on an open desert highway with no cops in sight. As I looked forward, I didn't see anyone else in that passenger seat other than him. The past few months had proved to me he was truly the best friend I could have ever asked for. (Don't tell Mara that.) He was my ride or die. The song in my heart. Christmas all year long. It made the answer easy.

"Yes."

The End

***

Be sure to visit The Holiday Ex-Files website—
www.theholidayexfiles.com

To read more about Mara and the Scott family, check out
How to Ruin the Holidays by Becky Monson.

If you enjoyed *The Holiday Ex-Files,* here are some other books by Jennifer Peel that you may enjoy:

All's Fair in Love and Blood
Love the One You're With
My Not So Wicked Stepbrother
Facial Recognition
The Sidelined Wife
How to Get Over Your Ex in Ninety Days
Narcissistic Tendencies
Honeymoon for One - A Christmas at the Falls Romance
Trouble in Loveland
Paige's Turn
My Not So Wicked Ex-Fiancé
My Not So Wicked Boss

For a complete list of all her books, see Jennifer's Amazon page.

About the Author

Jennifer Peel is a *USA Today* best-selling author who didn't grow up wanting to be a writer—she was aiming for something more realistic, like being the first female president. When that didn't work out, she started writing just before her fortieth birthday. Now, after publishing several award-winning and best-selling novels, she's addicted to typing and chocolate. When she's not glued to her laptop and a bag of Dove dark chocolates, she loves spending time with her family, making daily Target runs, reading, and pretending she can do Zumba.

***

If you enjoyed this book, please ra
You can also connect with Jennife
Facebook
Instagram
TikTok
Pinterest

To learn more about Jennifer and her boo
www.jenniferpeel.com

Made in the USA
Las Vegas, NV
06 January 2022